House Of Games
A University Mystery

Brenda Donelan

House Of Games

Dedication

Dr. Donna Hess served as my advisor at South Dakota State University for both my Master's and PhD programs. She was a tireless researcher and a lifelong educator. When I went into teaching, I tried to model my classroom presentations on those of Dr. Hess. I could never measure up, but I tried. She made it look much easier than it really was.

One of my fondest memories of Dr. Hess was when a group of us graduate students were seated around a large table, working on a grueling written exam. Dr. Hess bursts into the room and proclaims, "I brought lunch." Then she brought in two giant crock pots of homemade soup and bread that was still warm from the oven. To her, we weren't just students.

Sadly, Dr. Hess passed away in 2019. She leaves behind a legacy of former students, many who went into teaching themselves and tried to live up to her example.

Table of Contents

House of Games

They seem like nice young people. I hate to do this to them, but I have no choice. It will all make sense...someday.

Chapter 1

Leaves crunched beneath her feet as she weaved between cars haphazardly parked in the lot nearest her building. Marlee McCabe was in her second decade of teaching at Midwestern State University, yet she never ceased to be irritated by the random parking by students, staff, and faculty. She looked over her shoulder and saw a wavering line of various makes and models of vehicles. The older cars belonged to the faculty, while students and the higher-ups in administration drove the newer vehicles, the oversized pickups, and monster SUVs. Parking spots were freely ignored even though the lot was repainted every summer with glowing yellow lines marking each spot. It was common to get boxed in by two other vehicles, one parked in front and one in back. As bad as it was now, it was nothing compared to what would occur when a few inches of snow blanketed the town.

Marlee shuddered, pulling her scarf a little tighter around her neck. Fall was her favorite season, but in northeastern South Dakota, it lasted about a week before mild temperatures turned to biting cold wind, and snow fell with reckless abandon. Tomorrow, they would celebrate Halloween, and then the town of Elmwood would immediately switch to winter. If the snow held off until after Halloween, she would be satisfied. Nothing worse than seeing snow-covered pumpkins on the front step as trick-or-treaters wearing costumes over their snow suits rang the doorbell, shivering as they held out their bags for candy.

"Candy," Marlee mumbled to herself. "We need more candy." She added it to the mental list of things to pick up at the store. Between herself and her boyfriend, Hector Ramos, they'd polished off three family-sized bags of assorted candy bars in the past two weeks. She'd warned her boyfriend that buying candy in bulk that early in October was a recipe for disaster, but he hadn't listened. Now, they were both suffering the consequences of overindulgence and sugar dependence. Feeling the ever-growing tightness in her waistband, Marlee knew behavior modification was needed. "After Halloween, I'm off sugar!" These promises to herself were frequent but not adhered to for any length of time.

As she pulled into her driveway, Marlee looked fondly at the three-story Colonial Revival-style house she and Hector had recently remodeled. At first, it was a money pit, rife with electrical problems, faulty plumbing, and a furnace that blew out shortly after purchase. In the past year, they, well mainly Hector, had overseen repairs and remodeling of much of the home. They bought the house with the intent to fix it up and create rentals on the top floor, providing them with a steady stream of extra income. The third floor was now made up of four separate bedrooms, each with its own bathroom. A sitting room with a refrigerator, microwave, and dinette set was at the center of the room for the guests to share. The private back staircase with keyless entry allowed guests to come and go as they pleased without walking through Marlee and Hector's private residence on the lower two floors.

A scarecrow was slumped on a hay bale near the front door, and Marlee took the time to raise it a bit as she walked in. *Attention to detail* was repeatedly stressed on home rental websites. It wasn't enough for the rooms to be clean and functional; the whole property had to look inviting.

"About time you got home," Hector grumbled as Marlee walked in the door. "Did you forget we're hosting a party tomorrow?" He was adorable, standing atop a chair running a dust cloth around the kitchen light fixtures. She felt the same tingle when she saw him now as she did when they first met over ten years ago. His once-dark hair had turned mostly silver, and the years had added extra pounds to his midsection, but Marlee found him even more attractive now. Hector's caramel brown eyes, creased at the corners, gave her a playful look behind his glasses.

"No, I didn't forget," Marlee assured him with a smile. She was the one who'd lobbied for the Halloween party as an open house to announce the opening of their bed and breakfast. Advertisements were put in the newspaper and splashed across social media. Marlee announced the event to her colleagues and students at Midwestern State University, and Hector casually mentioned it to fellow officers and staff at the Elmwood Police Department. They were expecting around thirty guests to filter through the home to celebrate the opening.

"I hope everyone has a good time," Hector said, fussing with a burned-out light bulb. "And I hope the guests on the third floor aren't too disturbed by the party."

"I talked to all of them, and not only are they not bothered by the idea of a party, but they're excited to attend. They were especially thrilled when I told them it was a costume party."

Hector shook his head. He hadn't been in favor of the costume-themed party, even though it would be held on Halloween. His vision for the event was a more dignified party with treats, snacks, and door prizes. Marlee, on the other hand, had a different notion. Now, they were decorating for a Halloween costume party, which included a murder mystery game. "Remind me again of how the murder mystery game works."

"Nine people will be selected to play specific parts, and they will be given a note card with the role they are to play. The rest of the guests, regardless of how many people are here at the time, will guess the identity of the killer and their motive for killing the victim," Marlee said as she excitedly recounted the rules of the game. "And the winners not only get a prize, but they get their names engraved on a plaque that we will hang in the sitting room on the third floor. I'm hoping we can make this a yearly event."

"Let's not get ahead of ourselves," Hector cautioned. "Let's see how it goes this year and then decide if we want a repeat. It could be a total flop."

Marlee turned to glare at her boyfriend. "I think that's what you secretly want to happen. You want the murder mystery party to fail, so we don't have to do it again."

Hector stepped down from the chair and laid down his dust rag, looking Marlee straight in the eye. "Duh."

They both burst out laughing. As much as she wanted to be mad at Hector's lack of enthusiasm, she couldn't fault him for his beliefs. Getting ready for the party was a huge imposition on their time. Marlee's approach to most things in life was half-assed. That included cleaning, preparation, and upkeep of their home. "If the party doesn't go over well, then we'll wait a bit before deciding to do it again, okay?"

Hector nodded with a reluctant sigh. "But what will we do with all these decorations and props if we don't host the party again?" He pointed toward the skull-shaped candy bowl with a skeletal hand that reached out whenever one grabbed a piece of candy.

"That will never go out of style. We'll still be using that candy bowl when we're old and sitting in rocking chairs, regardless of whether we're hosting a Halloween party." Marlee smiled at Hector, knowing he wouldn't be able to resist her charm. They spent the remainder of the day and much of the following day cleaning and decorating.

At long last, Saturday arrived, and the party was upon them. One hour until the Open House was officially underway. Marlee turned on a battery-operated candle, placing it in the center of the dining room table, a recent switch from regular candles since there had been another incident involving Pippa and fire. Pippa was Marlee's aged Persian cat and had been with her long before Hector came into the picture. The fluffy gray kitty hated Hector with every fiber of her being and went out of her way to let him know it. Last month, he'd lit a lightly scented candle to mask the farty smell of cabbage soup. Pippa, resenting his very existence, leaped onto the counter, knocking over a roll of paper towels that came dangerously close to landing on the candle. After that, they'd agreed that cats and open flames were not a good idea.

Hector and Marlee stayed up late the previous night, putting the finishing touches on the Halloween decorations. When they had decided to open their top floor for rentals, they had no idea of the work that would go into it. Both assumed light cleaning and a couple of extra loads of laundry each week would be the extent of their involvement. Sure, there would be a slow-draining bathtub or a sticky closet door needing to be fixed from time to time, but those things would be mere annoyances, something Hector could fix on the same day. Breakfast was not part of the package, although the shared living space upstairs had a coffee pot, tea kettle, microwave, and mini fridge. Juice, soft drinks, and prepackaged breakfast bars were available for the guests.

What they hadn't counted on was the endless barrage of questions that a family from Nevada had sprung upon them two days ago. "Where is the closest Chinese restaurant? How far is it to the park? When does pheasant hunting season end?" All these questions could be easily answered with a quick Google search, which Marlee wanted to point out, but Hector noted that it would seem rude to the guests to tell them to "look it up" themselves. "They aren't your students. You have to be courteous to them," Hector noted.

"I am courteous, but when did people become unable to look up information for themselves? I'm doing them a favor by instilling self-reliance," Marlee countered. In the end, they agreed to put together a listing of restaurants, local attractions, and event centers around the area. The information packets were left in each room, hopefully, to head off any questions. The same information was uploaded to their business website, along with links to various establishments.

Of the four guest rooms on the third floor, only three were currently occupied. The fourth had been reserved, but a cancellation earlier that day had freed up the room. The first room, which they called the Green Room, was occupied by Leanne Desmond, a single woman in her forties traveling from Fargo, North Dakota. She was in Elmwood to meet a man she had met on an online dating site. Paul Rowley was housed in the Blue Room. He was in his late thirties and drove from Mobridge, South Dakota, to meet Leanne after several weeks of online chatting. They had arrived and checked in separately on Friday and had their first face-to-face meeting that night at Maverick's Steakhouse and Lounge. Although she'd vowed to stay out of their business, Marlee was fully invested in the story and sent frequent texts to both parties in hopes of finding out more about the progression of their romance.

Professor Jerome Vernon had the distinguished title of the first paying guest at Marlee and Hector's establishment. The seventy-ish professor, on sabbatical from a university in Wisconsin, was ensconced in the

Gray Room and spent his time either at one of the libraries or a local coffee shop. Professor Vernon had checked in the previous week and was booked for another two weeks. He referenced a research project he was working on yet never disclosed any details about the research or even a general topic. Marlee, being familiar with the quirky inner workings of the professorial brain, suspected that he wasn't working on any project at all. Rather, he was just enjoying his free time but made himself feel better by insisting he was working on a project. Her own sabbatical had started the same way: a month of avoiding work while insisting she was deep into her research. When she couldn't take the pressure of avoidance any longer, she buckled down and got to work, and she suspected Professor Vernon might be doing the same.

While Leanne and Paul were only booked for the weekend, Professor Vernon had his room for two more weeks. Online payment and keyless entry to the house and the individual rooms made Marlee's contact with the guests infrequent, which was her original intention. But now, she found herself wanting to know more about the guests, their backstories, and what brought them to Elmwood. She'd considered hanging out in the shared living room area upstairs just to see if any of the guests wanted to chat, but Hector had discouraged the idea. "The whole purpose of the keyless entry system was so that we didn't have to deal with guests face to face. Now you want to insert yourself into their lives."

"I know, I know," Marlee said with a sigh. "I thought I'd be irritated by people roaming through our house, but now I want to know what they're up to."

Hector took her hand and gave it a squeeze. "Do you think you're a bit at loose ends since your promotion to Full Professor?" Marlee had received notice of her promotion over the summer, and it had gone into effect at the start of that semester. Now that she no longer had to strive for promotion to the next level, Hector suspected she felt rudderless and in need of a new goal.

"Yeah, maybe," she acknowledged. "I feel kind of lackluster about teaching now. I still enjoy my students, but I'm in a slump."

"You could talk to your dean about it. Or your Supper Club friends. They might have some insight. Are they all coming to the Open House tonight?" Hector asked.

"Yep, Bridget is coming over shortly to help us with the final preparations. Diane and Kathleen will be here at 7:00, and Shelly and Gwen will be coming later. They have another party to attend and will hit that one first so they can spend most of their time here. Speaking of time," she said, glancing at the wall clock, "I need to get into my costume."

Hector rolled his eyes and grumbled under his breath. Originally, he wasn't going to participate in dressing up, but Marlee convinced him that if he put on his red plaid shirt and tool belt, he could go as the lumberjack from the Bounty paper towel commercials. Since it needed little effort on his part, he agreed. She would be going as a witch, per usual. This was her costume every year. Years ago, she had invested in a long, black velvet dress, matching cape, and an elaborate pointy hat.

"I'm going to run up to the room and throw on my costume before anyone arrives." Marlee turned and made for the stairway to the second floor. She changed into her witch's dress and hat and laced up a pair of black boots. Since she was still in the throes of menopause, the cape would not be needed until later, if at all.

Hiking up her dress, Marlee scooted down the stairs, ready for a beer before the guests started to arrive. Hector had already beat her to the fridge and was on his second Leinenkugel. He looked nervous, a rare trait for the confident detective. "What's wrong?" Marlee popped the top from her Bud Light bottle.

Hector took a healthy swig from his beer. "Just a little edgy, I guess. What if no one shows up? Or what if our B&B fails? We'll look like idiots."

Marlee was used to looking like an idiot but realized this was unfamiliar territory for Hector. "We know at least some of our friends are showing up, so we don't have to worry about that. And if the rental business never takes off, then we'll worry about that then. The place looks great. You did a fantastic job of decorating, and we're going to have a wonderful time tonight. Seriously, what's the worst that can happen?"

Marlee would soon regret her words.

House of Games

It was all planned and now this!

Chapter 2

Half an hour until the Open House was scheduled to begin, and everything was falling into place. Hector finished hanging fake spider webs across the light fixtures and was currently strutting around in his red plaid shirt, faded jeans, and tool belt. A pep talk and two beers was all it took to restore his confidence. Marlee had hired two students from her Criminal Justice Club to act as wait staff, passing hors d' oeuvres and serving drinks to the guests.

Marlee's cousin, Bridget McCabe, arrived with a flourish. She sprang up the front stairs wearing a green bejeweled bikini top, green leggings, and sparkly eye shadow. Her hair was in a tangled up do and speckled with glitter. "I'm a mermaid," she said, answering the question that was sure to be asked. "I can't walk up the stairs with my tail, so I have to put it on in here." She sat on an antique stool and shimmied her lower half into a shiny green fabric tube. "There, now I'm all set," Bridget said with a smile as she pulled herself upward with the help of the staircase banister.

"You're going to freeze in that skimpy outfit," Marlee chastised, more than a little jealous of her cousin's trim figure.

"Already thought of that," Bridget chirped. "I have a green top I can throw on if I get chilly." She motioned toward her purse. "What can I do to help you get ready for the party?" She shuffled toward the kitchen, her stride about four inches.

Marlee rolled her eyes. *Some help she'll be.* "I think we're all set. Now we just need guests."

Bridget reached for a wine glass on the countertop and helped herself to the giant box of Cabernet. "Can I pour you a glass too?"

"I'll have Sauvignon Blanc. Cab is my favorite, but I can't drink it much anymore since I was struck down by The Pause," Marlee said. "Hot flashes are a bitch."

"I haven't had much problem with that. Lucky, I guess." Bridget took a sip of her wine and sighed.

"Knock knock," called out a female voice before Marlee could offer up a retort to Bridget's good fortune. "Are we too early for the party?"

Marlee hurried to the front door and welcomed Leanne and Paul, the guests from the third floor who were on a first date weekend. They were smiling and holding hands, a sign the date was still going well. She was dressed as a princess with a flowing blue dress and matching gloves, topped off with a jewel-studded tiara. Paul's costume wasn't much of a stretch from his real life as a rancher, as he was wearing an Orange Denver Broncos jersey and jeans. "You're right on time," Marlee said, offering them a drink. Her two students, Ethan Wiley and Nadia Deen, were in the kitchen, moving the food from the catering tins to serving platters. "The food will be out in a minute."

"How long you been running this place?" Paul asked as he accepted the bottle of beer handed to him.

"We just opened last week, so please bear with us while we work out some of the kinks."

"Oh, no. I didn't mean that. I was only wondering about setting up an operation like this in Mobridge. My parents have a big, older house and are looking to retire to Arizona soon. I could fix it up and run it as a bed and breakfast."

Leanne scowled, taking a sip of white wine. "I thought we were talking about you moving to Fargo. You can't run a B&B in Mobridge if you're over four hours away. And there's no way I'm leaving my job."

"Just a thought," Paul said with a shrug.

"What did you guys do today?" Marlee interrupted, hoping to offset a disagreement so early in the budding relationship. "Did you make it out to the pumpkin patch this afternoon?"

"We did!" Leanne exclaimed. "It was lovely. We went on a hayride then warmed up in the farmhouse with apple cider and pumpkin bread."

Paul nodded in agreement, but Marlee couldn't read his body language. She was unsure if he had an enjoyable time or was just playing along with the Hallmarkish activities to stay on Leanne's good side. "Then we went out for an early supper, and here we are," he said.

"Meatball?" Ethan asked as he held a tray of steaming hors d'oeuvres along with cocktail napkins and toothpicks. He was dressed as a pirate, and the only thing distinguishing him as a waiter was the platter of food. "They're made with good ole South Dakota beef," he said as he tried to adjust his eye patch with his free hand.

"That's what I like to hear," Paul said with the most enthusiasm Marlee had heard from him so far. He skewered two meatballs on one toothpick and shoved one in his mouth. Leanne shook her head, passing on the local fare. "You don't like meatballs?" Paul eyed his date with suspicion.

"Still full from dinner," she said, taking another sip of white wine. "Besides, I try not to eat too much meat."

Paul's jaw dropped, exposing a partially masticated meatball. "What do you mean? You can't eat too much meat. No such thing."

Hector entered the room during the conversation and extended his hand to both Leanne and Paul. "I'm guessing you're in the cattle business," Hector said.

"Yep, third-generation rancher in Walworth County. Dad handed it to me, and when my son gets out of college, he's going to take over the ranch." Paul puffed out his chest as he popped the second meatball into his mouth.

"Where does he go to college?" Hector asked, stabbing a meatball for himself.

"Oh, he's only twelve, so it will be a while before he goes to college and then takes over. Until then, he's learning from me and my dad. By the time Landon graduates college, he'll have the latest knowledge and skills to keep the place afloat."

A clatter on the front steps diverted everyone's attention. Twelve people, most of them known to Marlee and a few strangers, stood in the open doorway. "Come in, come in," Marlee said, welcoming the guests. She quickly introduced Hector and herself to those who didn't know them. "Thank you so much for coming to our Open House. Please enjoy some food and drinks." Nadia and Ethan swirled by with platters of meatballs and mini egg rolls, taking drink orders as they moved through the living room. They also collected each guest's cell phone to prevent interruptions and distractions during the murder mystery game.

Within half an hour, the party was a roaring success. The living room and kitchen were crowded with guests laughing and chatting. The drinks were flowing, and the appetizers were a hit judging by the amount already served. Marlee beamed at Hector when she caught his eye, and he smiled back. The Open House was filled with friends, colleagues from the university and the police department, neighbors, and a handful of people she didn't know. To Marlee's delight, everyone was dressed in a costume, even if it was just a funny hat or graphic T-shirt. Most of the men put in minimal effort, throwing on a sports jersey like Paul or a plaid shirt and tool belt like Hector, but two men were dressed in tuxedos and wearing masks that hid their faces. They looked straight out of the cast of *Phantom of the Opera.*

The women at the party put more thought and effort into their costumes than their male counterparts. There were the usual costumes available for women: slutty nurse, slutty cat, and slutty bar wench. A few made their own costumes from clothes they had on hand, but two went all out. The two females, dressed in ball gowns and masks, accompanied the two males in tuxedos and masks. Neither Marlee nor Hector could figure out their identities. The four of them stayed together, talking among themselves and avoiding the other guests.

When Marlee approached the small group, she introduced herself, and they all nodded but did not reveal their identities. *That's odd*, she thought. It was a costume party, but most of the costumes did little to conceal the identity of the wearer. This foursome, however, was taking the masquerade seriously. If they were having fun, she didn't care. Besides, they were probably some of Hector's friends from the police department, and for whatever reason, he didn't want to tell her their identities. Or maybe the mayor's office. Her train of thought was interrupted when Nadia called her attention to the dwindling supply of appetizers.

"Just pop some of these in the oven," she said, gesturing to the freezer. "There are tater tots, chicken drummies, and cheese balls. If you find any other snacks in there, just throw them in the oven, too. Nothing's off limits. Except the walleye Hector caught this summer." Marlee was concerned that they were running out of food already yet pleased with the number of people attending the Open House. Both Ethan and Nadia had server experience. Ethan worked full time at Perkatory, a local coffee shop, while Nadia was employed at Perkins, a family dining chain restaurant. Marlee felt comfortable turning them loose in her kitchen to make do with whatever they could find to serve the guests.

Bridget shuffled into the kitchen. "How long until you start the murder mystery game?"

"Ten minutes, why?"

"Because I have to go to the bathroom, and it takes a while to maneuver in and out of this tail," Bridget whined. "Don't start without me, okay?"

"I might start talking about the game, but we won't draw the names for the participants until you get back," Marlee said. "Only nine people can play roles in the mystery. Everyone else acts as a detective."

Marlee went to the living room and stood on the stairs, hoping to gain the attention of the audience. Once enough people quieted down, she began to speak. "As many of you already know, we're going to be playing a murder mystery game tonight. We need nine people to play the roles involved in the mystery. Everyone else will function as a detective and can ask questions at the end. Those of you playing the assigned roles will be given notecards to fill you in on the character's backstory and possible motives for the murder. You will have to do a fair amount of ad-libbing during the game." She held up a plastic pumpkin and scraps of paper, instructing those who wished to be considered for a role to write down their name and put it in the bucket. One by one, people began lining up to sign their names and throw them into the pumpkin.

By the time Bridget waddled back from the bathroom, Marlee had finished explaining the rules of the game and collecting the names of those interested in playing a role. Marlee looked at her cousin, urging her to get her name in the pumpkin before the drawing. Bridget shook her head. "I want to be a detective," she said. About twenty people had "applied" for a role in the murder mystery, leaving the remainder to act as detectives.

One by one, Marlee drew out the names of the participants and announced their roles. To limit the confusion, each character would go by their occupation or the name of the person playing them. "Leanne, you'll be playing the part of the dinner host," she said handing over a notecard with the information to play the role. "The vacuum cleaner salesperson is Shelly McFarland," she said with a laugh, handing a notecard to her Supper Club friend. Professor Vernon, one of the guests from the third floor, was chosen to play the actor, while Hector was selected as the lumberjack.

"Hey, the role matches my costume," he said, playing along. Hector knew the basics of the game and that he was going to be playing the victim. It would require him to carry out his part until it was time to play dead. No one other than Hector and Marlee knew of his impending victim status.

Paul was chosen to play the kindergarten teacher and Leanne smiled at him as he took his notecard and returned her look with a grin. Even though Ethan and Nadia were technically working, Marlee told them they could play too. Both were chosen for parts; Ethan was the college student, and Nadia was the lawyer.

The next scrap of paper had only the letter "F" on it. When Marlee announced that F would play the role of the librarian, one of the unknown men in the tuxedo and mask stepped forward and accepted his notecard. The last name to be drawn was "Owl," and when that name was announced, one of the unknown masked women in the ballgown stepped forward. She would be playing the role of the chef. Marlee still had no idea who they were but was happy to see them taking part in the game.

"Everyone else is considered a detective. You won't have any role other than to keep your eyes and ears open for the next twenty minutes or so. Eventually, there will be a victim and then you can ask questions of the participants. Everyone understand the rules?" Marlee asked.

Hearing no objection, she ushered the nine participants to the dining room and urged them to sit in their places, designated by a placard. The nice dishes and stemware had been set out to replicate a fancy dinner. Cloth napkins in a subdued burgundy plaid were situated on the plates. Hector had overseen setting the table. She wasn't sure if it was done correctly, but it was close enough. Most of their friends and colleagues were more comfortable at a potluck than at a fancy dinner party. Everyone was seated in their respective positions, and Marlee, continuing in her role as Master of Ceremonies, was ready to announce further instructions. Before she could utter another word, there was a god-awful screech as Pippa launched herself onto the table, hissing in turn at each of the guests.

"Oh my god! I'm so sorry. This isn't part of the show," Marlee said, grabbing the hissing Persian and removing her from the table. One moment, and I'll be right back." She jogged up the stairs and locked Pippa in the bedroom she shared with Hector. "That was naughty. You're staying in here the rest of the night." Pippa took no notice of the scolding as she sat down, hoisted her leg over her shoulder, and began licking her butt hole.

When Marlee returned to the dining room, everyone was laughing, even Hector. And he hated Pippa. No one seemed too disturbed by the cat on the table other than Leanne. Her mouth was downturned, and she was brushing imaginary cat hair from the tablecloth. She straightened the "Host" placard even though Pippa had been nowhere near Leanne's table setting.

"My apologies, everyone. My cat was supposed to be locked in the bedroom, but somehow, she escaped. Anyway, back to the murder mystery game." Marlee proceeded to set the scene. The Host (Leanne) had invited eight people to a dinner party. They were all acquainted with Leanne, but none of them knew each other. At least not that anyone was disclosing. "Leanne, as the host, you can now start the dinner party."

Leanne collected herself and only briefly referred to the note card specifying her role. "Welcome to my dinner party. I'm so glad you all could make it. Since none of you know each other, let's go around the table, and everyone can introduce themselves and tell us a little bit about who you are. I'll start. Everyone already knows me. I'm Leanne, and this is my house," she said with a flourish of her arm. "I have a secret to share with all of you but will not do so until everyone has had a chance to introduce themselves. Will you begin," she asked looking to Professor Vernon on her left.

Professor Vernon, used to speaking before audiences, stood up and introduced himself, making eye contact with everyone in the room. "I'm an actor and have been in films along with some of the greats: Elizabeth Taylor, Danny Kaye, and Elvis Presley. You might recognize me from my most recent advertisement for Colon-Ease. I'm the constipation guy. Leanne was a student of mine at Sunshine State College. At that time, I was on hiatus from acting and was teaching for the theater department. She was a horrible actor, but we stayed in touch after the class until I found out she'd filed a complaint about me with the dean. That's why I wasn't offered another contract after that semester and had to move on. Luckily, I still had my acting career."

"My name is Shelly, and I'm a vacuum cleaner sales representative for the Kirby company. We make the finest in vacuum cleaners, and I'll get you all my contact information so we can schedule a free carpet cleaning in each of your homes. It's free! There's no obligation to buy." A round of chuckles was heard as Shelly got into her role as a salesperson. "I've known Leanne for twenty years, maybe more. We were neighbors when we were kids. In fact, she and two of her friends used to bully me. They chased me home from school and destroyed my homework. One time, Leanne pushed me down, and she and her friends kicked me. It didn't stop until my mom got involved."

"Uh, I'm Paul, and I'm a kindergarten teacher," he mumbled, unused to public speaking. "I'm the caretaker for my aunt. She used to own this house until she fell behind on the taxes and it was sold at auction. Leanne swooped in and bought it for a song." His voice drifted into nothingness, and he looked to his left.

It was Hector's turn, and although he was used to his real-life position of authority as a detective, he seemed uneasy as a pretend lumberjack. "Leanne and I know each other because I did repair work on her roof two years ago. She was pleased with my handiwork skills and has hired me to work on other fix-it projects. We also dated for a few months until she dumped me. I still don't know why."

"I am Owl, and I am a chef," said the unknown masked woman in the ballgown and tiara. "In fact, I was Leanne's personal chef for three years before she fired me. I have not seen her in over a year and have no idea why I was invited."

Owl looked to her left and motioned to Ethan that she was finished. "Hi, I'm Ethan, and I'm a college student. I met Leanne earlier this year when her car struck me in a crosswalk. My injuries were severe, and I'm still recovering the full use of my legs. To date, Leanne has not accepted any responsibility for the accident. Her insurance company denied my claim, and I'm in deep debt because of both my college expenses and my mounting medical bills."

When it was Nadia's turn, she looked around the room, sizing up everyone. "I'm Nadia, and I'm Leanne's attorney. She is my only client, and I dedicate all my time to her legal needs. I will be providing more details to all of you once Leanne shares her secret at the end of the introductions."

The masked man in the tuxedo was next. "I go by my first initial, F. I am a librarian and live in the world of thoughts, words, and books. Leanne recently made a generous donation to the local library, and we agreed to name the new wing of the library after her. Once the wing had been dedicated, Leanne withdrew most of her donations and refused to provide any more money. I have yet to understand why she acted in this unethical manner."

Everyone at the table turned to look at Leanne now that the introductions were complete. "I've not always lived my life in the most ethical way. I've cheated people, cut them out of my life with no explanation, harassed them, and taken advantage of their kindness and friendship. That ends today. You see, I'm dying and have a short time to live. I have wronged all of you and want to make amends before I pass. That is the reason you were all invited. I have an envelope for each of you stating how I will make amends, be it money, a written apology, or some other action. My hope is that you will forgive me for my poor character and think of me in a positive light now that I've made amends. To that end, I'd like to propose a toast." Leanne picked up her glass of red wine and said, "To all my friends; however I've wronged you, I want to make it right. Cheers!"

"Cheers!" The glasses clinked as everyone at the table joined in the toast. Everyone had red wine and took either a tentative sip or a generous gulp, depending on their preference for Cabernet.

Leanne continued with her apology tour, saying that she was a changed woman and not just because she was dying and afraid of going to Hell. All at the table, including the bystanders, were listening to Leanne when suddenly Hector stood and clutched his throat. He began frothing at the mouth and then collapsed on the floor.

Marlee had to hand it to Hector; he'd played his part well. They practiced earlier that day, and he knew exactly what he needed to do and how he needed to do it. No doubt he'd seen enough dead bodies on the job that he knew how to expertly play one. He lay on the floor near his dining room chair. Hector was on his back and both hands had fallen to his sides. As he fell, he'd wiped away the froth so that it wouldn't irritate him while the others tried to solve the mystery of his death.

"Oh my god," shrieked Leanne, right on cue. "What happened to Hector? Is he dead?" Some of the others at the table stood and went toward Hector's lifeless body, while others remained seated. Everyone leaned toward Hector's body, hoping to see if any obvious clues or guilty reactions would give the answer to who killed him and how.

Then the lights went out, leaving the house in complete darkness. Even the battery-operated candle in the middle of the table had gone dark. And then a gunshot rang out.

House of Games

They call it "taking one for the team."

Chapter 3

"Wait, that's not part of the show!" Marlee yelled. She regretted her stipulation that everyone hand in their cell phone when they entered the party. Not only was the electricity out, but they couldn't use the flashlights from their cell phones. The room was in complete darkness, with only a faint glimmer coming in from the streetlight at the corner of the block.

"Everyone, stay where you are," Hector shouted, now on his feet and taking command of the situation. He pulled out his cell phone and activated the flashlight. Clearly, he hadn't followed the no-cell-phone directive Marlee had put in place. "Is anyone hurt?"

Murmurs and a couple of giggles could be heard but not pinpointed due to the darkness of the room. "I'm serious, people! This isn't part of the game. A gun just went off, and I want to know if anyone is hurt." He shone the flashlight around the room, seeing a sea of confused and scared faces.

At that point, the lights in the house came back on. Everyone was in full view of everyone else. Hector was holding a gun that he'd picked up from the floor as he rose to his feet while Professor Vernon lay on his side in a bloody heap. If the reality of the situation had been in doubt up to this time, that was no longer the case. Screams and shouts rang out as people scrambled to move away from the professor's collapsed and bloody body. Marlee reached over to feel for a pulse and found none.

"He's dead," she said, her mouth agape. "Who has a gun?"

Everyone was shocked and looked around the room, waiting for someone to give an answer. Hector placed the gun on the dining room table as he called 911, demanding an immediate response from EMTs and the police. Within minutes, sirens were heard in the distance. The wailing of the police cars and ambulance was deafening as the vehicles arrived out front.

A party guest dressed as a clown pulled open the front door and the EMTs and police swarmed inside Marlee and Hector's home. Paramedics raced to Professor Vernon, attempting to revive him. It was no use. He was dead, and there was nothing that could be done for him. He lay on the floor as the puddle of blood on the rug grew larger and darker.

What seemed like a never-ending stream of police officers blocked off every entrance to the house, preventing anyone from coming or going. Rogers, the commanding officer at the scene, barked orders at the officers as they barricaded the party guests from the dining room. "No one leaves until you've been told to do so. Understand? An officer will interview each of you and they will tell you if you can leave or if you need to stay here. Most of you will be directed to come down to the police station for further interviewing. It might be tonight, or it might be in a day or two. Either way, we expect everyone's cooperation. No detail is too minor. Tell us everything you know about this man's death, and we'll sort out what's important." With that, Rogers gave a curt nod toward the crowd of about fifty and resumed conversations with two detectives on the scene.

It all happened so fast. Marlee's head was spinning as she tried to make sense of what she had just witnessed. A man was shot at their party during an electrical blackout. Who could have done this? And why?

She moved toward Hector, now being interviewed by his fellow officers from the Elmwood Police Department. As she neared him, an arm shot out, preventing her from approaching her boyfriend. "Ma'am, stay back," a uniformed officer directed. "Wait over here until you're told to leave." He motioned toward the kitchen as he turned to direct another party goer away from the area.

"But I live here," Marlee whispered to no one in particular. All she wanted to do was to get closer to Hector, to see that he was okay. He had been the pretend victim of the murder mystery party, but now he was a witness to the actual death that occurred. Since she couldn't stand near Hector, she waded through the sea of people and found her cousin, Bridget.

"What just happened?" Bridget asked, her eyes wide and glancing from one corner of the room to another. She had her arms wrapped around her, chilly in just a bikini top from the waist up.

Marlee grabbed a lightweight plaid blanket thrown over the back of a chair and pulled it around Bridget's shoulders. "I don't know. The murder mystery dinner was going as planned, everyone was following their notecards and playing their roles. Then the electricity went out and there was a gunshot. When the lights came back on, Professor Vernon was on the floor, bleeding."

Bridget nodded along in agreement with her cousin's recounting of the events. "That's what I saw too. Why would anyone shoot that old man?"

"I don't know. And I have no idea where the gun came from. We didn't have any guns as props in the murder mystery game. And if we did, it wouldn't have been a real one."

Two uniformed officers approached the McCabe cousins and directed them away from each other, no doubt to prevent them developing a shared story. Marlee knew this was customary practice in law enforcement investigations. Separate the witnesses and question them individually rather than in groups. This prevented the witnesses from contaminating each other's memories. When a group is questioned together, they come up with a shared story which may not reflect the actual occurrences each saw or heard.

After collecting Marlee's name, address, and other pertinent identifying information, the uniformed officer asked what she had seen and heard. Marlee gave a quick recount of events, just as she had told her cousin moments before.

"Why did the lights go out? Was it part of the murder mystery dinner?" The officer continued to scribble in his notepad, only looking up to ask a new question.

"No, it wasn't. I have no idea why the electricity went out. Everyone was enjoying the game, and then, poof, it was dark. That's when the gunshot happened. I never saw the gun before the game or during the game, and I don't know who brought it with them."

"Tell me what you know about Professor Vernon," the officer said, purposely leaving the question as wide open as possible to allow for any information, including assumptions, that Marlee could provide.

"He checked in last week and was booked for two more weeks. He was in the Gray Room upstairs and was our first guest. We had three other short-term guests last weekend and then no one other than Professor Vernon until Leanne and Paul checked in yesterday, separately. They met through an Internet dating site, and this weekend is their first date," Marlee recalled.

"Why was Professor Vernon staying in Elmwood for three weeks?"

Marlee sighed. She didn't know much about him since he'd booked and paid for the room through a travel site. He was sent a code to allow him onto the back staircase, which led up to his room, which also required a special code to enter. "I only talked to him twice, and that was just a quick visit. Professor Vernon is on sabbatical from Badger State University in La Crosse, Wisconsin. I'm not sure what brought him to Elmwood at the end of October. He said he was working on a research project, but when I asked him about it, he was vague. I got the sense that he'd told everyone he was doing research here but was just relaxing somewhere away from home for three weeks until he was ready to buckle down and work on his research."

"Why would he lie about doing research?" asked the officer.

Marlee sighed. "I don't know that he was lying about it. That was just the sense I got from talking to him. Like he wanted a little break before he got down to the real work, I'm a professor too and usually we can't stop talking about the research we're working on. The only time I didn't want to discuss it was when I was avoiding it."

"Sounds like you're making a lot of inferences based on your own experience." The officer had stopped jotting down notes and was now just looking at Marlee, sizing her up.

"That's true. I recognize that I'm reading a lot into his situation," Marlee admitted. "He told me on the second occasion that I talked to him that he was spending his time at the town library and a coffee shop. He left early most mornings, around the time Hector and I left for work. The guests are not provided breakfast, so there's never a time they might all be gathered in one spot. There's a common living area upstairs for the guests to share, so they may bump into each other there or on the back staircase as they are coming and going."

The uniformed officer continued with general questions, most of which Marlee could not or would not answer. She'd already been called out for letting her own assumptions color her view of Professor Vernon, and she wasn't about to open herself up much to the officer again. As the officer was closing his notebook, a detective approached them and said he'd take over.

"Can you show me Professor Vernon's room?" Shane Wallace was a newly minted detective on the Elmwood Police Force. He had come up through the ranks, serving as a uniformed officer in town for years before his promotion. Hector had recommended him for the position and had been informally mentoring the new detective for the past few months.

"Follow me." Marlee led the way through the kitchen and took the stairs up to the second floor, where her bedroom was located. Then she punched a series of numbers into a closed door that led them to the third floor. "Guests are not allowed on the second floor. They really aren't supposed to be on the main floor, either. That's why we have the separate entrance in the back that leads up to the top floor where the guest rooms are located."

She punched in the code to the Gray Room and opened the door for the detective. The gray and navy-plaid comforter coordinated nicely with the gray-painted walls and white trim. The room was neat and tidy other than the surface of the small corner desk. It was covered with papers, a notebook, pens, and a laptop. Professor Vernon had asked that daily room service not be provided until he requested it. *Maybe he really was working on his research*, Marlee thought as she looked at a desk eerily similar to hers the previous year when she was writing a paper.

"I overheard you tell the officer that you didn't think the professor was working on his research. Why did you come to that conclusion if he said he was at the library every day? And did you know about his paperwork here?"

"I didn't know about whatever work he was doing here," Marlee said, gesturing toward the desk. "I assumed he was doing some type of reading or research at the library, just not on his sabbatical project. Maybe he was researching family genealogy, or learning to speak German, or something else. I thought he was pursuing an interest but not doing actual academic research."

Detective Wallace gave her a quizzical look. "Explain that to me a bit more."

She realized that he probably wasn't familiar with the academic world from a professor's perspective, so she launched into a brief overview. "After a certain number of years at the university, a professor is eligible to apply for a sabbatical. That means they are relieved of their teaching and other academic duties for one or two semesters to pursue research or specialized training. The professor must have a well thought out plan for the research, as many of the applications are rejected."

"So not everyone gets a sabbatical. And once a professor gets one, do they have to report in weekly to show their progress?"

Marlee chuckled. "No, the professor is expected to have their research completed or nearly finished by the end of the sabbatical. Often, they will use the sabbatical to travel to another place for research. I went to Dublin to conduct a comparative study between prison systems in Ireland and the United States. That research was the basis for two papers I had published, which helped me secure my promotion to full professor."

"It's a big deal, then. Is that what you're telling me?"

"Yes, it's a ginormous deal. Without the release time from classes, committees, advising, and the rest of academic expectations, most of us would not have the time or the energy to conduct a thorough research project. To have the time off to work on a project, one that's your passion, is a very big deal."

Detective Wallace seemed unimpressed with Marlee's impassioned position on research and sabbaticals. "Must be nice to get several months off to work on whatever you want."

She let the remark slide. Marlee was used to non-academic types making quick judgments about the work and responsibilities at a university. Most people assumed it was easy work, not realizing the effort it took to conduct research and write peer-reviewed papers. Some research projects spanned decades.

The detective put on plastic gloves and began to look around the Gray Room. Marlee stayed, watching as he rifled through the loose pages on the desk. Looking over his shoulder, he said, "You can go back downstairs. I'll be in here for a bit."

Being dismissed was bad enough, but it added insult to injury when it was in your own home. Marlee stepped out of the room, but instead of going back downstairs as directed, she fussed around the kitchenette area of the third floor. She ran hot water in the sink, added a squirt of Dawn, and placed utensils and coffee cups in to soak. Crumbs from a guest's snack were on the counter, so she brushed those into her palm and dumped them into the trash. As she tidied up, Marlee craned her neck, peering into the Gray Room to keep an eye on the detective and his progress.

Detective Wallace sifted through the papers on the desk, lifting them up one by one and looking them over before returning to the original places. When he got to Professor Vernon's yellow legal pad, Marlee observed him rip off the top sheet of paper and put it in his inside jacket pocket.

That's weird, Marlee thought. *Why wouldn't he put evidence in a plastic bag to preserve it?* As she was pondering the detective's actions, he caught her eye.

"Didn't I make myself clear? I told you to go back downstairs and wait with the others. This whole third floor is off limits until further notice," he barked.

"Okay, okay," Marlee threw up her hands in defeat. "Jeez," she mumbled as she walked out the door and down the stairs to the first floor.

"What's going on up there?" Bridget asked once Marlee was back in the kitchen.

"Detective Wallace is looking through the Gray Room and asked me a bunch of questions about Professor Vernon. Then he kicked me out and said the whole third floor was off-limits. That guy is on a power trip," she said, recalling that she hadn't particularly liked him when she met him that summer at a fellow detective's barbeque. "And I don't think he's very professional. He ripped off a sheet of paper from a legal pad in the room, folded it, and put it in the inside pocket of his suit jacket. That's in violation of every rule regarding the handling of evidence."

"Why would he do that? Surely, he knows better," Bridget commented.

"Yeah, I don't think it was a lack of knowing proper protocol. He didn't think I was still on the third floor. I'm not sure if he knows I saw him put it in his pocket. Then he saw me and ordered me to come back down here." Marlee looked around the kitchen and the living room, noting that most of the partygoers were gone. "Where did everyone go?"

"The officers got their names and contact info and sent them home. Everyone was able to get their cell phones back. The ones who were at the table or up front watching everything before the gunshot are still here," Bridget said. "They told me I could leave, but I wanted to see how you were doing."

"I'm in shock. Who had a motive to shoot Professor Vernon? It had to be somebody at the table, right?"

"Maybe. However, it could be anyone who was at the party. The lights went out for about two minutes, so anyone could have shot him and then dropped the gun under the table," Bridget commented.

"So, if someone wanted to kill Professor Vernon, they had to rely on the chance that the electricity would be off all over town? That seems hard to believe. Nobody knows when it's going to be off unless it's a scheduled outage for some specific reason," Marlee said.

Bridget looked around to make sure no one else was listening. "I just overheard a couple of the officers talking. There wasn't a power outage all over town. Not even just in your neighborhood. Someone cut the electricity here in your house long enough for someone else to shoot the professor and stand there looking shocked like everyone else."

The murder mystery game. The lights going out. Brilliant! I only wish I could write the ending to this story.

Chapter 4

"No way! Two people were in on this?" Marlee couldn't believe her ears. "One person went to the basement and flipped the breaker while another shot Professor Vernon. Then, the breaker was flipped back, and they both resumed their positions." It was the only logical assumption for the illogical occurrences.

"That's what it sounded like to me from what I overheard," Bridget insisted. "It sounds crazy, I know."

"Who from the party was missing while we were conducting the murder mystery game? That must be the person who cut the electricity. They snuck down to the basement and flipped the breaker. Then, after they heard the gunshot, they flipped it back on and came upstairs. It would have been easy enough for someone to do this undetected since we were all engrossed in the game at first. Then, after the gunshot, we were all in shock over Professor Vernon's death. Did you see anyone leave?"

Bridget shook her head from side to side. "No, it was just like you said. We were all really into the game, and then when the gun went off, everyone was hyper-focused on that. At first, we all thought that was part of the game and that the gunshot was fake."

"I remember when the lights went out and the gun fired that some people were laughing. They thought it was all scripted. Everyone did, except Hector and I, because we knew the whole plot of the murder mystery storyline. No one else did," Marlee said. "What do you remember before the lights went out?"

"Hector had just taken a drink from his glass and fallen to the floor. The others seated at the table were the couple who were on their date, Professor Vernon, Shelly, Ethan, and Nadia, and then the two who went by F and Owl. I was standing at the foot of the table, across from Leanne, who was acting as the dinner party host. Next to me stood Diane and Gwen from Supper Club and a lady I recognized as a secretary from one of the departments at MSU. Can't think of her name right now. We were all front and center, so I don't know who was behind us. I was intent on solving the mystery, so I was only paying attention to the table and the people seated around it." Bridget frowned as she tried to dredge up any other memories from earlier in the night.

"I was acting as Master of Ceremonies to explain the game and get the ball rolling. Once Leanne started talking as the host of the dinner party, I moved off to the side of the room. But, like everyone else, I was focused on the table. Mostly, I was focused on Hector because he really overplayed his role when we practiced this afternoon. I had to tell him to tone it down and 'die' quickly without several minutes of moaning and frothing at the mouth."

"Do you know everyone who was here tonight?" Bridget asked.

"Most of them, but there were a few I didn't know. And a handful of people Hector invited, either from work or the gym, that I hadn't met. But you know what? There was a guest book just inside the door, near the sign-up sheet for the door prizes. Let's go take a look."

Marlee and Bridget tried to look nonchalant as they walked from the kitchen through the living room. The guest book lay on the end table near the front door. When no one was looking, Marlee reached for it and tucked it between the folds of her velvet witch's dress. She and Bridget then scampered back to the privacy of the kitchen without the watchful eyes of the uniformed officers. As Marlee glanced over her shoulder she saw Professor Vernon, still on the dining room rug with three crime scene technicians around him. Hector was off to the side, being questioned by officers.

The guest book had three full pages denoting names and cities of residence. Marlee's memory wasn't that great, so she doubted she would be able to remember the names and locations of the people she didn't know. It was not an issue, as Bridget took out her cell phone and snapped pictures of the entries on all three pages.

"How did you get your phone back? Everybody was supposed to hand them in when they came to the party so no one would be disrupting the murder mystery dinner with calls, photos, and texts," Marlee said with a frown. Bridget was always trying to circumnavigate the rules, especially when the rules had been put in place by Marlee.

"The cops handed them back to us after we finished our interviews and were told that we could leave, so don't worry, I didn't disobey your 'no phone' rule," Bridget snarked. "So, no, it wasn't the cell phones that disrupted your murder mystery party. It was the actual murder that caused the disruption."

"Okay, don't get your tail in a twist. I was just asking. Everybody is so on edge tonight," she grumbled, thinking of the uniformed officer and then the detective who had snapped at her and now Bridget. Realizing the reason for everyone's impatience, she muttered, "Um, understandably, of course."

The only people remaining in the home were Marlee, Bridget, Hector, and a slew of law enforcement officers and crime scene technicians. And Professor Vernon's dead body. Marlee could feel the bile rising in her throat as the reality hit her. Someone had died in their home. Correction: someone had been killed in their home, and it was carried out by at least two other people known to her and Hector.

Detective Wallace walked into the kitchen and gave Marlee a vicious stare upon spotting the guest book. "That's evidence. Give it here," he demanded, holding out his hand.

"Aren't you going to put it in a plastic bag and tag it?" Marlee asked, detailing proper police procedure when collecting evidence.

"Of course I am," he sneered as he reached for a folded plastic bag inside his jacket pocket and slid the guest book off the counter into the bag.

Marlee took a deep breath, knowing this was an opportune time to confront the newly minted detective on what she had seen earlier in the Gray Room. He'd ripped a sheet of paper from the top of Professor Vernon's legal pad and stuffed it in the inside pocket of his suit jacket without first placing it in a bag and then labeling it as evidence. On one hand, Detective Wallace would be compelled to either deny or justify his actions. It would let him know that Marlee knew he'd breached proper procedure with evidence. On the other hand, what was she hoping to achieve through this confrontation? It would only serve to irritate, embarrass, and possibly alienate the detective.

She decided to err on the side of caution and keep her observation to herself. Besides, she had another way to figure out what was on the legal pad. "I'm guessing you're going to seal off the house for tonight and want us to stay somewhere else."

The detective nodded absent-mindedly as he wrote on a label, affixing it to the bagged guest book. "That's right. You won't have access to the place for a while. We'll let you know when you can come back."

"I'll need to pack some things for Hector and me and get my cat and her carrier. Is it okay if I run upstairs and get what I need?" Marlee asked.

"Yeah, but be quick about it."

"Bridget, you'll have to help me get the cat carrier down from the hall closet. Hector usually gets it, but he's still being interviewed," Marlee said, grabbing her cousin by the arm and pulling her along toward the staircase.

Once they were on the second floor, Bridget said, "I thought you kept Pippa's pet carrier in the garage. Why did you move it upstairs?"

"It is in the garage. I'm using that as an excuse to run up to the third floor so I can look at the legal pad in the Gray Room," Marlee explained as they continued up the steps to the third floor. She punched in the code and opened the door.

"Ah, I bet I can guess what you're going to do," Bridget said with a chuckle. "I've seen this on a hundred police shows. You're going to use a pencil to shade the next piece of paper on the legal pad. The indentations from the first page will show up, and then we can see what was handwritten on the top page."

Marlee grinned at her cousin. "Very good. You should apply to be a detective." They rounded the corner to the Gray Room, finding the door closed and bright yellow tape securing the door. Removing the tape would be an immediate red flag to police and crime scene techs that the room had been entered and possibly tampered with after being secured by Detective Wallace. "Crap! I didn't think he'd have it sealed off so soon."

"Now what?" Bridget asked. "We can't just rip off the Crime Scene tape and reattach it, can we?"

"No, we can't," Marlee said dejectedly. "That piece of paper must have something important on it, or else the detective never would've taken it. And why would he stuff it inside his pocket like he didn't want anyone else to know he'd taken it? If he had just bagged and tagged it as usual, I never would've given it a second thought."

"I thought Hector was his mentor at work. Surely, Wallace knows better than this," Bridget said. "He must have gathered evidence a hundred times before."

"I'll talk to Hector and see what he says. It's sloppy police work at best and concealing evidence at the worst. Either way, it's not a good look for Detective Wallace," Marlee said. "Hector won't like this at all, especially since he recommended Wallace for the job."

They returned to the second floor, and Marlee began packing a couple of days' worth of clothes for both her and Hector. Pippa jumped onto the bed, nuzzling her arm and purring. "Hey, kitty. We're moving out for a day or two. What do you think of that?"

"You can all stay at my place," Bridget offered. "No sense in paying for a hotel when I have extra room.

She smiled at her cousin appreciatively. "Thanks. We'll try not to make pests out of ourselves." With a huge sigh, she zipped up the oversized tote bag and went into the bathroom to gather their toiletries. She placed them in a separate tote and slung it over her shoulder. Marlee grabbed Pippa around the middle, and they made their way back to the first floor, with Bridget lugging the largest bag.

"I guess Hector moved the cat carrier to the garage," Marlee said within hearing range of Detective Wallace and two uniformed officers. "Bridget, would you grab it while I gather up Pippa's things?"

Bridget returned with a large pet taxi, a purple fluffy blanket covering the bottom. She set it on the floor in the kitchen, and Marlee attempted to place a now-growling cat inside. Pippa braced her front paws against the sides of the pet carrier, preventing Marlee from getting her inside. It took some maneuvering, but the grumpy Persian was eventually stuffed into the cage without any physical harm to Marlee.

After gathering up Pippa's wet food and dry kibble, food and water dishes, toys, and litter box, she hauled them out to her Honda CR-V and placed them in the rear. She'd wait until they were ready to go before placing Pippa in there, as it was late October and too chilly for an indoor kitty to be in an unheated garage. Marlee came back inside, glancing around the corner to see Hector still talking to officers. "*Cop talk,*" she thought as she moved around the kitchen, gathering her vitamins and Hector's protein supplements. He was a dedicated detective with decades of service and no incidents. Of course, he would want to thoroughly discuss a man being killed in his own home. "*Maybe I should just tell him I'm leaving and that he can come over to Bridget's when he's finished talking about the case.*"

Marlee cautiously entered the dining room, hoping to avoid getting her ass chewed again by Detective Wallace. "Um, excuse me. Hector, I just wanted to let you know Bridget said we can stay at her house tonight. I was told we would have to be out of the house for tonight at least. I have Pippa, and I'm headed over there now. See you in a bit."

"I wouldn't wait up," Detective Wallace said matter-of-factly. "Hector is coming down to the station to give his statement."

"Why? Didn't he just tell you everything that he saw?" Marlee was confused. She assumed they, along with some of the other party guests, would have to go to the police department within the next day or two to give full statements, but she didn't understand why Hector needed to go right now.

"Can I have a minute?" Hector asked the other detectives and officers on the scene. After getting a nod from Detective Wallace, he came over to Marlee. She noticed the lines between his eyes were pronounced, a giveaway that he was stressed. Of course, he was stressed, a man was just shot at their home.

"What's going on?" Marlee asked, placing her hand on Hector's upper arm. "Why can't you wait and go tomorrow?"

"Because of the gun that was used to shoot Professor Vernon. It was my service weapon."

They'll get theirs. That's one thing I'll be sure of before I go. Nobody messes with Professor Jerome A. Vernon!

Chapter 5

"Your gun? That was your gun under the table? How did it get there?" Marlee's mind was swimming with questions. Hector kept his service weapon either on him or in the locked gun cabinet in a closet on the first floor. No one had a key to the gun cabinet, not even Marlee. Unless Hector took it out, there was no way the gun would be anywhere but locked inside the cabinet.

Hector ran his hand through his thick salt and pepper hair. "I don't know. I locked it in the gun cabinet Thursday night when I got home from work. No one else has the key. The gun under the table looked a lot like mine, but I wasn't sure. After the squad arrived, I checked my gun cabinet, and it was locked, but nothing was inside."

"Wait, they don't think you shot Professor Vernon, do they?" Marlee gasped. How could Hector's fellow officers believe he'd shoot someone in his own house? And not only were the officers part of the same brotherhood and sisterhood as Hector, but he had seniority over nearly all of them.

Hector shrugged. "I hope not, but you have to look at it from their perspective. My gun was found at the scene of the murder, and I'm the one holding it when the lights came back on. They will check for fingerprints on the gun, and, hopefully, someone else's besides mine are detected. One of the crime scene techs already swabbed my hands for gunpowder residue, and they'll take my shirt for testing once I'm down at the station. These are all steps I would've taken if I was called in to investigate."

Her understanding of police procedure was outweighed by her emotions. "They seriously can't think you shot Professor Vernon. How dumb do they think you are? Nobody would shoot a guest with their own service weapon and then be found holding that same gun."

"You'd be surprised. People can be pretty dumb," Hector said. "I have to go now. They're waving me over. I'll call you when I know what's going on." The weight of the matter added years to Hector's handsome face. Earlier that day, he'd been almost giddy as he finished hanging the last of the decorations, anticipating the fun that their guests would have that night. He had acted grumpy and put upon, but he'd been enjoying himself and the upcoming party. And now he was a tired, middle-aged man, about to be hauled down to the police station for questioning.

Marlee teared up as she watched Hector climb into the back of a police car as Detective Wallace and another detective climbed into the front seat. *At least they didn't handcuff him*, she thought. That would just add insult to injury. Marlee knew he wasn't under arrest, just being taken in immediately for more questioning. She tried to look at the matter from a neutral perspective rather than the highly personal perspective she and Hector were living.

"Doing okay?" Bridget asked. She'd moved beside Marlee and had watched as Hector was driven away in the squad car.

She took a deep breath. "I have to keep my head clear and figure out what happened."

"No, you need to pack up your cat and leave. I told you both more than once that the house is a crime scene and you need to vacate. Right now," hissed the uniformed officer who initially interviewed Marlee.

Marlee threw up her hands. "Okay, no need to get huffy puffy. We're on our way out." She drove around the block after backing out of the garage, as she wanted to see the front of the house.

"What are you doing?" Bridget asked as they cruised by for the second time.

"I don't know. There's something that isn't sitting right with me."

"Besides the murder, you mean?"

"Yeah, obviously. It's something I can't put my finger on. More of a feeling that I can't put into words," Marlee mumbled, trying to make sense of it. "It's like I know something but it's at the back of my brain and needs to be uncovered." Pippa's mournful wails interrupted the conversation, and it was agreed that they'd drive to Bridget's house without further ado.

Fifteen minutes later, Bridget held open the door from her garage leading into the house as Marlee hauled in Pippa and all her kitty supplies, plus the bags of clothes and toiletries she'd packed for Hector and herself. It took four trips from the car to the living room, and once Marlee was finished, she plopped on the floor beside the cat carrier. "Do you have any alcohol?"

"Of course," said Bridget, springing into action like a firefighter at the scene of an arson. She returned to the living room with two wine glasses and a bottle of

Cabernet. "I know you've been avoiding red wine, but it's all I have."

"I'll make an exception for today," Marlee said as she whipped the velvet dress off over her head to offset the impending hot flash that menopause plus red wine and a variety of other delectable substances now caused. Dressed in a dark tank top and gray shorts, she moved toward the coffee table and filled her glass. "Damn, that's good."

Bridget scooted closer to the coffee table and filled her glass. "Someone died at your party. On Halloween. During a murder mystery game. If this was a storyline in a novel, I'd find it contrived and unbelievable."

Pippa's howls reminded everyone she was still in her carrier and needed to be released so she could inspect her new surroundings. Marlee reached over and let her out. She and Bridget had agreed that Pippa would be locked in the living room rather than allowed to roam the whole house as she did at home.

"I know. The whole thing sounds like it's part of the murder mystery game, but it's not. Someone was shot by another person at the Open House. And now Hector is in the hot seat because it was his gun supposedly used in the murder. Everybody must know he didn't do it, but it still looks bad. How would his gun get out of his locked cabinet? It makes Hector look like he's sloppy about gun safety and that he lied about the gun being locked up. And as a detective, it just doesn't look good to have someone killed in your home during a party."

"You said Hector's gun was 'supposedly' used in the shooting. You think there might be another weapon?" Bridget scrunched up her nose at the idea of two unseen firearms floating around the party.

"Most likely, it was Hector's gun, but we don't know for sure. The gun will be sent to the crime lab for ballistics testing to determine if it was indeed fired and if the bullet matches the one found in Professor Vernon's body. If the gun wasn't fired or the bullet doesn't match, then Hector's gun wasn't used in the commission of the crime."

"And if his gun was used, then the question is who fired it," Bridget said.

"Right. So now the police are not only questioning Hector further but testing his clothes for gunpowder residue and possible blood, tissue, or other blowback when the bullet entered the professor's body. Since Hector picked up the gun after the shooting, some gunpowder residue could have transferred to his hands." Marlee took a deep breath and sighed. Not only was she worried about Hector, but she felt a deep sense of responsibility for Professor Vernon's death since it occurred at her house while he was a paying guest.

"Poor Professor Vernon," Bridget said, reading her cousin's mind. "Who would shoot him? He seemed like a harmless old man."

Marlee rose to her feet with the aid of the coffee table. "Do you have any poster board? We need to put together a crime chart. Actually, we need two charts. One with a drawing of where everyone was located at the table. The other will be a typical crime chart with suspects listed and the linkages noted between them and the victim."

Bridget ran to a spare bedroom that doubled as her office and returned with two white poster boards and a container of colored markers. "I bought these supplies last time there was a murder in town."

"That's a sad commentary on our life and the town of Elmwood," Marlee said as they moved to the breakfast bar. Sitting side by side on bar stools, the cousins began to recall the locations of everyone sitting at the table during the murder mystery party.

"Leanne was at the head of the table since she was acting as the host for the murder mystery party," Bridget said.

"Yes, and she went around the table clockwise having everyone introduce themselves," Marlee recalled. "Next to Leanne was Professor Vernon, then Shelly, the third guest was Paul, and Hector was the last person on that side of the table. On the other side was Owl, then Ethan, and Nadia, with F sitting to Leanne's right."

"Yep, that's how I remember it too. And you were standing off to the side after your emcee duties were finished and Leanne began. I was at the foot of the table, straight across from Leanne. Diane and Gwen from Supper Club were beside me, and so was some lady that works at MSU, but I don't know her name. Everyone else was behind me, so I didn't know the location of anyone else. I was concentrating on figuring out whodunnit in the murder mystery game."

"I was focused on Hector and making sure he followed the plan. He tends to go off script, and I didn't want him to mess up the whole thing. To his credit, he did a fantastic job," Marlee said as she opened Bridget's refrigerator and gazed inside. "I didn't get much of a chance to eat earlier. Do you have anything other than vegetables?"

Bridget rummaged around in the fridge and found some fancy cheese, then paired it with crackers she found in the pantry. "Will this do?"

"You bet," Marlee said as she sliced off a generous hunk of Gruyere, sandwiching it between two water crackers. "I think better when I have snacks." She then reached over Bridget's arm for the wine bottle. She began pouring wine into the glass and then stopped. "You know what I just realized?"

"That we're almost out of wine?"

"No, that people at the table had all moved once the electricity came back on. Nobody was sitting in the same spot. Hector was standing near his chair. I think some of the others were standing by their chairs, too, but I can't remember for sure."

"Oh, wow. I can't remember either. It was so dark after the electricity went out, but I could hear people moving around. And then the gun fired, and I remember hearing more movement. At that point, I still thought this was part of the show."

"Before the power went out, somebody had to sneak down to the basement to flip the breaker. And then, in the cover of darkness, somebody else fired the gun," Marlee recalled. "Did you see anyone go to the basement? Or anyone hanging around by the door to the basement?"

"No, I don't remember anyone acting suspiciously before the party started. Everyone seemed excited to be at the Open House and ready for the murder mystery game to begin. We were all joking around and talking about our costumes. Let's put together a list of everyone we personally know who was at the party," Bridget suggested, setting aside the poster board with the depiction of the murder mystery game table.

The cousins started a list of the people known to them who were at the party. Within ten minutes, they'd accounted for fifty-one people. "The ones we don't know are the four people that were overdressed and wearing masks. Owl and F were two of them. I never heard the names of the other two. Then there were two men that Hector knows from his gym. His workout buddies, he calls them." Marlee tried to recall their names but couldn't remember even though Hector talked about them all the time. Since he'd started working out regularly at the gym that's all he could talk about, and Marlee tended to tune out that line of conversation since she wasn't in an exercise mood lately. Or ever.

Bridget pulled out her phone. "Now, let's look at the photo of the guest book and see who we don't know." They hunched over the phone, looking for unfamiliar names. "Just because someone was there doesn't mean they automatically signed the guest book. Some may have skipped on purpose or forgot about it."

"True," Marlee agreed. "I hate signing guest books. The only time I sign in is when I want to prove that I really did attend. Like for a funeral. If I'm going to a funeral, I want credit for being there."

"That's kind of shallow, don't you think?" Bridget gave her cousin a disapproving look.

Marlee ignored the dig. "There aren't any signatures for Owl, F, or the other two who were with them. Why wouldn't they sign in? Did they come to the party with intentions to kill?"

Marlee grabbed Bridget's phone to take a closer look at the photo of the guest book. "Actually, I'm not seeing any names that I don't recognize. That means some people didn't sign in, most notably the four in formal wear. Maybe the four who were overly dressed up are known to me and I didn't recognize them because of their costumes."

"But that doesn't make any sense. All you have to do is look at the names on the guest list and identify the costumes each were wearing and when you saw them."

"I guess it's possible someone may have been there dressed in one costume and then came back dressed as one of the four unknown people," Marlee said. "But why?"

"To kill Professor Vernon?" Bridget guessed.

"This is a very elaborate plan to kill him. And why shoot him at a party with fifty potential witnesses? It seems like there are a lot of other ways to kill someone without going to the trouble of getting Hector's gun out of the locked cabinet without anyone knowing, sneaking down to the basement and cutting the power, shooting Professor Vernon during the power outage, and then blending in with everyone else at the party. I mean, if someone just wanted to kill Professor Vernon, they could shoot him outside the house or at the library or when he was leaving the coffee shop. Every scenario that I can think of is less complicated than what actually happened."

"None of it makes any sense," Bridget agreed.

A loud knock at the front door startled them. They were both on edge after the earlier events of the night.

Bridget peeked out the front window near the door. "It's Hector," she said, relieved as she opened the door.

"Are you okay? I'm so glad you're back," Marlee said as she rushed into Hector's arms. "We were worried about you."

"It's a big mess," Hector said as he sunk onto the couch. "I'm suspended from work until further notice."

House of Games

What would I do differently? I wouldn't have put so much trust in the wrong people.

Chapter 6

"Suspended?" Bridget's eyes were wide with disbelief. "How can they suspend you when you're innocent?"

Marlee sunk onto the couch beside her boyfriend and put her arms around him. "I'm so sorry." There wasn't much more she could say. It really should not have been a surprise to any of them that Hector would be relieved of his work duties, albeit temporarily, while the matter of Professor Vernon's murder was sorted.

"I knew it was going to happen. Hell, it's what I would have done if I oversaw the investigation, and a fellow officer had a murder carried out at his house with his own weapon. Still, it's a kick in the nuts. They all know me and know my only involvement was picking up the gun after I found it on the floor," Hector shook his head in disbelief. The rational part of him understood why he was put on administrative leave, but his emotional side could not understand it.

"What do you think happened? Bridget and I've been running through all kinds of motives and scenarios. We started working on a crime chart and a diagram of the seating arrangement at the murder mystery table. Still, we can't make sense of it."

Hector helped himself to the fancy cheese and crackers Bridget had set on the coffee table. She'd poured him a glass of Cabernet, and even though he wasn't much of a wine drinker, he drained the glass in four big gulps. "Well, it's my gun for sure. The serial number on the weapon I found under the table matches the one recorded for my gun so that part of the mystery is solved. But there's no way I just left it lying around the house. It was locked in the gun cabinet, and no one else had a key."

Marlee nodded in support of her boyfriend. "Never once have you left your service weapon lying around the house. You either have it on you, or it's locked away. Someone broke into your cabinet and retrieved the gun, then used it to shoot Professor Vernon. It makes me wonder if you were set up."

"Who would set up Hector?" Bridget asked. "I'm sure there are plenty of people mad at him since he helped send them or their loved ones to prison, but who would go to these lengths?"

"Yeah, if someone wanted revenge there are less complicated ways to do it. They could have planted drugs in my vehicle or claimed that I used excessive force during an arrest. This plan is sophisticated and depended on split-second timing," Hector said.

"And it involves more than one person," Marlee announced. "Bridget said she overheard a uniformed officer say that the electricity didn't go out all over town or even around our neighborhood. It was just our house. Somebody flipped the breaker in the basement, waited until they heard the gunshot, and then a couple of minutes later, flipped the breaker back and came upstairs to join the rest of us in figuring out what happened."

"Wallace brought this up when he was questioning me at the station, but I didn't know if it was true or if he was just throwing out different scenarios to see what I'd say," Hector said. It was customary practice in law enforcement to lie to suspects in hopes of gaining more information than they intended to reveal. On television shows the police will tell a suspect that another suspect has ratted them out and pinned the whole crime on them. Sometimes, that will make the original defendant come clean about some of their involvement while trying to mitigate their overall culpability.

"It's what I overheard, so I don't know if it's fact or speculation. It makes sense. The timing it took to coordinate the power outage with the gunshot would take more than one person, don't you think?" Bridget asked.

"That right there tells me it's someone who is familiar with the house. The breaker is tucked away in a corner behind the washer and dryer. Someone wouldn't just walk into the basement and be able to see it. They would have to spend time searching. Or already know where it's located," Hector said, nodding toward his empty wine glass.

Bridget reached for another bottle, uncorked it, and filled the glass to the rim. "So, either it's someone who has been here since you bought the house or someone who had been in the house when it was owned previously. That doesn't exactly narrow down the suspect list. Do you know who the owners were before you two bought it?"

"We bought it from brothers who live in New York. It belonged to their parents, and it was the home where they grew up. When the parents both passed away, it became part of their estate, and the sons sold it since neither had plans to move back to Elmwood," Marlee said. "I can't remember their names. We never met them. I don't think they ever came back to do any work on the house; they just got it done. And all the paperwork for the sale was done online and through our realtors. They were motivated to sell and were open to negotiating when we offered a price lower than what they were asking."

"I spoke with one of them on the phone after the sale. I had questions about the furnace, and he was able to answer them. Seemed like a decent guy on the phone," Hector recalled. "We knew it was a fixer-upper when we bought it, but older houses have all kinds of quirks that require the previous owner's knowledge."

"That was before the old furnace blew, and we had to get a new one. It was December or January when that happened," Marlee said. "I remember it well because we were without a furnace for a night, and we camped out in the living room with space heaters."

"That new furnace set us back quite a bit," Hector commented, forgetting for a moment about his legal predicament.

Getting back on topic, Marlee brought the table diagram to the coffee table and splayed it out before them. "Does this look right to you? Bridget and I thought this was how everyone was seated when the murder mystery game began."

He nodded. "Looks right. People moved, though, once the electricity went out and the gun went off. I caught a glimpse of a man over by the kitchen when the lights came back on, but I don't know who it was. I only saw his back. We should put together a diagram of where everyone was when the lights came back on."

"We already talked about that, but neither of us could remember. I know almost everyone who was seated at the table was standing when the lights came back on. I was focused on you and the gun and then Professor Vernon when I saw he was on the floor," Marlee said.

"And I was at the end of the table, right across from where Leanne had been sitting," Bridget said with a glance toward Hector. "Diane and Gwen from Supper Club were near me, but I don't know who else was behind me. I thought that was all part of the murder mystery game and was intent on figuring out who had supposedly poisoned you."

Hector removed his glasses and began polishing them with the tail of his untucked white T-shirt. "When we first started the game, I remember seeing Diane standing beside you, Bridget, but then I lost track of everyone. I'm usually very observant, but tonight I was focused on playing my part as instructed, so the game went off without a hitch."

Realizing that none of them had a good handle on where most of the party attendees were, Marlee switched gears. "Did Wallace or any of the other cops give you any ideas as to why Professor Vernon was killed?"

"They questioned me about him. How long he'd been staying here, when he was scheduled to leave, and what he's been up to during his stay. I didn't have any first-hand information; everything I know about him is what you told me," Hector said, gesturing to Marlee.

"Tonight was the first time I'd met him in person, just to introduce myself and welcome him to our home. I asked if he found the accommodation acceptable, and he said everything was fine. He asked if burning a candle in his room was allowed, and I said we didn't permit that because of a possible fire hazard. And that was it. A few minutes later, the names were drawn for the game, and we sat at the table."

"I really wish Bettina was in town this weekend," Marlee said. Bettina Crawford was a detective with the Elmwood Police Department. Not only was she Hector's trusted colleague, but she was one of Marlee's best friends. Her ex had the kids, and she had taken a much-needed weekend off to travel to the Black Hills with her new boyfriend. Although always professional, Bettina would be able to provide extra details from the case that Hector was not privy to since his suspension.

"Me too," Hector said. "She should be back in town tomorrow. I know she's back at work on Monday. She'll be limited in what she can say. I don't want her to risk her career just to leak information to us."

"Of course not," Bridget agreed. "But we know that Bettina has a way of doing her job but also letting us know what's going on."

Hector turned to look at Bridget and Marlee. "Oh, really? Is that how you two find out so much about the past murders?"

"No, it's just good detective work on our part," Marlee said, throwing Bridget a disgusted look. The last thing she needed was Hector getting on her case about how she and Bridget obtained their information when informally investigating a case that Hector and his team were officially investigating. He often tried to squelch Marlee and Bridget's efforts to find out what happened, insisting that the police had the ultimate authority and the McCabe cousins and their amateur sleuthing, were more of a nuisance than a help.

By this time, they were all exhausted and had not come up with any new conclusions about the shooting of Professor Vernon. Marlee and Hector retired to the guest bedroom while Bridget went to her own room. Pippa remained locked in the living room and made her displeasure known by constant wailing and scratching at the door. Marlee finally got up and let her into their bedroom, much to Hector's displeasure. He and Pippa held a mutual dislike of each other. After Marlee got into bed and turned out the lights, Pippa jumped atop the bed and curled up beside her.

It was nearly nine o'clock when Marlee rolled out of bed on Sunday morning. As upset as she'd been the night before, she doubted she'd get much sleep at all. That wasn't the case, as she drifted off almost immediately and never woke in the night, not even to pee. The aroma of coffee from Bridget's fancy schmancy coffee machine enticed Marlee out of bed, and Pippa trailed close behind.

Bridget was busy playing host while Hector sat at the breakfast bar and enjoyed a cup of coffee and a blueberry scone, straight from the oven. "You baked scones?" Marlee was incredulous that her cousin had the time and energy to bake after their ordeal the previous night.

"They're from a mix. I just added water and stirred," Bridget confessed. It was for the best. Bridget was not the greatest cook, even though she tried. Something as simple as a scone mix, she could manage, but anything involving chopping, dicing, and sautéing did not end well.

"They're good," Hector said with a nod of affirmation. "I've already had three. Good thing you finally got up or else you'd be out of luck for breakfast."

"How long have you been up?" Marlee asked as she slid onto the bar stool next to Hector.

"About two hours. Pippa started growling at me around 7:00 a.m. when I dared to look in her general direction. I knew it was time to get up since I don't trust that cat. I suspect someday she's going to chew my face off when I'm asleep."

"I'm sure you would wake up before she chewed it all off," Marlee said, dismissing her boyfriend's complaint. "Did you get any sleep at all last night? Or were you worrying about Professor Vernon's case?"

"I dozed but didn't get any real sleep," Hector said. "I still can't believe that a man was shot to death in our home. I texted one of the guys from work to see if he heard anything new, but he hadn't. Or at least there's nothing new that he can tell me at this point."

It was unusual for Marlee to be completely cut off from inside information from the police department. Between what little Hector told her and what she could suss out from Bettina Crawford, Marlee could usually piece together a plan of action on who to interview and what documents to obtain. But now she was without inside information, at least until Bettina returned from vacation later that day.

"Hey, did you know the four people who were really overdressed for the occasion? The two men wore tuxedos, and the women had on fancy ball gowns. One of the women was Owl, and a man was F. They were at the table playing the murder mystery game."

Hector shook his head from side to side. "No, I thought they were friends of yours from campus."

"No, I don't know them. And going by F and Owl seems strange. Why not give us their real names?" Marlee asked.

"Yeah, what brought them to the party? Are they even from Elmwood?" Bridget questioned. "They seemed a little fancier and more sophisticated than most of the people around this area."

"I thought so, too," Marlee said. "They had on costumes and masks for a Halloween party, but a Halloween party held at a ritzy venue in a big city. Not at a B&B in Elmwood, South Dakota. They were very much out of place and sort of kept to themselves. Other than Owl and F joining the game, I didn't see any of the four talking to anyone else at the party. Not even me. I would've thought one or more might have talked to Hector or me since we were the hosts of the party. When I introduced myself and welcomed them to the Open House, they all just nodded. Didn't say a word."

"I planned to talk to them after the murder mystery game was over," Hector said. "I was curious about them too."

Bridget poured herself another cup of coffee and leaned against the countertop as she thought about the four mysterious party guests. "Do you think they owned the tuxes and ball gowns, or did they rent them for the party?"

Marlee looked at her cousin wide-eyed and impressed. "That's a great question. Where would one even rent something like that here in Elmwood? Maybe a bridal shop or a place that carries dressy clothes for high school proms?"

Bridget reached for her laptop and began tapping on the keyboard. "I see two shops here in town that sell or rent formal wear. Tiaras and Tuxes is on Murphy Street, and Irene's is on Main. Let's go check them out."

"Can't go today," Hector said. "It's Sunday, and they won't be open."

"They won't be open for regular business, but if the tuxes and gowns were rented, they are probably due back soon. Somebody would have to be at the shops to receive the returned clothing," Marlee said. "Even if the doors aren't open, I bet there's a number we can call to talk to someone about returns."

Bridget did a little more tapping on her keyboard and found the websites and phone numbers for both places. Marlee got up to refill her coffee cup and reached for her phone. "I'll call Irene's first." On the third ring, the phone was answered by a woman with a raspy voice who identified herself as Irene.

"I'm wondering about returns of formal wear," Marlee said, deciding as she talked how much information she would reveal to Irene.

"Everything is due back by 5:00 this evening. There's a $100 late charge per day for each garment and if the items are not returned within three days your credit card will be charged for the full cost to replace the item plus a convenience fee."

Irene sounded like a no-nonsense type of gal, so Marlee decided to be straight with her and not try to concoct a ruse. "I had a Halloween party last night and there were two men dressed in tuxedos and two women in fancy ball gowns. One dress was blue and the other was burgundy. Does that sound like anything that was rented from your shop?"

"That's an odd question. Why do you want to know?"

"Because no one here at the party knew who these four people were and I'm trying to track them down. Somebody left a small clutch purse behind, and I suspect it was one of the ladies," Marlee said, adding a little BS to the story just to make it more palatable. "I contacted several of the others who were at the party last night and the purse doesn't belong to any of them."

Irene paused for a moment before replying. "Yes, they were returned either last night or earlier this morning."

"Did another employee receive the clothing from them?"

"No, I don't have overnight staff. They dropped the garments in the depository in the back of the building."

"Depository? Like at a library? The slot where you return books without going inside?" Marlee asked.

"That's exactly right. If there are no stains or rips, the person gets their deposit returned. I charge a $1,000 deposit per garment on top of the rental fee. When the garment comes back on time and in good condition, the deposit is refunded to their credit card," Irene said.

"And were the two tuxes and two gowns in good condition when they were returned?"

"Two were and two were not. One tuxedo and the blue gown had flecks of blood on the front. It was hard to see on the tux, but it's there. They will lose their deposits for these two items, I'm afraid. It takes extra time and expense to remove blood stains."

"Who rented these pieces of formal wear? Do you have their names from the credit cards?" Marlee held her breath as Irene clicked away on her keyboard for what felt like an hour.

"All four pieces were rented by one person. The name on the rental document is J.A. Vernon from La Crosse, Wisconsin," Irene reported before ending the conversation.

House of Games

He was careless, but I bet he won't make that mistake again.

Chapter 7

"Professor Vernon is the one who paid for the rentals of the tuxes and gowns," Marlee reported to Hector and Bridget. The phone slid from her hand and clanked on the Formica countertop.

"Why would he rent fancy clothes for four people to attend the party? How did they know each other?" Hector asked. "It doesn't add up."

"And Irene said there were flecks of blood on one of the tuxes and the blue gown. I'm guessing it's blood spatter. When the bullet hit Professor Vernon's body, there was a blowback of blood and maybe tissue. Blood and tissue could land on the shooter or anyone close to the shooter or victim."

Hector grabbed his own cell and dialed his office. "Yes, I know I'm suspended. But I just found something out by accident. Marlee called Irene's, the formal wear place on Main Street." He relayed the rest of the conversation between Marlee and Irene and suggested that an officer go pick up the clothing at once before Irene sent it to the dry cleaner.

"That was quick thinking," Marlee said admiringly. "Did Wallace seem receptive to your help?"

"Not until I mentioned the gist of your call to Irene. Then he was all ears. I left out the part you made up about trying to track down the owner of a purse that was left behind. He didn't ask why you had called Irene's, but I bet he will when he talks to you next time."

"What's the big deal about the clothes having blood on them? I mean, any of us near the table could have blood from the gunshot, couldn't we?" Bridget asked.

"Not necessarily," Marlee said, launching into an abbreviated version of her talk on gunshot evidence from her Crime Scene Investigation class that she taught every fourth semester. "The blowback would have a small range, meaning the shooter or someone standing near the victim or the shooter would be affected. I was standing over on the edge of the room. There's no way I would have any blowback on me. It wouldn't reach that distance. The crime scene techs will have to figure out the angle of the bullet wound to figure out the distance from which the gun was fired."

"One other thing we're forgetting is gunshot residue. If any of the four unknown guests shot the gun, then there may be gunshot residue on their clothing. That's one more reason Wallace needs to get those clothes from Irene right away and have them tested," Hector said.

"Getting back to Professor Vernon, why would he rent formal wear for these four people? I didn't notice him talking to them. In fact, I don't recall seeing them talk or mingle with anyone else. They stayed together until the murder mystery game began. Then Owl and F played the game while I'm guessing the other two watched," Marlee said.

Bridget twirled her nearly empty coffee cup from side to side. "Maybe one or both of them ran to the basement and cut the power."

"They were pretty conspicuous in their dressy attire, but we were all so focused on the game that multiple people could have roamed around the house without our knowledge," Marlee said. "And then, after the gunshot and the lights came back on, everything was total chaos. Twenty extra people in gorilla costumes could have been in the room and I don't think I would've noticed."

"We need to talk to your Supper Club friends," Hector suggested. "We need to know what they saw. And we need to hear from them right away before their memories get distorted."

"Actually, how about if I ask each of them to write down what they saw and email it to me? That way, we'll have something on paper and can follow up with questions in person."

Hector agreed to his girlfriend's suggestion. It was always best to get each witness's statement independent of others so that one's memory isn't tainted by the story of another. If four people witness an accident involving a car that sped away and three of the people announce that the car was gray, the fourth witness will usually go along with the group even though they saw a blue car. It's because they assume that their memory was wrong, and if three other people said the car was gray, then it must be gray.

Marlee called Diane, Shelly, Kathleen, and Gwen and asked each of them to provide a written account of everything they could remember from the night before.

"I know you're busy, but can you please do it right away?" They all agreed, even though they were up to their ears in grading tests and papers. There were only five weeks of classes left in the semester and then finals week, so this was crunch time in the academic world. No one had time for extra chores, so it spoke volumes to Marlee that she could count on her friends to drop everything and provide information to her right away.

Within two hours, all four Supper Club members had provided a detailed description of their place in the dining room when Professor Vernon was shot. The four individual stories mirrored each other with one glaring exception. Shelly McFarland indicated that F, the librarian, flipped off the battery-operated candle on the table before the game started. Neither Diane, Kathleen, nor Gwen mentioned it, and Marlee made a mental note to ask them specifically if they saw F switch off the candle. She didn't expect Diane to have witnessed it since she was standing at the foot of the table next to Bridget in what was essentially the front row. Gwen, on the other hand, was a few steps back and had a better overview of the other spectators.

"You know who I completely forgot during all the chaos? The couple on their first date weekend; Leanne and Paul. Where did they go after they were questioned? I mean, they had to vacate the house too. I don't know if they were even allowed to retrieve anything from their rooms. I don't remember seeing them when Bridget and I came downstairs after packing our clothes and toiletries." Marlee wrung her hands, upset with herself for putting her paying guests at the back of her mind.

"You have their numbers because you were texting to make sure everything was fine with the room. And you were fishing for details on their romantic weekend," Hector reminded her.

Marlee called Leanne Desmond, and she picked up on the third ring with a tentative, "Hello?" After exchanging quick updates about their current lodging situation at the Super 8, Leanne said she and Paul were just on their way to Pizza Ranch for lunch.

"Is it okay if we meet you there?" Marlee asked. She hated to crash their date, but she needed to know what, if anything, Paul and Leanne witnessed last night before Professor Vernon was murdered.

"Sure, that's fine," Leanne assured her. "We're on our way now and will save a table."

Marlee drove her CR-V, Hector in the passenger seat and Bridget in the back, the short distance to the Pizza Ranch. It was a local favorite, known more for its delicious broasted chicken than their mediocre pizza. The parking lot was jam-packed with the Sunday after-church lunch crowd. She drove around the lot, finally parking on the side street.

Leanne and Paul must have arrived just before the lunch rush. After paying at the cash register, Marlee, Bridget, and Hector spied the couple at a large round table and were waved over. "I'm so sorry for everything that happened last night. This is definitely not what we had in mind when we organized the party with the murder mystery game," Marlee said, looking earnestly from Paul to Leanne and back again. She sincerely wanted to make things right with them, not just because it was the right thing to do but also because they also needed to avoid bad online reviews of their B&B.

"We know," Paul assured her as Leanne nodded in agreement. "We don't hold any of this against you."

"Thank you for being so understanding," Hector said. "Obviously we will refund your money for the whole stay."

Before getting into the details of the previous night, the group went through the buffet line. Marlee heaped a mound of whipped potatoes covered with chicken gravy on her plate, making little room for an enormous piece of chicken. *I'll get some vegetables later*, she thought, knowing that she wouldn't.

"Were you able to get any of your belongings out of your rooms?" Marlee asked as she picked chunks of white meat from the bone.

"Yes, the police let us get everything. I mean we only had one bag each, but it would be a major inconvenience if we had to go buy clothes and toiletries for today. We're going back to our towns after lunch," Leanne said.

"Have you already been down to the police station to give your statements?" Hector asked.

"No, we talked to the police last night at your house. We both told them everything we know," Paul assured.

"That was just a preliminary statement from each of you. You have to go to the station to provide more detail and answer questions," Hector advised. "Depending on the case, you may be directed to stick around town for a few days.

"Oh, that won't be possible. I have a big meeting at work on Tuesday and I need to be there bright and early tomorrow morning to prepare for it. It'll take all day to get ready," Leanne argued. "There's just no way around it."

Hector shrugged and, after finishing his last bite of food, left for round two at the buffet. Marlee knew Hector wasn't giving up that easily. No way would he allow witnesses, especially potential suspects, to dictate when they were available to the police. Minutes later, he returned to the table, a fresh plate containing chicken and two slices of pizza. She noted the gleam in his eye and knew Leanne and Paul would not be leaving Elmwood on their own timetables.

"What do you remember after the gunshot?" Bridget pushed food around on her plate, still full from the scones she had eaten just hours ago.

"I remember people gasping, but then also a couple of giggles. At that point, I thought it was all part of the game. I remember being impressed with the level of detail you'd put into this mystery game. Then the lights came back on, and soon after, I realized that the professor was dead for real and that it wasn't part of the game. At that point, I sort of forget who was where," Leanne said.

"When I realized he'd been shot, I moved closer to see if he was breathing. Someone was in front of me blocking my view. Couldn't tell you who it was, though," Paul recalled.

"Did either of you talk to the two couples who were dressed in formal wear? The two guys in tuxedos and the two women in ball gowns?" Marlee asked.

"No, I didn't talk to anyone other than Paul and the waiters. And you," she said gesturing toward Marlee.

"I made a comment to one of the men about the weather, and he ignored me. I can take a hint. By the way they were dressed, I could see that they thought they were better than us," Paul grumbled. "Some people just don't know how to have a civil conversation."

"Did you see anybody leave, either before or after the lights went out?" Bridget asked.

Both shook their heads, indicating they hadn't noticed anyone departing the dining room area. "Only when the EMTs and the police came did I see anyone leave the dining room," Leanne said. "By then, everyone was moving out of the way to see if the professor could be saved."

Another train of thought was poking around in Marlee's brain. "Did you talk to Professor Vernon much while you were staying at the B&B?"

"A little while we were in the kitchenette area. He came out of his room to heat up something in the microwave. Leanne and I were at the table, drinking coffee and chatting. We asked him to join us, but he said he needed to get back to his work because of a deadline," Paul said.

"Did he tell you what kind of work he was doing?" Marlee asked.

"He told me something about it, but it was way over my head," Paul said with a wave of his hand. "I finished high school but only went to one semester of college, so I'm not up on all the lingo."

"How about you?" Marlee turned to Leanne.

"No, I went back to my room then to use the restroom. He was taking his meal out of the microwave when I came back. Then he went into his room, and I didn't see him again until the party."

"Did you overhear him talking to anyone on the phone? Or hear any strange noises coming from his room?" Marlee was on a fishing expedition, knowing that the private professor kept his interactions with others to a minimum. At least that had been her impression of him during the past week since they first met.

"Not really. There were some people who came to visit him later that night. There seemed to be a disagreement, but they must have settled it quickly because the conversation became much quieter," Leanne said.

"Wait! Professor Vernon had guests in his room the night before he was murdered?" Marlee exclaimed.

Can I get some privacy, please? Everyone in this town has a hundred questions for me. Won't they be surprised when they discover the real answers?

Chapter 8

"Yeah," said Paul. "Leanne told me about it the next morning. Around 10:45 on Friday night, I remember thinking it was a bit late for the professor to have guests, but some people are night owls and keep odd hours. As a rancher, I'm early to bed, early to rise. Always have been and always will be."

Leanne threw Paul a look that Marlee couldn't quite interpret but sensed it wasn't positive. "I was watching Stephen Colbert when I heard muffled voices. At first, I thought Paul was outside my door, so I turned down the volume." She blushed as she mentioned what she thought to be a romantic overture. "But then I could hear a male and a female voice, then the professor, and then they went inside his room and shut the door. I heard it click. The voices were loud for a little bit, then quieted down. I couldn't hear anything they said, but they all sounded angry at first."

Leanne looked at Hector. "I'm surprised you didn't hear their footsteps. Not sure how many people were there, but at least two."

"We can't hear anyone walking up or down the stairs on the back entrance that you use to access the third floor, and we put extra padding under the carpet in the guest bedrooms on the third floor since our bedrooms are right below. It would have to be a huge noise to get our attention on the second floor. We tried to keep things as quiet as possible, not just for us, but also for the privacy of the guests."

"Did you hear them leave Professor Vernon's room?" Marlee asked.

"No. Either they were really quiet, or I was asleep," Leanne said. "I have the television on most nights. It helps me fall asleep."

"I was asleep too. Lights out and TV off," Paul stated in his typical no-nonsense fashion. "Didn't hear a thing."

They all made another trip through the buffet, and when they finished eating, they walked out to the parking lot. Just as they were saying their goodbyes, Detective Wallace rolled up in his unmarked car that everyone in town knew was a police vehicle.

"I need you two to come down to the station to give your statements," he said, pointing to Paul and Leanne. "Get in, and I'll bring you back when we're finished." Marlee looked at Hector and tried not to smile.

"Guess you were right," Paul said to Hector. "They do need us to go to the cop shop and talk some more."

Marlee, Bridget, and Hector walked to the CR-V and discussed what they had learned from their lunch visit with Paul and Leanne. "We know Professor Vernon had visitors and the conversation was contentious at first. Maybe it was the four people who were overdressed for the party. I mean, he knew them since he rented their formal wear from Irene's." Bridget said.

"It could have been all four of them or maybe even just two or three," Hector said. "Leanne said she heard male and female voices in addition to the professor's voice.

"What about our security camera? Does it cover the back staircase?" Marlee asked, looking at Hector.

"No," Hector said with a deep sigh. "I had planned to have it hooked up by now but got distracted with preparations for the murder mystery party and Open House. And I really regret not getting it done."

"It's not your fault, Hector," Bridget said soothingly. "You couldn't have predicted this."

"I've been a detective for more years than I can remember. If anyone should have been prepared for this type of thing, it's me. I can't count the times I've chewed out homeowners and business operators for not having working security cameras. So many times, the cameras are broken or haven't been hooked up. Now I've done the same damn thing."

"What about the neighbor? Does he have cameras? Or the people across the street? Any of them could've captured people entering the back staircase around 10:45 p.m. and leaving later that night or in the early morning hours," Marlee suggested.

Hector thought for a moment. "I don't remember seeing cameras on Chuck's house, but it's worth asking. Maybe he saw or heard something. I'll find out when we get home."

"Won't Detective Wallace get upset when he finds out you're informally interviewing the neighbors?" Marlee asked. "Maybe Bridget and I should talk to them."

He reluctantly agreed, noting that he was walking a thin line with Wallace. "I've already called him twice today, first about the returned formal wear at Irene's and then to let him know Paul and Leanne were leaving town."

Marlee drove by their house, which was still surrounded by yellow crime scene tape. There weren't any police cars or official-looking people at the home, at least not that they could see from the outside. Hector's Jeep was parked along the curb on the other side of the street. It was agreed that he'd take his vehicle back to Bridget's while Marlee and Bridget chatted with the neighbors about what they'd seen.

The people at the three separate houses across the street hadn't seen anyone coming or going from Marlee and Hector's home on Friday evening and hadn't noticed anything suspicious on Saturday night until the police arrived. One of the homes had a security camera, but it was only focused on their front door and didn't provide a street view. "We mainly use it to make sure nobody steals our packages when UPS delivers them," Emily Durkle reported. "I have it linked to my phone, so I get a notification when there's activity by the door. If a package is delivered, I run home from work and put it inside as soon as I'm able to get a spare moment. I work right around the corner, so it's only a minute away." She would have happily chatted their ears off all afternoon, but Marlee let her know they had to keep moving along. After providing her with a few superficial details about the shooting at their home the previous night, Marlee was able to pull herself away from the older woman.

Since Marlee's house was on a corner lot, there was only one next-door neighbor. His name was Charles DeYoung, and he was no fan of Marlee and Hector running a B&B in their neighborhood. Shortly after buying the house, they'd notified the retired man about converting the third floor of their home to guest rentals, and he'd approached the city about zoning restrictions. When Charles discovered that Hector and Marlee's intentions were completely legal, he tried to discourage the construction workers at their house by telling them they would never get paid. Then, some construction equipment went missing from their yard. One afternoon, Hector went over to have a chat with Charles, noting that they would no longer tolerate his interference. Marlee wasn't privy to everything Hector said, but he must have made an impact. Since then, Charles sneered whenever he saw them but left them and their contractors alone.

Marlee took a deep breath and rang the doorbell, steeling herself for what would likely be an unpleasant conversation. "Hi, Charles. I suppose you know about the tragedy that happened at our house last night."

He nodded, not bothering to greet her or Bridget.

"We're trying to help figure out what happened and were wondering if you have any security cameras that point toward our house or the street." She looked around the outside of his house as she talked, not seeing any obvious surveillance equipment.

"I knew your upstairs motel would bring the wrong kind of element to the neighborhood," Charles growled. "But I didn't think somebody would be murdered the first few weeks you were open."

Marlee ignored the jab, knowing nothing would be gained from engaging in a verbal war with the cranky neighbor. "Do you have any cameras that might have shown someone coming or going from our house?"

"You had about sixty people coming and going last night, from my count," he snapped. "More than that if you count the police and the ambulance crew."

"It was an Open House. Everyone was welcome to attend. I put a flyer in your mailbox last week," Marlee said, thinking maybe Charles was pissed because he hadn't been invited to the shindig.

He made an unintelligible grumbling sound and shook his head back and forth. "I don't have any interest in what goes on over there. You couldn't pay me to come to your party."

Realizing that the conversation between Marlee and Charles was going nowhere, Bridget intervened. She introduced herself, leaving out the fact that she and Marlee were cousins. "I think the main thing to keep in mind is that someone was killed next door, and until that person is arrested, everyone may be at risk."

Bridget's logic resonated with the old man and threatened his sense of safety. "No, I don't have security cameras. But you can bet I'll be getting some now." With that, he closed the door in their faces, and they walked down the stairs.

"Well, that's everyone who might have seen something," Marlee said, disheartened that not one single neighbor had seen anything out of the ordinary the last two nights.

"What about the house across the back alley? Maybe they have a camera," Bridget suggested.

Marlee shrugged, thinking it wasn't worth their time yet wanting to cover all bases. "Okay, let's go talk to them. They just moved in a few weeks ago and I haven't even met them yet. Hector talked to them. Said it's a young couple, no kids."

They walked around the block and approached the front of the decrepit home. It was a fixer-upper, just as Marlee and Hector's home had been before they invested thousands of dollars in renovating and updating. She hoped the young couple knew what was in store for them, as she was still suffering from PTSD due to the constant attention their home needed that first year.

"Hello," Marlee said, introducing herself and Bridget to the young woman who opened the door. "There was an unfortunate tragedy at my house last night," she said, pointing in the general direction of her home. "I was wondering if you have any security cameras that might have caught suspicious activity in the back alley between our homes. We're trying to help find out what happened."

"No, we don't have any cameras yet. My husband has been talking about installing them. Is this a dangerous neighborhood? We just moved here from Seattle." She twisted her wedding ring back and forth and shuffled from one foot to the other.

"No, it's safe here. This type of thing is very abnormal," Marlee assured her new neighbor, purposely leaving out the murder investigations she herself had been involved with over the years. No need to startle the newcomers. "Did you happen to notice any people coming or going in our side door on Friday night or early Saturday morning?"

She indicated that she hadn't but said she'd talk to her spouse. "My husband's nineteen-year-old brother has been staying with us this past week. I'll ask him, too."

Marlee provided the new neighbor with her phone number and asked that she call or stop by if her husband or teenage brother-in-law saw anything worth mentioning. "Hope to get to know you better under more pleasant circumstances. If you need anything while you're settling into the neighborhood, let us know."

Defeated, the McCabe cousins returned to Bridget's place. Hector had been there unsupervised for over an hour and had taken it upon himself to winterize the windows on the front of her house. "Just a bit of caulk around the edges will keep the drafts out," he assured Bridget.

"I'm enjoying having a handyman around the house," Bridget said with an appreciative smile. "Let me think of some other chores for you while you're here."

Marlee gave her cousin the side eye. Although Bridget and Hector were just friends, she always sensed an undercurrent of romantic interest between the two. They both denied it, yet Marlee suspected if she were to die, it would not be long before Hector and Bridget found themselves together. Marlee trusted them both implicitly. At the same time, she kept her eyes open.

They stepped inside and were greeted by Pippa. Well, not so much greeted as assaulted. The fluffy gray Persian leaped from the couch, launching herself right in the path of Hector. "Dammit, Pippa," he admonished as he tried to shoo her away with a gentle nudging of his foot. "That cat is always flying at me out of nowhere."

"She's upset," Marlee cooed, leaning over to soothe the finicky feline. "First, she's forced out of her house, then we bring her to a new place, then we leave her alone. It's no wonder she's out of sorts. She will calm down eventually."

"I wouldn't fucking bet on it," Hector growled under his breath. He was all too familiar not only with Pippa's unsavory behavior but also with Marlee's endless excuses for the cat's breaches of etiquette.

Marlee scooped up Pippa, who was no longer hissing. The kitty rested in her arms and began purring, meanwhile, glaring at Hector over Marlee's shoulder. They went through the kitchen, and all sat at the dining room table. Bridget brought over a bottle of Cabernet and three glasses. "Sorry, Hector. I'll pick up some beer for you later,"

"No need. We can go back home later today. I talked to Wallace again and he said the scene will be cleared by this evening."

Marlee made a face. "Do we really want to go in there tonight with Professor Vernon's blood in the dining room? Maybe we should get a cleaning crew to come in and shampoo the rug." Although she'd been involved in investigating murders in the past, this was the first time she had to deal with the practicalities of living at a crime scene.

"I thought we'd just roll up the rug and trash it. It wasn't that expensive, and it's easier to get a new one," Hector said.

"That's a good idea. I know I'd think about poor Professor Vernon every time I looked at that rug. Let's get something completely different."

"Agreed. There will still be plenty of cleanup once the crime scene techs are finished. There'll be fingerprint dust everywhere; our things will have been rummaged through, and don't forget, we still have to clean up from the party," Hector said, making a face.

As the three moaned and groaned about the impending clean-up duties awaiting them at their house, Hector's cell rang. "It's Wallace," he said, getting up from the table and pacing around the house.

Marlee hated it when Hector tried to keep the information to himself before sharing it with her. Granted, his job as a police detective necessitated this most of the time, but he was on suspension now, and there was no expectation that Detective Wallace would be sharing confidential information with him that he couldn't tell Marlee and Bridget. Old habits die hard as Hector moved back through the living room and out the front door.

Ten minutes later, Hector returned to the table. "Well, I just got my ass chewed by the guy I've been mentoring for the past few months. Wallace is really getting a big head now that he's lead on the investigation."

"What was he mad about?" Marlee asked.

"Obviously, he knows we've talked to Irene at the formal wear rental shop and that we've met with Paul and Leanne. He just had a call from a concerned neighbor about you two going door to door in the neighborhood, asking questions. Wallace is not happy and threatened to get the Chief involved if we don't back off," Hector said.

"Even though we've technically helped him quite a bit already?" Bridget asked, incredulous that their assistance wasn't appreciated. "I mean, Leanne and Paul would have left town if we hadn't met with them and tipped Wallace off about it. And who knows how long it would've taken him to figure out that the formal wear rented by the four unknown guests came from Irene's and that it was returned with blood on it?"

"I know, I know," Hector agreed. "I can also see his point. If I were him, I'd be saying the same thing."

"Now you know how we feel when you tell us to stay out of it." Marlee gave Hector a self-satisfied smirk. "How does it feel to be told to butt out when you're actually doing a lot to advance the investigation?"

"Look, Wallace is just doing his job, and I think he's doing it well. It's always easy to look in from the outside and see what looks like mistakes. We have no idea if he already knew about Paul and Leanne leaving or about the tuxes and gowns returned to Irene's. He knows a lot that he can't tell us," Hector admonished.

Marlee slapped her forehead. She couldn't believe she forgot to tell Hector what she'd seen in the Gray Room the previous night. "Hector, you might not be quite so understanding when I tell you what I saw Wallace do at our house. I showed him to Professor Vernon's room, and he had basically dismissed me. Well, I don't like being told what to do, especially in my own home, so I just sort of lingered around in the common area. I peeked in and saw Wallace rip off a sheet of paper from a legal pad on the professor's desk. He folded it and put it in his inside jacket pocket. When he saw I was still on the third floor, he rudely kicked me out. I don't know if he knows I saw him hiding evidence."

"Oh, come on, Marlee!" Hector barked. "You can't possibly think that Shane Wallace hid evidence. He's the lead detective on the case, not a suspect. He probably just needed to write something down and didn't have any paper on him." He shook his head in disgust and stormed out of the dining room, slamming the front door as he went outside. Moments later, they heard an engine start and saw Hector's Jeep drive away.

House of Games

And they thought I wouldn't recognize them. Pfft! Do they think I'm daft?

Chapter 9

"What just happened?" Bridget was dumbfounded by Hector's reaction to Marlee's claims about Detective Wallace.

Marlee was taken aback as well. Hector was the one of them with the cooler head who could see beyond emotion. She was the one who flew off the handle and reacted when presented with unsavory information. Of course, Hector usually wasn't a witness or possibly even a suspect in a crime. "I don't know. He's normally the calm one. I guess the suspension and the murder and everything else is really getting to him."

Bridget topped off their wine glasses before they moved to the living room to ponder Hector's blowup. "He's used to being in control and now that he's on suspension, he has no power and no access to confidential information."

Marlee nodded. "And I'm sure he's feeling some embarrassment from being suspended even though he did nothing wrong. It would be hard to face coworkers, especially those ranking below him. Plus, Hector has been mentoring Wallace. Anything Wallace does, positive or negative, reflects on Hector. I'm sure the last thing he wants to hear right now is that the officer he's been mentoring is cutting corners and not following proper protocol in securing and storing evidence."

"Where do you think he went?'

"Probably just driving around until he cools off. Maybe to the gym. He always has his duffel bag in his vehicle so he can exercise whenever he gets time." She was proud of him and his new commitment to fitness. Hector hadn't lost much weight, but he was toning up, and she noticed a newfound swagger, which she found attractive.

"Are you one hundred percent sure you saw Wallace rip the paper off the legal pad and stuff it in his jacket? I mean, you said you were looking at him from an angle. Maybe it wasn't what it looked like." Bridget approached the topic carefully, knowing Marlee wouldn't appreciate the challenge to her version of events.

Marlee walked into the kitchen and returned with a stack of blue Post-it notes. She turned and placed them on the coffee table in front of her cousin. Then she angled herself in the opposite direction, ripped off the top Post-it note from the pad, and stuffed it in the pouch pocket on the front of her hoodie. "What did you see?"

Bridget sighed before narrating back exactly what Marlee had reenacted. "Okay, I'm sorry. I thought maybe your view was obscured or that there was another explanation."

"No, that's what I saw. There are two explanations. The first and most egregious is that he tampered with evidence. The second is that Wallace improperly collected and stored evidence. Either way, it doesn't look good. Wallace is either incompetent or crooked."

"And that's why Hector is so upset," Bridget said. "The detective he's been mentoring throws a shadow on both of them and their investigations."

"Yep," Marlee confirmed. "And if Wallace is acting improperly in this case, how many other cases has he handled like this?"

"I can't think of a motive for tampering with evidence," Bridget said. "What would Wallace have to gain by taking the sheet of paper from the professor's notepad?"

"I wish we knew what was written on the notepad. That might give us a clue as to why Wallace hid the paper in his jacket pocket. And maybe he didn't have anything to gain by stashing the paper. Maybe he was trying to conceal something or protect someone."

"But what? Or who?"

"I think our next step is to do a deep dive into the background of Detective Shane Wallace. Let's see if we can find any connection between him and Professor Vernon," Marlee said, reaching for her laptop and doing a general Google search on Wallace. "Looks like he's from Northfield, Minnesota, and was kind of a big deal on the high school basketball team. He was also in football and track. Here's a yearbook photo of him." She turned her laptop so Bridget could see the scowling teen with cystic acne and a Caesar haircut.

Marlee turned the laptop back toward her and resumed her search. "Wallace went to Badger State University in La Crosse, Wisconsin, on a basketball scholarship but dropped out two years later when a shoulder injury derailed his basketball participation. Two years after that, he graduated from Keystone

Community College with a degree in Criminal Justice Studies. He worked store security at Target while in college and then went into the police academy in Minnesota."

"That's a lot of detail. You're getting all that from Google?" Bridget asked, wondering why her own searches on people provided scant information.

"Nah, I switched over to a subscription site. For $19.99 a month, I can find out background details on just about anyone."

"Is it legal?"

"Yeah, it's legal. I used it when I worked as a probation officer. After I left probation, I continued using the service. Technically, it's for law enforcement and investigative personnel, but no one has ever contacted me to say I can't use it, so I guess that means there's no problem."

"That seems unethical," Bridget countered. "I think you're going to get into trouble."

"No, I won't," Marlee assured her Nervous Nellie cousin. "I'm signed up as a private investigator. I just did a quick switch from probation officer to PI on their website, and all is good."

"You're not a private investigator!" Bridget snapped. "You're a college professor. But you keep forgetting that."

"You sound like Hector, always trying to limit what I can do. For your information, I have the paperwork downloaded to get a PI license. If I run into any trouble using this website, I'll just get my license and all will be good."

"Let me guess. Hector doesn't know about any of this, does he?"

Marlee rested her forefinger on her chin and looked off into space. "Hmmm... I can't remember if we've talked about it or not. Anyway, back to Detective Wallace. His first job out of the academy was with the Fergus Falls Police Department in Minnesota, and then he moved to a smaller PD in the same state. Doesn't look like it was a promotion, so I don't know why he was transferred. It could have been Wallace's choice to move, or he may have been transferred against his wishes. I'll need to follow up on that. Then he ends up in South Dakota as a deputy in the Lyman County Sheriff's Office."

"That must be where he met Hector," Bridget said.

"Yeah, Hector said they knew each other since they worked in neighboring counties. Then Wallace got a position as a uniformed officer here in Elmwood and was recently promoted to detective. That brings us to today. Once Hector cools off, I'll ask him more about Wallace's background."

"I'd give that some time if I were you," Bridget cautioned, still reeling from Hector's earlier blowup.

"No shit," Marlee agreed. She continued tapping away on her laptop, securing more up-to-date information on Detective Wallace. "He's on his second marriage. She's from Elmwood, so that may be part of the reason he moved here; no kids with her but two from the first wife. She has custody, but he gets visitation. He and his current wife own a house over on the east side of town in a newer development area. The wife works as a nurse at the hospital. They each have a vehicle that they're making payments on. A mortgage, but nothing outlandish compared to what they're earning. No bankruptcies. A reasonable amount of debt, mostly from college tuition."

"It's scary how much you can find out about people. I'm surprised you can access all that information so quickly."

"Almost all this information is readily available to anyone if they know where to look. The paid site has it all gathered and makes it quicker than individually looking for financial records and such. Now I'm going to look up Professor Vernon and find out more about him," Marlee said.

Within the next half hour, Marlee reaped a plethora of information on Professor Jerome Vernon. She already knew he was a professor of English on sabbatical from Badger State University in La Crosse, Wisconsin. Marlee discovered that before he checked into their B&B. She was so excited to have their first paying guest, and she wanted to learn more about him, so she checked out his webpage on the university's website. His research interests focused on Creative Writing, and he'd authored an off-Broadway play and several academic papers on writing for the theater. A quick review of Rate My Professor revealed generally favorable ratings by his students. Only two indicated a substandard experience in his class, with one writing that the professor was too strict about deadlines.

What had not been listed on the academic website or any of the informal search results was that the professor was a registered sex offender in the state of Wisconsin.

"Oh my god, Bridget. I think I just figured out a motive for someone to kill Professor Vernon. It's because he's a sex offender. Either the shooter was getting revenge on him specifically or just hated all sex offenders and wanted him out of the way."

I'm in too far. I can't go back now.

Chapter 10

"A sex offender? How can he teach at a college as a registered sex offender?" Bridget asked, aghast that Professor Vernon would be employed in a position where he was around young people all day.

"I'm not finding the specifics of his crime, but I'll keep digging," Marlee said, hunched over her laptop, typing as fast as her stubby fingers would allow. "My guess is that either the university doesn't know, or his offense didn't involve college-aged students."

"What does that mean? I wouldn't want him around my students, regardless of what exactly he did. He should be banned from all teaching institutions," Bridget insisted.

"His victims may have been specific, like young children. Something that doesn't pertain to college-aged students or at least doesn't put them at risk from being in his classes."

"What about office hours? He could shut the door when a student comes in to talk to him about an assignment and then assault them without anyone else seeing him," Bridget said. "Or what if he was leading an off-campus tour or taking students to conferences with him? I just can't imagine any university thinking it's acceptable to have him around students. Even though most of them are over eighteen and considered adults."

"I don't disagree with you, Bridget. It seems like a significant risk for the university to take. That's why I think they may not even know about it. If it was a recent offense, Professor Vernon may not have brought it to the attention of his dean and maybe no one is checking up on him. If he's not on probation, then he may not have any restrictions other than registering as a sex offender every year." Marlee recalled her own experience as a probation officer over a decade ago when she worked with sex offenders. Most of them had been convicted of sexual contact with children. The contact included touching and fondling but not intercourse. Those who were convicted of sexual abuse had committed an act involving penetration, either against a child, someone unable to consent, or against their will.

"How many other perverts are working on college campuses that nobody knows about?"

"Good question. Of course, not everyone with kinks and perversions is a sex offender. Some folks are just into some wacky things, sexually. If everyone is an adult and able to consent, then it's not a problem," Marlee said.

"Now I'm going to be wondering about the other profs in my department at Marymount," Bridget said with a shudder. For nearly eight years, she'd been a professor of Film Studies at Marymount College, the other institute of higher learning in Elmwood besides Midwestern State University. Marymount was a private college, attracting students from wealthier and higher achieving backgrounds, while MSU was a state school with few restrictions on acceptance.

"Here's a quick rundown of what else I found on Professor Vernon: never married, no kids, lives a modest lifestyle, has rented the same apartment for over ten years, drives an older car, and has no debt. Other than the sex offender status, his background is fairly boring."

"Whatever he did to be convicted of a sex crime probably wasn't his first offense," Bridget said.

"That's right. Most people commit several other crimes before they're caught. It's been estimated in some studies that an average sex offender may have dozens of victims before they are caught. And that's if they're caught at all. The other thing to keep in mind is that whatever Professor Vernon was convicted of may have been plea-bargained down to a lesser charge," Marlee said.

"So, his offense was worse than what he was punished for?"

"Yep, in a typical plea agreement, a defendant admits to a lesser offense, which means a reduced penalty. It's a win-win for the prosecution and the defendant. The defendant gets a lesser penalty, and the prosecution doesn't have to prepare for a trial. Often, the prosecution may not have a strong enough case to guarantee a conviction, so accepting a plea to a lesser charge is at least securing a fraction of justice."

"Doesn't seem like there's much consideration for the victim and what they want."

"That's one of the biggest criticisms of the justice system," Marlee said. "Victims are often forgotten or the last to be considered. That's why I spend a certain amount of time in my criminology classes focusing on the impacts of crimes on victims. Sometimes, it's physical or financial, but frequently, the mental and emotional harm are the worst."

Marlee's cell rang before she could launch into further discussion of victim rights within the criminal justice system and the need for reform. After a quick conversation, she clicked off her phone and turned to her cousin. "Bettina's back in town and is coming over. She has updates on the case."

"Thank God we have somebody working on the case that will give us some information— and keep an eye on Detective Wallace," Bridget said. "I mean, I know she can only tell us so much, but she'll do what she can to get to the truth of who shot Professor Vernon and the motive for doing it."

Marlee nodded. "I trust Bettina's police work just as much as I trust Hector's. With him on suspension indefinitely, we need Bettina's help more than ever. I'll be very interested to hear what she has to say about Wallace and his work here in Elmwood."

"I hope she doesn't explode like Hector did when you brought up Wallace stuffing the paper from Professor Vernon's room into his pocket. Is a challenge to any officer's work a threat to all of them? I've heard of the thin blue line of cops sticking up for cops, but wouldn't they want to know if one of their colleagues was doing something illegal, unethical, or just sloppy?"

"I'd hope so, but cops are a strange bunch. They have a stick-together attitude that we don't have in academia. If I were doing something illegal or unethical, my colleagues in my own department would be the first to point it out so that it didn't disgrace the university or the discipline of Criminology," Marlee said.

"Yes, yes," said Bridget, bobbing her head up and down. "And likewise, if I know of something fishy going on in my department, I'd be the first to turn it in, too."

"Cops have an us versus them philosophy. They're attacked from all sides: prosecuting attorneys, defense attorneys, judges, victims, defendants, and the public. Some of it is justified, and some isn't, but they feel the need to stick together. Even if one of their own is in the wrong, they consider their fellow officers to be family. And family doesn't turn on family."

Bridget suppressed a giggle. "I feel like I just watched an episode of *Blue Bloods* where this very issue was discussed."

"It's a common theme that comes up in television shows because it happens all the time in real life." A loud pounding interrupted their conversation, and Bridget jumped up to see who was at the front door.

"Took you long enough," grumbled Bettina Crawford as she walked in the door and kicked off her shoes. The middle-aged Native American woman had been a detective with the Elmwood Police Department for ten years, although she and Marlee were friends back when she was a uniform officer in Sisseton and the surrounding tribal areas.

"Come on in," Bridget said, taken aback at Bettina's abrupt manner. "What's wrong with you?"

"Sorry, long day. The weekend getaway with Randy turned sour yesterday, so today's drive home from the Black Hills was awkward."

"Oh, no. Can things be fixed, or was it a breakup?" Marlee poured Bettina a generous glass of wine and handed it to her.

"I don't know. Right now, I feel like we're done. I can't stand the sound of his voice or his face." Bettina happily grabbed the wine and took a sip. "I'm not on duty. This is just me here visiting as a friend."

"Have you been updated on Professor Vernon's murder?" Marlee asked, anxious for information that would lead to the arrest of suspects and enable her boyfriend to go back to work.

"Somewhat. I talked to Wallace on the drive back, and he gave me a quick overview. I heard about Hector's suspension, and it's to be expected in a case like this," Bettina said.

"That's what he said. In fact, he said he would've done the same if the roles were reversed," Marlee recounted her conversation with Hector when he came back to Bridget's house the night before. "I know he's not pissed about being suspended because it's protocol in a case like this, but he's still upset and embarrassed."

"No doubt. I'd be upset, too. Let's hope things move along quickly so he can get back to work. Wallace is going to drive me crazy on this case," Bettina reported.

"How so?" Marlee asked as both she and Bridget leaned in a bit closer to the proverbial tea Bettina was about to spill.

"He keeps asking the same basic questions repeatedly like he's never investigated a murder before when I know for a fact that he's been involved in a few. This is the first time he's lead on a murder case, so he wants to do everything right. And I get that. I'd want to make a good first impression, too, but c'mon— there's such a thing as being too cautious."

Marlee and Bridget exchanged looks. Bettina's complaint against her coworker fell in direct opposition to what Marlee witnessed Wallace do with evidence in Professor Vernon's room. "What is it?" Bettina demanded, noticing the looks the McCabe cousins gave each other. "What's going on?"

"I'm not sure how you'll handle this," Marlee began. "I told Hector what I saw, and he blew up and left the house. That was over an hour ago."

Bettina raised her eyebrows and gestured for Marlee to talk.

"Okay, but don't kill the messenger," Marlee said and then went on to recount seeing Wallace in Professor Vernon's room and watching as he stuffed a piece of paper in his jacket pocket.

"That's not proper evidence collection. Are you sure he didn't put it in a bag first?" Bettina countered.

"Nope, I know what I saw, and I'll swear to it in court, if necessary," Marlee said, adamant in her claim. "It was either sloppy police work or an attempt to hide evidence."

Bettina shook her head in disbelief. "I've worked with Wallace long enough to know that he's a pro when it comes to evidence collection. He wouldn't break protocol or chain of evidence. Whatever was on that sheet of legal paper can't be used as evidence because it was improperly collected and stored."

"So that means he was hiding it so it wouldn't become part of the investigation. The information on the paper is damning to someone, and Wallace didn't want it to be part of the evidence in this case," Marlee said.

"Wallace is a pain in the ass with all his questions, but I just don't see him hiding evidence. He's a stickler for rules. Hector has instilled that in him since he started here in Elmwood. Besides, what would be on the paper that would tempt Wallace to hide it?" Bettina asked.

"It must have been incriminating or embarrassing to someone. But what would it be? Professor Vernon didn't know anyone here in town. At least not that we're aware of. So how would he have anything incriminating or embarrassing on someone? And what would be so bad that it got the professor killed?" Marlee questioned.

"That may not be true," interjected Bridget. "Remember, Professor Vernon is the one who rented the tuxedoes and ball gowns for the four unknown guests at the party. We don't know for sure where they're from, but Elmwood could be their home."

Marlee and Bettina both nodded at Bridget's comment. She had a point. But that still didn't explain why Detective Wallace would stick his neck out by stealing and hiding evidence. "Any news on the fingerprint testing on the gun or the blood spatter and blowback?" Marlee asked.

"It's Sunday, so the lab is working with a skeleton crew. We should have answers tomorrow or Tuesday," Bettina said. "Wallace is the lead detective on this case, but I'm going to follow up on everything he says and does. Especially given the information you just told me."

"We did a little poking around ourselves, and Marlee found out that Professor Vernon is a registered sex offender," Bridget reported. "In the state of Wisconsin."

Bettina's eyes got wide. "I hadn't heard that yet from Wallace. I'll give him a call and see what he knows about it, if anything." She moved from the couch to the kitchen for more privacy as she placed the call.

She returned to the living room moments later, and the news she had to share was devastating. "The lab finished the fingerprint testing, and there is only one set of identifiable prints on the gun that killed Professor Vernon. The prints are Hector's."

Just because I'm old doesn't mean I've lost my value.
This really is the biggest gift I have to give.

Chapter 11

Marlee was not surprised by the fingerprint match. Of course, Hector's prints would be on the gun, as he picked it up when he found it on their dining room floor. Plus, it had been determined to be his service weapon, so his fingerprints would be all over the gun. It would be suspicious if they weren't. But the prints of the shooter should be on the gun, too. "Only Hector's prints? No one else's?"

"Some smudges, but nothing that could be used to identify anyone other than Hector," Bettina said.

"That's more than a little suspicious," Marlee said. "I would have expected some unidentifiable fingerprints. Whoever fired the gun rubbed their prints off as best they could and then tossed it on the floor near Hector, knowing he would find it and pick it up."

Bettina paused, not saying what everyone was thinking.

"Unless Hector was the one who fired the weapon," Bridget blurted out.

"Hector did not fire the gun, Bridget! What's the matter with you?" Marlee chastised her cousin, who seemed intent on solving the case even if it involved throwing Hector in the slammer. She turned toward Bettina, "Um, no one thinks that, right?"

"I know Hector didn't shoot anybody. If he had, even if it was an accident during a game, he would have come clean immediately and acknowledged what he did. That's just who Hector is: forthright and ready to accept the consequences of his actions," Bettina said, but then there was another lengthy pause. "But not everybody knows Hector as well as I do. I'm not saying that anyone in the department thinks he shot the professor, but the optics on this don't look good for him."

Marlee read between the lines. "You mean the public is going to find out about Hector's prints being the only ones on the gun and demand an arrest be made."

Bettina nodded. "I'm afraid that's what will happen, especially if we don't find something to implicate another person in the shooting."

"He's clearly being set up," Marlee said, jumping to her feet. "Somebody got his gun out of the locked cabinet and then shot Professor Vernon when the lights went out during the murder mystery game. And it was a two-person operation because one was in the basement flipping the breaker."

"Okay, let's say Hector is being set up," Bettina acknowledged. "Who at the party wanted Hector to take the fall for the murder of an elderly professor? And why was Professor Vernon the target? Or was he? Maybe it could have been anyone at the party, game participant or guest, who was shot. Besides, there are one hundred easier ways to set Hector up than during a party at his own house."

"If we go with that idea, then the focus is on Hector, not Professor Vernon. Instead of the professor being targeted for some reason, Hector was set up to take the fall for murder. It could have been the murder of anyone," Bridget summarized.

Bettina nodded as Marlee retrieved the crime charts and made a space for them on the coffee table. She flipped over the crime chart with the seating arrangement from the murder mystery game. Marlee wrote Hector's name in the center. "Let's say Hector is our victim in the sense that he's being set up for the murder. Who has a reason to want Hector in prison?" Marlee grabbed a marker, poised to write down a series of names.

"Wouldn't every single person Hector has helped put in prison have a motive to set him up?" Bridget asked.

"Every single one of them, plus their families and friends. There may also be some victims of crime who believe Hector didn't do enough to help them find justice. The possibilities are endless," Bettina replied.

"Are there any cases that really stand out in your mind where someone might try to retaliate against Hector?" Marlee asked Bettina, still ready to write down names.

"I mean, it could be any of them, but two that stand out in my mind are the Amdahl brothers. They were co-defendants in a drug case that we worked. It then went through federal court because of the amount of drugs involved," Bettina recalled.

"I remember that. They were in their early twenties and were transporting meth and heroin from Minneapolis to Elmwood and other towns in South Dakota and North Dakota. They were on their way to Fargo when they were busted."

"What is it about them that makes you think they could be involved in this? Aren't they in prison now?" Bridget asked.

"One is in Sandstone in Minnesota, and the other one is serving his time in Oxford in Wisconsin," Bettina said. "It's not them specifically, but their mother who could be involved. She made threats against Hector several times, and at one point, we suspected she had a hit out on him, but we couldn't prove it."

"What?" Marlee asked. "Hector never told me about this."

"There's a lot Hector doesn't tell you," Bettina said.

"He and I are going to have a very serious conversation when he gets home," Marlee said, adamant that her boyfriend should be more transparent about the dangers of police work.

"You know he can't tell you everything," Bridget said, and Marlee nodded.

"Is there anybody connected to law enforcement that has it in for Hector? Another detective or one of the uniformed officers? Did he step on somebody's toes at work or get a promotion that they wanted?" Marlee was fishing for any ideas as to who might want not only to get Hector fired but also imprisoned.

"Somebody is always butt hurt about something," Bettina acknowledged, "but I can't think of anyone mad enough at Hector to pull something like this."

"I hate to ask, but what about Detective Wallace?" Marlee said, gesturing for Bettina to hold off on commenting. "Hear me out. I know Hector has been mentoring him and was the one who recommended him for the detective position. Maybe he's jealous of Hector and wants him gone, thinking it will improve his status in the department."

"No, I can't see Wallace doing that. Anything is possible, and what you told me about him stashing evidence in his pocket is troubling, to say the least, but I really don't think he'd want to harm Hector. Besides, it doesn't improve Wallace's status that much in the department. We'd have to promote someone to fill Hector's position as a senior detective, but Wallace doesn't have enough seniority to be considered. Basically, Wallace loses his mentor and friend if Hector's off the force. It would hurt Wallace more than help him."

"I agree that it's farfetched. I just thought that if he was capable of improperly handling evidence, then maybe he could set up this whole scheme." Marlee frowned, realizing her theory had plenty of holes.

"I'm going to check the evidence log and see what was bagged and tagged from the professor's room. It will be interesting to see if Wallace logged the piece of paper you say he stuffed in his jacket or if there is no record of any papers seized," Bettina said.

Marlee could see that Bettina was more concerned about Detective Wallace's behavior in the professor's room than she was letting on. "Do you have any other concerns about Wallace?" Marlee asked.

Bettina paused as she chose her words. "Nothing that I'm prepared to talk about right now, but I'll be keeping my eyes and ears open where Wallace is concerned. And as for this investigation, I'll be double- and triple-checking everything he does."

By the time Bettina left, both Marlee and Bridget felt satisfied that the investigation of Professor Vernon's murder would be in good hands, not because of Wallace, as lead detective, but due to Bettina Crawford, who would be following up on his every move.

"You know who I think we should talk to?" Bridget said, clearing the wine glasses and empty bottles from the coffee table and walking toward the kitchen. "Ethan and Nadia. They were both playing the murder mystery game. And, since you'd hired them to act as servers, they may have insight into the four unknown people. Maybe they know who they are or overheard something while passing around the drinks and hors d'oeuvres."

"You're right," Marlee exclaimed. "Let's go now. I'll send Hector a text letting him know where we are. I'm surprised he hasn't cooled off and come back by now." She tapped a short message to her boyfriend that Bridget's backdoor was unlocked and that they would be out for a bit. She intentionally left it vague. If she mentioned they were going to talk to Ethan and Nadia, he would do his cop thing and insist that she not meddle in police affairs. Bettina said Hector withheld information from her about threats against him at work. They'd be talking about that later. But in the meantime, he didn't need to know everything she did either.

After deciding that the amount of wine they drank was insufficient to impair their driving, the duo set off for Perkatory, one of several local coffee shops. Ethan Wiley worked nearly full-time at the coffee shop, balancing his heavy workload with his first year of graduate studies at Midwestern State University. She liked him, not just as a former student but also as a friend. He was a good kid who had a tough background but nonetheless did all that he could to make a stable life for himself.

Ethan was busy blending coffee drinks when they arrived, but Teddy, the owner and resident conspiracy theorist, stood at the counter to greet them. "Ah, I see you two have come back. Not going to cause any trouble in here, I hope," he said, alluding to the scrap Marlee had gotten into with a couple of moms and their babies when she was overly stressed and under-caffeinated. And maybe just a bit menopausal. It had been months since that happened, but Teddy had a memory like an elephant, and he used that one incident to form his opinion of Marlee forever.

"We'll behave," Marlee said as she and Bridget each ordered a hot tea from Teddy and paid him in cash. She'd given up trying to apologize for or justify her poor behavior in the shop months before and just accepted that was the owner's impression of her.

Teddy took the twenty-dollar bill and handed Marlee her change. "Glad to see someone using cash. I'm thinking of only accepting cash. The kids," he said, tossing his head toward Ethan, "tell me it won't work because most people only use credit or debit cards. It's a big takeover. They don't want us to use our own American currency."

Marlee backed away, unwilling to engage with Teddy in his current conspiracy obsession. He always brought up some injustice that he thought "they" were imposing on him but never articulated who "they" were.

She knew better than to probe the depths of those shallow waters.

As they waited in line, Ethan prepared their teas and handed the steaming mugs to them. "I'll come over in just a minute."

They settled into a booth near the front of the coffee shop so they could watch the other customers. When Marlee went there to concentrate on grading or writing, she always took the table at the back that faced the wall to limit distractions. Today, she had plenty of work to do, but figuring out who killed Professor Vernon came first.

Ethan slid into the booth beside Bridget, offering a plate of lemon blueberry tarts. "Technically, these have been in the display case too long and should be thrown away."

"Yum, thanks." Marlee was not above eating outdated food. She did it all the time and was rarely sick from it. She scooped up a large bite with her fork and inched it toward her mouth, but Bridget waived them away, saying she was too full from their lunch at Pizza Ranch. Marlee fumed inside. Her slim cousin was always food-shaming her, and one of these days, she was going to let that skinny little turd have it.

"What's going on with the case? I talked to the police last night, but they said they'd call for me to come down and make a statement at the station. I still haven't heard from them," Ethan pushed up his glasses with the oversized frames.

Marlee and Bridget took turns bringing Ethan up to speed. "When you were passing the hors d'oeuvres and drinks, did you talk to the two ladies in ball gowns and the two guys in tuxes?"

He thought for a moment, again pushing up his glasses. "No, I didn't. They never said anything to me, just accepted glasses of red wine when I went by with a tray of them. None of them ate any of the appetizers. At least none that I served. Maybe they took some from Nadia's platter. Who were those people anyway?"

Marlee shrugged. "We don't know. Hector didn't recognize them either. In fact, no one we've talked to so far knew them. It's like they popped in from out of town." She relayed the information about them already returning their formal wear to Irene's and about the blood found on one dress and one tuxedo.

"And Professor Vernon is the one who rented their formal wear," Bridget added. "He must have known them, but we don't know how. Did you see him talking to any of them?"

"I did!" Ethan exclaimed. "I didn't hear anything, but the professor was talking, and the four of them were all leaning in to listen like they didn't want to miss a word of what he was saying."

"Did any of the four talk back to him at all or react to anything he was saying?"

"Not that I saw. It was a quick interaction, and then the professor handed something to one of the men, maybe an envelope or a folded piece of paper, and walked away, leaving the foursome standing there. That's it," Ethan said. "Do you think one of them killed him?"

"It's possible," Marlee said. "At this point, every single person at the party is a potential suspect. Did you see anyone go into the basement before the lights went out?"

"The door to the basement was left open a crack at one point, and I closed it, but I didn't see anyone go down there or come back. But I was in and out of the kitchen so much it's hard to keep track of who was where."

Marlee nodded. "We're all having the same problem. There were too many people to keep track of. Do you remember anyone being gone for any length of time? Anyone who disappeared for ten or fifteen minutes?"

He thought again and then shook his head. "Not that I remember. I'll think on it a bit and see if anything comes to mind."

"You mentioned to me the other day that the professor was coming in here regularly to work on something," Marlee said to Ethan. "Did you get a glimpse of his laptop? Did he say what he was working on?"

"He didn't bring in a laptop. I remember him writing on a yellow legal pad, which I thought was kind of odd because it would be so much faster to type out his thoughts rather than writing them by hand, but I guess he was old school. And no, he never said anything about his work. I remember his handwriting was illegible, so I probably couldn't have read his notes anyway."

"So, you sort of saw his notes," Bridget said.

"No, his signature when he signed his credit card bill. I could hardly read his name at all, but it kind of matched the name on his credit card. A lot of people just scrawl their names very quickly, so I didn't think much of it. Maybe his handwriting is impeccable after all," he said with a shrug.

"Ethan, you were sitting at the table playing the murder mystery game. Who do you think shot the professor? Do you think it was someone at the table? Or was it someone else who was standing close by?" Marlee asked.

"It would have to be someone sitting at the table, right? If he was shot in the stomach, then the shooter would have aimed at him from under the table. If he was shot in the chest, then the bullet would have come from above the table."

"The gunshot happened a few seconds after the lights went out," Marlee said. "If the lights were out, how could the shooter be sure they had a good aim? They may have lined up the shot before the lights went out, but how could they be sure Professor Vernon would remain in the same position? He could have leaned to the right or left or stood up."

"That's right, we don't actually know if he was sitting or standing when he was shot," Bridget said. "I assumed he was seated, but we don't know that for sure. He could have jumped up from his chair as soon as the lights went out. Or he could have turned in the chair to ask the person beside him what was happening."

"After the gunshot, there was silence and then screams, and then some people laughed, thinking it was part of the game. When the lights came back on a few seconds later, Professor Vernon was on the floor, and Hector was standing over him holding a gun," Ethan recalled. "At this point, I'm still thinking it's part of the game too. I mean, it seemed a little overdone with Hector supposedly dying from drinking poisoned wine, then an electrical outage right before a gunshot, then the professor is supposedly shot dead. I thought you'd gone too far with the theatrics, but we were all having fun, and I was happy to play along."

"The only planned part was Hector being the victim of the murder mystery game. Whoever flipped off the electricity in the basement is in cahoots with the person who shot Professor Vernon. We have two people who need to be held accountable for murder," Marlee said.

House of Games

End game. I have to keep my eye on the end game. Don't get too bogged down in the pain and emotion. And leave intellect out of it, too.

Chapter 12

For the next twenty minutes, Marlee, Bridget, and Ethan batted around various theories on who had killed Professor Vernon and why. Their brainstorming session was interrupted when Teddy approached the table. "You still working?" The cranky coffee shop owner barked at Ethan.

Ethan sprang out of the booth with a general apology to his employer for neglecting his work duties and to Marlee and Bridget for abandoning their discussion. "It's our fault, Teddy," Bridget said as they, too, rose from the booth.

"Yeah, we were just leaving because Ethan told us he needed to get back to work," Marlee said, trying to cover for her former student.

"I'm tryin' to run a business here," Teddy grumbled as he walked back toward the counter where absolutely no customers were waiting.

Once back in her vehicle Marlee said, "Teddy's always got a stick up his ass. I'm not sure why Ethan stays. Even though he won some money last year, I know he's intent on saving every cent so he can get his doctorate. But he could still find a better place to work." Her cell buzzed with a text, interrupting her verbal takedown of Teddy and his abrasive personality.

"Hector's back at your house. Wallace gave clearance for us to move back home," Marlee said with a smile.

Bridget frowned. "I was enjoying your company. It gets kind of lonely around my house."

"You can pack your jammies and come stay with us tonight."

"Ha ha," she fake-laughed. "Nice try. You just want help cleaning up from the crime scene and the party."

"That too," Marlee acknowledged. "But it would keep you from being so lonely."

"I think I'll pass. Still have tests to grade and need to get my students' final project information to them. Now that we're into November, it's going to be hectic on campus."

Marlee grimaced. She too had papers to grade, recommendation letters to write, and a committee assignment hanging over head. This was in addition to the lectures she needed to fine tune for the week's classes. "Don't remind me."

Hector had managed to capture Pippa and wrestle her into the pet carrier by the time they arrived at Bridget's house. He had the bite marks on the back of his hand to prove it. Pippa was pacing in her cage, a constant low growl emitting from her throat. "Looks like that didn't go well for anyone," Marlee joked.

Although he didn't seem to be fuming any longer, Hector was a long way from a joking mood. Marlee gave him a pass. She could overlook his moods occasionally, just as he overlooked hers. "I'll pack our clothes," Marlee said, moving toward the guest room.

"Already done and in my Jeep. All we have to do is load the cat and cat supplies, and we're ready to go," he said, not making eye contact with either Bridget or Marlee. Bridget had not been there when Hector blew up earlier, but he knew Marlee would have told her about it. He was embarrassed by his behavior and, in true male fashion, decided to ignore everyone's feelings rather than apologize for his behavior.

Hector drove his Jeep back to their house, and Marlee followed in her CR-V with Pippa in tow. They both stood in the driveway, looking at their house before going inside. "This is really bizarre," Marlee said.

"I know. I've been to hundreds of crime scenes, but I always got to leave when the investigation was over. This gives me a whole new perspective on how crime victims feel," he said.

She grabbed his hand and squeezed it. "We can always go back to Bridget's."

"No, I think the sooner we get the place cleaned up, the better we'll feel," Hector said, his can-do attitude taking over. "Can you leave the cat in our room or in her carrier until we've made some progress? I don't want her tracking fingerprint dust and who knows what else all over the house."

"Good call. I'll let her run around in our bedroom. That should be enough freedom to keep her calm for a bit," Marlee said knowing full well that the kitty would raise hell until she had full run of the first and second floors.

They met in the dining room, both staring at the bloodied rug underneath the table. They moved the table and chairs and rolled up the area rug, stashing it in a corner of the garage for now. Blood had soaked through the rug, and stains were visible on the newly refinished hardwood floor. The last thing she wanted to deal with was cleaning up Professor Vernon's blood. Seeing it on their area rug and now the floor made the murder even more real. As much as she wanted to avoid the gruesome task, Marlee didn't want Hector to be further traumatized by cleaning up the remaining blood. She took a deep breath and started scrubbing.

Hector had insisted that they invest in stripping and finishing the wood floors right after they moved in. She'd been against the idea, noting that they had tons of bills to pay off and plenty of other things in the house that needed immediate attention. Refinishing the floors seemed like a cosmetic procedure that could wait. Now, she was thrilled that Hector had gotten his way. The protective coating on the old wood floors made cleaning up dried blood a breeze. *The manufacturers should use that in their marketing campaign*, Marlee thought.

Meanwhile, Hector had collected the remains of the party. Wine glasses and small plates were in the dishwasher, while old food, beer bottles, napkins, and other debris were taken out to the trash receptacle in the garage. Getting everything cleaned up and back in order on the first floor went quicker than either of them expected. By 9:00 p.m., they were both exhausted but had a tidy living room and a kitchen with the rest of the dirty dishes stacked and ready to go through the dishwasher the next day.

"Pizza?" Marlee asked, looking at Hector. He agreed, and within half an hour, they were eating a large thin-crust bacon and green pepper pizza. They ate mostly in silence, as so much had happened in the past twenty-four hours. Marlee was ready to process it all but knew Hector needed to take his time. And since he was suffering the harshest consequences from the professor's murder, Hector's wants superseded her own.

With only two pieces of pizza left, Hector began to open up. "I didn't mean to jump all over you about what you said about Wallace. It was a shock, and I'd had about all the shocks I could handle at that moment." This was his apology, and Marlee nodded her acceptance of it. When she and Bridget got into an argument there were effusive apologies and mea-culpas from both, regardless as to who was really at fault. With Marlee and Hector, there was a brief acknowledgment of less-than-stellar behavior on his part, and that was it. No more was to be said.

"Bettina stopped over at Bridget's while you were out. We told her what we knew. She said Wallace had updated her on the phone while she was driving back from the Hills with her boyfriend. Or ex-boyfriend. Anyway, sounds like she's up to speed on the case," Marlee said.

"Did you tell her about Wallace and what you saw him do in the Gray Room?"

Marlee hesitated and then nodded. "Bettina didn't say much, just that she'd keep an eye on all the evidence." She thought it was best to keep it brief as it related to the topic of Detective Wallace. Hector may still be in a snit over her earlier claims and didn't want to jeopardize the rare moments of peace they'd had in the past day. Besides, Bettina could speak for herself and tell Hector directly what she was going to do.

"Should we go check out the third floor or should we just go to bed?" Hector asked. He looked beat. The lines on his handsome face were more pronounced and his eyes were red. Marlee noticed he took his glasses off multiple times to rub his eyes, a sure sign of fatigue.

"Let's just go to bed. We can deal with cleaning the third floor tomorrow," Marlee said. "I'll cancel my two morning classes, and in my evening class, they have a test, so I can be around here most of the day."

Hector nodded, relieved. They walked up the stairs to their second-floor bedroom. Marlee opened the door and saw Pippa sitting on their bed, a fresh furball puked up on Hector's pillow. She distracted him and grabbed the pillow, shooing Pippa off the bed. Hector walked right by the bed to the ensuite bathroom to brush his teeth. When he returned, a fresh pillowcase was on his pillow, and Pippa was nowhere to be seen.

Morning started earlier than intended. At 5:00 a.m., Hector's cell phone rang, and he leaped out of bed as he answered it, ready to head out on the latest investigation. It was only as he was pulling on his jeans that he realized he wouldn't be going into the station or arriving at a new crime scene. He was on suspension, and, as he realized it, he sank onto the side of the bed, cell phone still held to his ear.

"Who is it?" Marlee asked, sitting up and rubbing her eyes.

"False alarm," Hector said.

"What kind of false alarm?"

"Deb is on dispatch and called me before realizing I was suspended. That was an awkward conversation," Hector said.

"What was it that she was calling about?"

"A   break-in   at   Irene's."

"The formal wear place we've been talking about? That can't be a coincidence," Marlee said. "I hope Wallace had already taken the gowns and tuxes from the four unknown guests. That had to be what someone was looking for, don't you think?"

"That's my guess. Either those clothes or the records, paper or computerized, showing that Professor Vernon paid for them. It must be something related to the professor's murder," Hector said.

"Yeah, I don't think breaking into a shop that sells and rents formal wear would be high on the regular burglar's list of places to hit. It's connected," she said with assurance.

Since they were both wide awake, they decided to get a jump on the day. Marlee made coffee while Hector stirred up the batter for pancakes. Bacon sizzled in the skillet beside him.

"What is it about crime that makes me so hungry?" Marlee asked, stuffing a forkful of buttery pancakes into her mouth.

"Same here." Hector poured syrup on his second stack of pancakes and helped himself to more bacon. "I'm not going to the gym today either."

"Your gym buddies will miss you," she said and then paused as she remembered a new detail from the Open House. "Hey, I just remembered. What were the names of the two guys from the party? Your workout friends."

"What workout friends? None of my gym people came to the party."

"Yeah, they did. One guy was wearing a Minnesota Vikings jersey, and the other was wearing a Minnesota Twins jersey. You remember," Marlee insisted.

"No, they aren't friends of mine. I thought they were some of your people from the university," Hector said.

"I don't remember seeing them before, that's why I thought they were your friends," Marlee said, dumbfounded that now there were two more unknown people at their party.

Hector's fork slipped from his fingers, making a loud clang on the plate. "We have two more suspects in Professor Vernon's murder."

House of Games

Brenda Donelan

Nobody uses good ole pen and paper anymore. It's how I started writing, and it's how I'll finish. I can't stand using a computer to write a story. It sucks the creativity right out of me.

Chapter 13

"Holy shit," Marlee muttered, struggling to get her mind around the possibility of two new suspects in the murder of Professor Vernon. "All this time, I thought they were your gym buddies. They look like guys you would work out with."

"I only saw them briefly but assumed they were your colleagues from MSU. One of them could have sneaked into the basement and cut the electricity."

"And the other one could have been the shooter," Marlee interrupted. "We need to talk to everyone from the party to find out who saw these two men. And find out where they were seen right before the electricity went out and when it came back on."

"This changes everything," Hector said, light coming back into his eyes. He'd been looking defeated since his suspension went into effect, but now he seemed hopeful and even a bit perky. "I'm calling Bettina."

"It's not even 6:00 yet. Will she be up?"

"Yeah, she was next on the list for the dispatcher to call. She's already at Irene's shop investigating the break-in." After placing the call, Hector turned to Marlee. "Bettina says nothing seems to be missing at Irene's shop. Definitely thinks it's connected to the unknown foursome at our party and the professor's murder."

"So far, we have the four overdressed guests and the two guys in the jerseys that are all unknown. Instead of narrowing down our suspect list, it keeps growing," Marlee said.

"Other than the Minnesota sports jerseys, what do you remember about the two guys I thought were your friends from MSU?"

"Both were medium height and weight. Both middle aged. Average looking. I think they were wearing jeans and tennis shoes. What do you remember?" Marlee asked, confident that she had given a good overall description of the two unknown men.

"The guy in the Vikings jersey was around five foot ten inches and one hundred and eighty pounds. He had short dark brown hair, slightly receding in front. No glasses. No visible scars or tattoos. I'd say around thirty-five years old. He was wearing black drawstring athletic pants and black New Balance tennis shoes. The guy in the Twins jersey was a little bigger, maybe six foot tall and two hundred pounds. He had short brown hair too, but it was a bit lighter than the other guy's. And it wasn't receding in front. He was maybe a couple years younger. He had on dark-wash jeans and dark brown loafers. No glasses, tattoos, or scars. They had the same nose. Looked like brothers to me," Hector said.

Marlee couldn't hide it. She was impressed with Hector's powers of observation. She always thought of herself as having a keen eye, but his skills left her in the dust. "Wow, could you describe them for a sketch artist? If no one knows these guys we will need a good description to go on and you have their looks memorized."

He grinned, the first smile she'd seen in well over a day. "Yeah, if no one knows who they are, I can give a description to our artist."

"What were all these randos doing at our party?" Marlee asked, frustrated with the number of unknowns who had attended.

Hector raised his eyebrows and gave her a look. "It was an Open House. That means the house or business is open for anyone to come."

"I know, but what was their motivation for coming? Our friends came to support us and so did my work colleagues and there were a few neighbors. And of course, our B&B guests were here, but who else would think to attend something like this?"

"Free food and drinks?"

"Maybe, but it was just appetizers, cheap beer, and boxed wine. It's not like we were serving prime rib and lobster. Other than those tied to the university, I can't think of anyone who would go too far out of their way for basic finger food and cheap alcohol. Academics and students will go to anything for free food," Marlee said recalling one of her department colleagues praising the free snacks at Tractor Supply Company.

"I think there are some older people that make the rounds for free food. It's part of their social life, going from business to business and meeting up with their friends. My secretary's mom does it all the time and rarely has to buy lunch anymore."

"None of our unknowns fall into the older age range. The two guys wearing jerseys were in their thirties, and the four overdressed people were probably in their late forties?" Marlee looked to Hector for confirmation on the ages of the foursome, and he nodded.

"The foursome wasn't completely unknown. The professor knew them well enough to pay for the rentals of their gowns and tuxes. That doesn't help us much, but we know there was at least some connection to someone here at the B&B. Our best bet is to reach out to everyone at the party and ask if they know who the two guys are. Somebody may have brought their friends along and didn't mention it."

"I'll email my friends and ask if they know those two guys or have any ideas about their connection to our party," Marlee said, already tapping out a message to her Supper Club friends and work colleagues. "I gave your descriptions of the guys and asked everyone to get back to me ASAP on this." No sooner had she sent the email than replies started coming in. Everyone who replied remembered the two guys in the Minnesota sports jerseys, yet no one knew them.

"This is strange," Marlee said as she sent a text to both Paul and Leanne. Although they had been on a date over the weekend while staying at the B&B, one of them may have had friends who lived in the area and invited them over. Marlee didn't recall the two guys talking to anyone, but she wasn't paying any attention to them either, assuming they were Hector's gym buddies.

Leanne texted right back, indicating that she remembered the two guys but didn't know their connection to the party. "Leanne didn't know them," Marlee reported to Hector. "I'm guessing if Paul knew those guys, then he would have introduced them to her, so we can cross both Paul and Leanne off the list as knowing them. Who else can I contact besides the people we're still waiting to hear from?"

"Ethan Wiley and that other student who was serving the appetizers. What was her name?"

"Nadia Deen. I spoke with Ethan about what he saw at the party last night, but I haven't talked to Nadia at all. Guess I sort of forgot about her. I'll go talk to her in person about last night and also if she knows those two jersey guys. I'll swing by Perkatory later and talk to Ethan again," Marlee said, mentally organizing her day. "I don't have to be on campus until 6:00 tonight, so there's plenty of time today to check in with everyone."

She reached for the crime chart to look it over again and remembered that she had not talked to Hector about Professor Vernon's status as a sex offender. "We discovered it last night while doing an Internet search of him," Marlee said. "I told Bettina, and she was going to look into it since there weren't any details about his offense online."

Hector shook his head in disbelief. "There's another wrinkle to the case. Should we go up to third floor and take a look at his room?"

Not only was she curious about the professor's possessions and any possible clues to his murder, but she also needed to clean up his room to get ready for the next guests who were arriving mid-week. "Yeah, I guess we should."

They climbed the stairs via the back entrance, looking for anything that might be a clue. The stairway was empty, as she expected, since the police would have seized anything of importance left on the stairs. She held her breath as Hector pushed open the door to the third floor. The police had not made as much of a mess as she'd expected. All four rooms had been rummaged through, but everything was intact. Marlee had watched too many cop shows where the police overturned furniture and trashed the place they were searching. She supposed that happened but was thankful that the Elmwood Police Department had been respectful of their property.

They walked to Professor Vernon's room first, standing in the doorway. It was impossible to believe that the quirky man inhabiting the room for the past week was now dead. His brown hard surface suitcase was folded shut in the corner next to a pair of brown shoes.

"Before we go in, can you show me exactly where you were when you saw Wallace take the piece of paper?" Hector asked. The accusation toward his fellow detective was still nagging at him, and Marlee knew he was looking for a logical explanation.

"I was over here by the sink," she said, walking over and taking up the position she was in earlier. "Then I looked over my shoulder, and I saw Wallace rip a piece of paper from a legal pad on the desk, and he turned slightly, then folded it and put it in his inside pocket," she said.

"Okay," Hector said calmly. "Now, can you go in the Gray Room and, without touching anything, act out what you saw Wallace do?"

Marlee took a deep breath and walked into Professor Vernon's room. The sun wasn't up yet, but the sky was getting lighter. Hector reached around the doorway and flipped on the overhead light. "Was the light on yesterday when you showed Wallace to the room?"

"Yes, I turned it on as soon as we walked in. Otherwise, it would've been dark except for the light from the shared living area." She motioned toward the small table lamp that was always left on so that guests could find their way to their rooms and the kitchenette as needed. "I turned the light on in here, and Wallace looked around a bit and then told me to leave. Well, I don't like being ordered around in my own house, so I moved out to the living area to tidy up a bit. There were some used mugs on the counter that needed washing and crumbs that hadn't been wiped up. Mostly, I was dinking around to see if he found anything of importance in the professor's room."

"Now act out what Wallace did in the room," Hector said.

Marlee turned and mimed picking up a legal pad on Professor Vernon's desk, ripping off the top sheet of paper, folding it, and stuffing it inside her imaginary suit jacket. Then she looked around to make sure no one saw, just as she'd observed Wallace doing. When she finished, she turned back toward Hector to gauge his reaction.

"And you were standing by the sink when you saw him take the paper?" Hector asked.

"No. I was at the sink then went in to get a better look. I moved a little closer and saw him take the paper without bagging and tagging it."

"Did Wallace know you saw him?" Hector asked.

"I don't know. I moved back right away, but that's when he realized I was still on the third floor and he ordered me to leave," Marlee recalled. "I'm not sure how he realized I was still there. Maybe he caught a glimpse of me, or I made a sound."

Hector moved into the spot near the sink where she said she'd been standing the previous night when she saw Wallace and the paper. "Now, do the whole thing again. Just like you did before."

Marlee rolled her eyes as she turned to reenact Wallace's actions. When she was finished, she turned to look at Hector. "Did I pass your test?"

Hector threw up his hands in mock surrender. "Hey, I only wanted to see how the whole thing played out. Besides, you know eyewitness accounts are often unreliable. We've all done it. Thought we saw something and then realize our mind filled in some blanks with things that really didn't occur."

"I'm very familiar with false eyewitness accounts," she said, more than a little irritated. In her Intro to Policing class, she showed a thirty-second clip of a film and then asked the students to describe the people in it and what action played out. The versions were wildly different from student to student, yet they were all presented with the same video. Marlee knew Hector was rationally sorting out what happened, still unable to make sense of his trusted colleague acting in an unprofessional and possibly illegal manner.

"I clearly saw everything you acted out, just as you said it had happened," Hector acknowledged, trying to soothe her hurt feelings. "I thought the view might be obstructed, or it was too dark to see what happened in the room, but that's not the case."

"So, what now? Do you ask Wallace straight out what he was doing?"

"Unfortunately, I do nothing since I'm on suspension."

"When I told Bettina about the incident, she said she would look at the evidence log to see if the paper from the legal pad had been added. If it has, then not following proper procedure for evidence collection seems to be the main issue with Wallace. If it hasn't been logged in, then we have a tampering situation," Marlee said.

"Agreed, but I just can't understand Wallace doing either. He knows better than to shove evidence in his pockets. And let's say he did take it to destroy it. What's his motive? He doesn't know Professor Vernon or anything about his research," Hector said.

"We don't know that for sure," Marlee pointed out. "We're assuming there was no connection between the detective and the professor, but they may have been acquainted. Or something the professor had written down was something that Wallace didn't want anyone else to see." She walked back over to the desk in the Gray Room and picked up the legal pad, turning it from side to side, hoping to see indentations from the writing on the previous page.

Hector moved closer and looked over her shoulder. "I can't see anything, can you?"

She shook her head and flipped through the thirty or so remaining pages in the legal pad. "Nothing." She reached for a pencil and began shading the top sheet of paper, hoping that indentations would show up, darkened from the pencil lead. Nothing was visible and Marlee slammed the pad and pencil down. "Now what?"

"Do you want to look through all his papers and notebooks on his desk and try to figure out what he was researching? While you work on that, I'll strip the bed and throw the bedding and towels from all three rooms in the wash."

"It's a deal," she said, pulling out the desk chair, ready to delve into the work Professor Vernon had been working on prior to his death. She rolled up her sleeves and started looking at the book on the top of the pile. It was a South Dakota Codified Law book. Judging by the titles, the whole stack was related to the rules of law within the state. Marlee noted the markings on the spines of the books. They'd been checked out from a library, and a peek inside confirmed that they were from the community library in Elmwood.

Moving on, Marlee reached for a notebook with a hardcover. Inside were notes on amending current legislation and bringing initiated measures up for a vote in South Dakota. The Professor had similar notes for the states of Wisconsin, Minnesota, Iowa, and Michigan. She pushed it aside, noting that it would be the first thing she'd dive into in depth. But first, she wanted to get an overview of everything on the desk before immersing herself in one thing.

A manilla folder at the bottom of the pile of books and notes proved to be revealing. Inside were printed emails to and from Professor Vernon regarding his sabbatical research. He had been given a semester release from his duties at Badger State University to write literary fiction. His premise was to explore the themes of love and loss from the perspective of an elderly man on his deathbed. After conducting necessary research on the topic, the expectation was that he would publish a book or papers for academic journals, thus contributing to the overall body of knowledge on the subject. The emails were peppered with the usual academic speak, Professor Vernon insisting his proposal was cutting edge and would bring great prestige to his department and the university. His dean, on the other hand, was not convinced. According to the printed emails, Professor Vernon had only narrowly received the support of his dean for the research. Marlee knew that without the support of his dean, there was no way the Sabbatical Committee would approve his request.

She was confused. Her knowledge of creative writing in the literary field was limited, as that was not her area of expertise; however, Professor Vernon's research proposal seemed to hold water. He had a thoughtful plan for conducting his research and writing his book. She couldn't decipher why his dean was being such a stickler. Marlee had been in academia long enough to notice political game-playing when she saw it. It appeared Professor Vernon was not on the best terms with his dean, and the dean was making life tough for the professor; a game as old as time.

She reached for her phone and googled the name of the Dean of Arts and Sciences at Badger State University. Dr. Ralph Spangler was new to the deanship, having accepted the position only a year ago. He had come from the University of Minnesota where he was a dean for seven years. Before that, he'd been chair of his department and a full professor. Marlee wondered what prompted the move to La Crosse, Wisconsin. Since he moved from one deanship to another, it wasn't a promotion. In fact, it may have been a pay cut since Badger State University was significantly smaller than the University of Minnesota. Some states valued education more than others. Unfortunately, South Dakota wasn't one of those states. Low wages in the state led to brain drain, which led to the same fateful decisions being made over and over again.

Marlee knew if she didn't put her phone away, she'd be going down an online rabbit hole soon. As much as she wanted more information on why Professor Vernon and his new dean didn't get along, she knew it was not the most important task at hand. If time allowed later, she'd dig into it. Academic feuds fascinated her, especially since they were usually so petty.

The rest of the papers in the professor's manilla folder held more printed emails, much the same as those she'd already read. Of interest, it appeared that Dean Spangler had only agreed to support Professor Vernon's request for a sabbatical after the professor had contacted the university president. *I bet the Dean would've had it out for Professor Vernon for the rest of their careers since the professor went over his head,* Marlee thought. Now, that would no longer be an issue.

A ripped half sheet of paper fell to the floor. It had been tucked between pages she'd already rifled through, yet she had not seen it. Marlee picked it up and read over it three times, making sure she understood what she was reading. This scrap of paper that had been overlooked by both Marlee and the police held the reason for Professor Vernon's death.

House of Games

Me: *"You can't fire me. I have tenure."*

Him: *"Your incompetence is shedding a bad light on this university. We have to do something."*

Me: *"I won't go without a fight."*

Him: *"There's nothing left to fight about. You're getting your sabbatical, and when you return, you'll announce your retirement effective immediately."*

Me: *"Like hell, I will."*

Chapter 14

"This is ridiculous," Hector scoffed after reading the scrap of paper from Professor Vernon's folder. "He hired someone to kill him because he was dying. That kind of thing only happens in movies. Bad movies."

"I agree. It's unbelievable, but look again at what's written. Instructions on how and when he wanted to be killed. The professor was directing someone to shoot him while he was in Elmwood. The top half of the email is ripped off, so we don't know who it was written to. But he typed his name at the end."

"This could be a story he was writing for fun. Or an idea for a screenplay. Maybe he had dreams of writing the next Hollywood blockbuster. There's no indication that this is a directive for someone to actually shoot him," Hector insisted. "And anyone could have typed his name. It doesn't mean he wrote this."

Marlee reached for the manilla folder and took all the pages out. She sat down and went through every single piece of paper, looking for the top half of the paper. Not finding it, she turned to the stack of books and began fanning through the pages to see if it had been used as a bookmark. Still not finding it, Marlee turned to the professor's hard-backed notebook. The top half of the paper was not there either.

"Shit!" She slammed down the notebook. Marlee had been through all the books and papers on the desk, so now she turned toward the clothes still hanging in the wardrobe. Professor Vernon hung up two pairs of khaki pants, four plaid button-down shirts, and two dark blazers. Typical wear for an aging professor. *Probably the same things he wore when he started teaching thirty years ago,* she thought as she searched the pockets of his pants and jackets. Finding nothing, she moved toward his suitcase. It was empty except for a few days' worth of off-white underwear, thread-barren undershirts, and well-worn socks. Nothing was in the lining at the top of the insides of the luggage.

"Maybe it is a hoax. Or a creative writing project, like you said." Marlee sank down onto the bed.

"What advantage is there to having someone shoot you versus dying of a disease?" Hector pondered. "It shouldn't make any difference in insurance or benefits paid to loved ones. I guess it would be quicker and less painful to have someone kill you than wait for a disease to wrack your body for months or even years."

"We still don't know where he was shot. I assumed he was shot under the table, and the bullet hit him in the stomach. It's incredibly painful but not always fatal. Plenty of people get shot in the stomach and recover," Marlee said, recalling an article she recently read on gunshot wounds.

"That's right. There's no guarantee that a bullet to the stomach would kill him. And how would the shooter have known that they even hit the professor? The gun didn't go off until the lights were out. For all they knew, they may have missed him entirely or shot someone else."

Marlee nodded along. "Yeah, the whole electrical outage and shooting were orchestrated down to the second. I wonder if Professor Vernon knew that was when he would be shot. I wonder if he knew someone was pointing a gun at him. If so, he could have kept his position after the lights went out, allowing the shooter to keep their aim under the table."

"We need to find out who his next of kin is. He wasn't married and didn't have any kids, but there must be a sibling, niece or nephew, or distant cousin. Maybe a friend or a former student he was close to that he would have named," Hector said. "I'll see if Bettina has located anyone yet."

Bettina arrived at their home within fifteen minutes and asked to be taken directly to the Gray Room. "Where's this so-called murder directive?" she asked, looking around the room.

"Right there on the desk. I'm afraid both Hector and I handled it before we realized what it was. If there were any fingerprints besides Professor Vernon's, we probably destroyed them."

"At least you didn't crumple it up and put it in your pocket," Bettina mumbled to herself. She put on gloves before picking up and examining the half-torn page "Nothing here that shows whether this is real or fiction. As weird as this professor was, it could be either."

Hector joined them in the Gray Room after running to the basement to move the laundry from the washer to the dryer. "I don't know that an insurance policy is going to pay out more if the insured is killed by violence versus dying from cancer. Do you?"

"Nope," Bettina said. "Besides going to a lot of effort to make this happen, if it is legit, why here in front of fifty potential witnesses during your party? There are dozens of easier ways to kill himself or make it look like an accident if that was his intent. And why would he email the details to someone? That seems like something you wouldn't want written down anywhere, let alone printed off from email."

Marlee nodded along. "I was beginning to agree that this had to be some sort of creative writing project except for one glaring hole. The professor's actual murder was carried out by firearm while he was in Elmwood, just as the note directs. So that means that either the note is legit, and the professor's murder played out per his wishes, or someone inserted the typed note into his papers either before or after killing him, knowing it would be located. Which, I'm a little surprised that neither Wallace nor the crime scene techs found it when they searched the room."

"I'll add that to my growing list of Wallace's oversights in this case," Bettina said with a scowl. "One other option is that whoever killed the professor knew he was dying and added the note to his stacks of paperwork, but they did so knowing it would be found, and then the insurance company could rule the policy invalid since he participated in his own death."

"Some policies will pay out to the beneficiaries when there's a suicide, and some won't. It depends on the policy. Often, it comes down to how long the person had the policy. If they had it for ten or twenty years, then it will pay out. On the other hand, if it was bought in the past few months, then it looks like there was an intent to defraud the insurance company on someone's behalf." Marlee recalled the general ins and outs of life insurance policies as they related to suicides, as she'd researched this on another death in the area years ago.

"I think we're getting ahead of ourselves. We don't even know if he had a life insurance policy. If he didn't have any kids or anyone in his family that he was close to, then maybe he didn't see a reason to get it," Hector said.

"I don't know how state government works in Wisconsin, but in South Dakota, we have health insurance as part of our benefits package," Marlee said. "We can get life insurance through the state too, but it's an extra cost. Some of my friends said they get it while others don't, either choosing a cheaper option on their own or foregoing it altogether. I already had my own life insurance set up before I started working at MSU."

"Sounds similar to what we have with the City of Elmwood," Hector said, and Bettina nodded along. "Still assuming that the note is legit, maybe insurance wasn't the angle."

"What do you think the angle might be?" Bettina asked.

"No idea. That's where the detective work comes in," Hector commented with a wry half-smile. "Wish I could dig into this. Officially."

"As soon as we get you cleared, then your suspension will be lifted, and you'll be back at work bitching about it like the rest of us," Bettina assured him. "I know it's tough, but enjoy your time off a little bit.

Work on projects around the house. I'm sure you have some fix-it things to keep you busy. I'm keeping an eye on Wallace so the case won't go off the rails."

"Was the paper Marlee saw him put in his pocket logged into evidence?" Hector asked.

"No, it wasn't. I checked right away this morning and Wallace didn't log in anything from the professor's room. And now, with you two finding this email note, I'm wondering what else he missed. Until I've had a chance to go over this room myself, I'm going to seal it off with crime tape. I'll be back later today to see what else Wallace and the crime scene techs may have missed," Bettina said, shooing them out of the room. She used her gloved hands to place the ripped email note into a plastic bag and sealed it, attaching an evidence tag to the bag.

Hector and Marlee obediently left the Gray Room and watched as Bettina placed yellow tape across the doorway. "Are you bringing the crime scene techs back in?" Hector asked.

"Not unless I find something. They were in here yesterday and went over the room, so they should have fingerprints and all that. You two were already in here cleaning and looking through his things, so any evidence previously missed was probably destroyed. So far, Wallace has made a mess of this case," Bettina growled. "I'm keeping a detailed log of what Wallace has and hasn't done and will be turning it over to the higher-ups."

"After the case is closed?" Marlee asked, wondering why she would wait so long to bring Wallace's incompetence and possibly illegal activity to the attention of his superiors.

"Unless there are more fuck-ups on his part," Bettina said, walking down the back staircase. "In that case, then I'll turn over what I have immediately."

"Oh, and I have some preliminary findings from the lab and the autopsy. The Professor was shot in the chest at close range. His death was likely immediate since the bullet struck his heart," Bettina said as she opened the door to her unmarked police car. And Hector, gunshot residue was found on your hands but not on your clothing. There wasn't any blowback on your clothes either."

"Of course, there would be gunshot residue since I picked up the gun right after it was fired, so that means nothing," Hector said. "Good news for me is that there wasn't any GSR or blowback on my clothes. That puts me one step closer to clearing my name and getting my job back."

"Agreed. It was good news for you, and it helps us better understand the bullet's trajectory. The techs are working on that right now," Bettina said. She left with a promise to check out Professor Vernon's life insurance situation and follow up on his sex offender status.

"That creeps me out," Marlee said as she watched Bettina drive away. "I'm glad we didn't have any little kids staying here with a sex offender on the premises."

"Assuming his offense involves kids," Hector said. "Anyone could be his victim. We won't know until Bettina or Wallace find out more about it."

"I feel so much better with Bettina keeping an eye on Wallace. Not only do I trust her work as a detective, but I feel like Wallace won't be able to get away with much now that Bettina has him in her sights."

"Me too. I still can't believe that Wallace would be so sloppy or so unethical in his evidence collection," Hector said. "He knows better, and it's going to reflect poorly on the whole department regardless of why he did it. When this gets out, it's going to call into question every investigation he's ever worked on."

"As it should," Marlee said. "If he's incompetent or crooked, then innocent people might be in prison because of him."

Hector glared at her. "And plenty of those people in prison are there rightfully so. Wallace's screw-ups are going to cause us a bunch of extra work. Some of the cases he worked on here might be overturned and then we go back to trial."

"But you don't want innocent people in prison for crimes they didn't commit, right?" Marlee insisted. "I mean what kind of justice system do we have if the police are mishandling evidence?"

"You don't understand," Hector said as he stomped back inside, the door slamming behind him.

Marlee looked at her phone. It was almost lunchtime, and with Hector in a huff, she wasn't going to stay home and eat with him. She texted her cousin to meet her at Perkatory for a caffeine and carb-laced lunch. When she arrived, Bridget was already there waiting in line to order. She motioned Marlee over toward her, garnering them the glare of three people in line behind them.

"It's been a day already," Bridget sighed after they'd placed their orders and went to sit in a booth.

"Tell me about it," Marlee interrupted, purposely cutting off her cousin's impeding diatribe on the difficulties of professorhood in the last month before final exams. She launched into the new developments she and Hector discovered at their house that morning.

"Holy crap!" Bridget leaned in closer across the table. "Was the printed email Professor Vernon's attempt at a suicide note? Or directions on when and how to kill him?"

"That's what we're trying to figure out. It's also possible that it's not true at all. Maybe the professor was writing a story or a script."

"Every step of this case gets wackier and wackier," Bridget said, mouthing a "thanks" to the person who delivered their coffees and scones to their booth.

"Is Ethan working today?" Marlee asked. Her motive for coming to Perkatory was three-fold. First, she wanted to get away from cranky-ass Hector. Second, she wanted to update Bridget on what she'd learned since returning home the prior evening. And third, Marlee wanted to talk to Ethan some more about the party.

"Yeah, he's in the back. I'll grab him for you," the counter attendant said.

Ethan Wiley rounded the corner moments later, his own steaming beverage in hand. "Scoot," he said, motioning for Bridget to move over.

After exchanging pleasantries, Marlee got to the point. She described the two guys at the party dressed in Minnesota sports jerseys. "Do you know who I'm talking about?"

"Yeah, I remember them. They were only there for a little bit but drank several glasses of wine and ate a ton of appetizers. I was about ready to ask you if I should cut them off, but then poof. They were gone. Didn't see them leave or anything. Those two are the main reason we ran out of the catered appetizers and had to raid your freezer for more."

"How long would you say they were there?"

"An hour. No longer than that. I remember them coming in the front door right before we served the first round of appetizers. That would've been about 7:00 p.m. And I don't remember seeing them anymore when you asked for people to start signing up for the drawing for who got to play the murder mystery game," Ethan recalled.

"We started the game right at 8:00 p.m., so I announced it maybe ten minutes before the game was underway," Marlee said. "Does that sound about right?"

Ethan nodded, and Bridget agreed, adding her own recollection of the timeline. "I asked you if I had time to go to the bathroom before the drawing started, and you said I did if I hurried. That was at ten minutes to 8:00. I know because I looked at the hallway clock on the way to the bathroom. I really had to go, but since there was a line, I decided that I'd just hold it until the game was over."

"You have the bladder of a twenty-year-old, my dear," Marlee said to her cousin with equal parts admiration and derision.

Bridget brushed off the remark, unsure how to take it. "Did they say anything to you, Ethan? Or did you overhear anything?"

"Even though they ate and drank way more than would be expected at an Open House, they were very polite. They thanked me each time I offered them food and wine. That's all they said to me. Not that it makes any difference, but one of the men, the shorter one, had a very high voice. Very feminine."

"I don't suppose you saw them go to the basement?" Marlee asked.

"No, never saw them anywhere but the living room. Like I said, I think they left before the game was announced. I don't remember seeing them anymore after that."

Satisfied that she had elicited everything from Ethan about the two Minnesota jersey guys, she switched back to an earlier conversation they'd had about the time Professor Vernon had spent in Perkatory the past week. "You said he wrote out notes with a pen and paper, not a computer. Did he even have a laptop with him? You know, sometimes I bring my laptop with me but then leave it on the table or in my bag without using it."

"I never saw one on his table. He always had a bag with him, but I never noticed if he had a laptop with him. Why? What's so important about him having a laptop?" Ethan asked.

Marlee drew in her breath. She wasn't prepared to tell Ethan about the ripped email detailing how the professor wanted someone to kill him. Yet, she knew that to get information, she had to give information. "This morning, we found a sketchy email that had been printed off. We don't know for sure who wrote it or who it was to because the top half was ripped off." Although not entirely true, her statements were not entirely false either. "That's why we were wondering about the professor sending emails."

"He went to the library. He could have sent them from a library computer. Or he could have emailed someone from his phone. Either way, he'd need access to a printer. And guess what they have at the library for people to use? Printers," Ethan said, getting sassy now that he sensed he wasn't getting the whole story from Marlee.

With a vague promise to fill Ethan in on the note later, the McCabe cousins finished their coffees and scones and walked outside of Perkatory. "I have night class but will cut them loose after their test. If you think of anything, come on over after 7:30. You can keep Hector company if I'm not there yet. He was out of sorts when I left."

"Oh, no. What did you do now?"

"Hey, don't assume it was me. He's the one being unreasonable this time. But I'll ignore it since he's got a lot going on with the suspension and everything. I'm just warning you that he could be in a mood when you get there tonight."

Although she'd rather be punched in the gut than go back home and put up with Hector right now, she did so anyway because she was a patient and compassionate girlfriend. Also, she suspected he might have updated information on the case. Nearing their home, she saw a police cruiser and a vehicle she now knew to be Wallace's unmarked car.

"*Dammit! I wonder what he wants,*" she thought as she pulled into the driveway and entered the house.

"Hello," she called out in an overly friendly voice, moving from the kitchen into the dining room and over to the living room.

Scrunched together on the loveseat were Detective Wallace and a uniformed officer. Hector was straight across from them in a wing-backed chair. They all turned to look at Marlee as she walked in, yet no one said a word.

"What's going on?" she finally blurted. If someone didn't spill the beans soon, she would explode.

"Do you want to tell her?" Wallace asked Hector. "Or should I?" The detective seemed to be enjoying himself, given the smirk on his face.

Hector stood and walked toward Marlee, pulling her into the kitchen and out of earshot of the police. "I have no idea how or why, but..."

"But what?" Marlee asked, becoming more frightened by the minute.

"Wallace tracked down Professor Vernon's insurance policy and the beneficiary of the policy. It's me. I'm the beneficiary of his $100,000 life insurance policy."

I asked how long I had. He said, "Not long."

Chapter 15

"What the hell, Hector? How do you know Professor Vernon? What's going on?"

"I have no idea what's happening. I'd never met that man before in my life. There's no good reason for me to be the beneficiary of his life insurance policy. I'm as shocked as you are." Hector's words coincided with his expression. It took a lot to shake Hector, but this bombshell, along with the murder with his weapon and then his suspension from work, did it. He was more than a little shaken.

"So, what now?" Marlee asked, remembering the detective and uniformed officer in their living room?

"I'm going back to the station with them to talk about this some more. I've already told them everything I know. Somebody is setting me up." He took a deep breath, trying to steady himself.

"Don't tell them anything else. Especially since Wallace still has evidence that he never logged in. I'm getting you an attorney. Don't talk until Denny gets there," Marlee said, already reaching for her phone to call a man who had represented not only herself but also some of her friends when they found themselves on the wrong side of the law.

"I don't want that dirt bag anywhere near me," Hector said, his voice full of contempt for the bloodthirsty defense attorney. "If anybody wants me to be in trouble over all this it's him."

"I know you can't stand him. He's a despicable person, but a damned fine attorney. The reason you hate him is because you've been on opposite sides. His job is to advocate for people who are charged and ensure that procedure is followed and that their client's rights are protected. You're both in pursuit of justice but coming at it from different angles. In this moment, you're not a cop. You're a suspect."

Hector didn't respond as he walked outside with the uniformed officer and Detective Wallace. Since he wasn't under arrest, he was able to sit in the back of the detective's vehicle, uncuffed.

The vehicle wasn't even out of sight before Marlee called Bettina Crawford to find out more. She answered right away, saying she expected the call. Bettina did not want to be seen openly providing information to Marlee on Hector since he was the number one suspect. They agreed to meet at Marlee's office on campus, away from the prying eyes of the police force.

Marlee grabbed a bag of papers and the exams she would need for her night class. Since she would be on campus already, it only made sense to stay there until her class started in two hours. She slowly jogged up the stairs to her office, huffing and puffing outside the door as she fumbled for her keys. Once inside, she closed the door, leaving the lights off so no one would know she was there. Marlee slunk down on her office chair, her coat still on and book bag slung across her shoulder. It was all starting to sink in. Hector was in real trouble, and she didn't know what to do. It wasn't until she heard a light tapping on the door that she moved.

"It's bad," Bettina said by way of greeting as she hurried through the door, quickly closing it behind her. "You need to tell me everything about Hector's connection to Professor Vernon. And I mean EVERYTHING."

"The only connection I know of is the professor being a paid guest at our B&B and a murder victim during our Open House. That's it. I'm as shocked as everyone else that the professor supposedly named Hector as the beneficiary of his life insurance policy," Marlee insisted.

"It's not 'supposedly.' It's a fact that Hector Ramos of Elmwood, South Dakota, is the beneficiary of Professor Vernon's life insurance policy with Massachusetts National in the amount of $100,000," Bettina said.

"Right before he left with Wallace, Hector told me about it. He said he didn't know anything about it and had just met the professor at the same time I did," Marlee pleaded. "He was sincere. You know Hector. He would have been the first to bring it up if he knew the professor, especially after he was shot. And if he knew he would be the recipient of a considerable sum of money upon someone's death, I'm positive he would have told me. Especially since we were in so much debt getting our house repaired and renovated."

Bettina paced back and forth from the closed door to the window overlooking a leafless tree in the parking lot. "You're right. I do know Hector, and I know what kind of person he is. I know he didn't leave his gun unsecured at your Open House. I know he didn't shoot Professor Vernon. And I damned sure know he wasn't aware he was named beneficiary of the professor's life insurance policy. And you want to know how I know these things?"

Marlee raised her eyebrows, waiting for Bettina's explanation. "Let's for one minute say that Hector was going to kill someone because he was going to receive a large payout from their insurance company. He sure as hell wouldn't do it this way. Hector's not stupid. He wouldn't kill someone in his own home with his own gun during a party."

"The other thing to keep in mind is that an insurance company won't pay on a policy if the beneficiary is suspected of killing the insured party," Marlee said.

"Bingo. This whole thing reeks of a setup. Somebody went to a lot of trouble to get Hector in trouble, but they surely aren't a criminal mastermind. It's almost like they want to embarrass him as much as get him arrested for murder," Bettina guessed.

The shock Marlee felt came back in waves, as if she was hearing the news again for the first time. One minute, the shock nearly bowled her over, while in the next minute, she was able to look at the situation objectively. "But who would do this to Hector? And why? And why was Professor Vernon part of the whole scheme?"

"I can't answer those questions," Bettina said, "but I did some research on the Amdahl brothers. You know the drug traffickers who went to federal prison? We had a lead that their mother had put out a hit on

Hector following their arrests. Anyway, the brothers are still in prison, and both have another twenty-some years to serve. Their mother died last year. She'd been ill, but I don't know the actual cause."

"We can rule out that lead," Marlee said dejectedly. "Any good news?"

"I've got a little more information on the professor. First, his sex offender status in Wisconsin isn't as bad as it sounds. He didn't touch or rape anyone. In fact, he did what a lot of guys do. The professor was in Atlanta, Georgia, when it happened. He was walking back to his hotel from a writer's symposium. It was only a few blocks away, but he'd gotten a little tipsy and was headed in the wrong direction. He stopped to relieve himself near some shrubs that happened to be on the edge of an elementary school playground. It was nighttime, and no one was around, except for the police car that spotted him. He was taken into custody and charged with Indecent Exposure, which is considered a sex offense in the state of Georgia. Since he lives in Wisconsin, the judicial system transferred his registry requirements from Georgia to his home state. That's why he's on the sex offender registry," Bettina reported. "Luckily, he was able to explain his situation to the university administration and keep his job."

"That's about the best-case scenario. I'm relieved to hear that he wasn't molesting children or drugging college students and taking advantage of them. He used poor judgment, but I bet one hundred percent of men and a high percentage of women have peed when they were outside and needed a restroom. Especially when alcohol was involved."

"I couldn't find anything else in his background to indicate anything suspicious. Looks like he was just a drunk guy who didn't have the bladder control he once did."

"So, we can cross off someone shooting him as an act of revenge for a sex offense," Marlee said. "What about next of kin? Did you find out who he has listed as his contact person at the university or on his medical records?"

"Janelle Vernon, his niece. She works at the same university as he does. We're trying to reach her now," Bettina reported. "She hasn't called us back. We will have an officer from the La Crosse PD go talk to her on campus if she doesn't call back tomorrow."

"Wonder why she wasn't the beneficiary of his life insurance policy? I think most people would leave it to family, close friends, or a charity that they feel passionate about, like the American Cancer Society or a local Humane Society."

"People do strange things when it comes to money," Bettina said. "We're still digging to see if he has a will. And if so, who is set to inherit from his estate."

"I gathered that he worked in academia all his life, so he probably doesn't have a lot of wealth. On the other hand, he appeared to live frugally, and if he didn't have any children, he might have a good-sized portion of cash socked away in a bank account somewhere."

"We'll find out," she said. "I have to take off. I'm meeting Wallace to interview some of the people from your party."

"Who are you interviewing?"

"I'll tell you later after we've talked to them," Bettina promised. "I'll swing by your house later tonight."

Marlee puttered around her office until it was time to give the exam to her Criminology class. It was the last test before the final exam, so tension was high when she walked into the lecture hall. Three students were already waiting up front by the podium, wanting to speak with her before the test began. The first wanted to know if she could take the test later, as she hadn't had time to study. Marlee assured her this would be fine, but make-up exams were much more difficult. After consideration, the student decided she'd roll the dice and take the exam that night as scheduled. The two other students needed clarification on a point they didn't fully understand. She answered the questions to their satisfaction, and after a few brief announcements, Marlee handed out the exams at 6:10 p.m.

Every single student handed in their paper and left by 7:00 p.m. She wasn't sure if she'd made the test too easy or too difficult. Her exams for the night class usually took students well over an hour to finish. Normally, she would start grading the multiple-choice section of the exams that night, leaving the essay portion until office hours the next day. Having a murder in her home and her boyfriend as the prime suspect had changed everything. Hector and his freedom were her primary concerns right now, closely followed by getting justice for Professor Vernon. The grading could wait.

She hurried home, knowing both Bettina and Bridget would be coming over later. In anticipation of their visit, she ordered two large pizzas and checked to make sure there were two bottles of Sauvignon Blanc in the fridge. Hector wasn't home yet, and he hadn't texted her at all since he'd left with the police that afternoon. It wasn't like him. He was good at checking in, even if it was just a quick text message.

Bridget arrived first, and Marlee updated her on Hector being the beneficiary of the professor's life insurance. By the time Bettina made it, the pizzas had been delivered, and the cousins were sitting in the living room drinking white wine. They all scooped up pizza and chomped away as they talked.

"Was Hector arrested?" Marlee asked, worried that he still wasn't home. "He's been at the station a long time."

"No, he left around 6:00 p.m. I'm surprised you haven't heard from him. Probably meeting with his attorney."

"He should be home soon," Marlee agreed. "Can you tell us about the interviews you and Wallace did this afternoon?"

"The couple that was here on a date weekend, Paul and Leanne, we talked to them again. Not much new other than they are totally incompatible, and I'm sure this was their first and last date. They returned to their respective homes, and anything else we need from them can be done over the phone. Then we talked to your friend, Shelly McFarland, who is the only one who saw F, the librarian, turn off the battery-operated candle on the table before the game began. We caught up with Ethan Wiley at Perkatory, and he mentioned that you'd been in to talk to him a couple of times about what he saw at the party. Wallace was pissed that you're nosing around, so be careful. Ethan gave a lot of details and helped with the timeline of events but didn't give us anything new. Nadia Deen is coming down to the station tomorrow before her classes, so we'll see what she knows," Bettina said.

"What about the fancy-dressed people? Two of them were part of the murder mystery game, Owl and F," Marlee recounted. "I never found out their real names or the names of the other two people they were with."

"We're still looking for them. Apparently, the foursome left before the officers arrived and told everyone to stay there. Did you see them leave?" Bettina asked.

Marlee and Bridget both shook their heads that they hadn't. "Owl and F were participating in the game, so they were seated at the dining room table before the lights went out. I think they were still at the table when the lights came back on. At least I don't remember any empty spaces at the table where they were sitting. Honestly, I can't say for sure that those two specific people were still at the table when the lights came back on. I was too distracted by the gunshot because I knew it wasn't part of the game." Marlee said.

Bridget scrunched her face, hoping to stimulate her memory of the night. "Same here. I don't remember there being vacancies at the table, yet I can't swear that Owl and F were there."

"The squad cars arrived within five minutes after the lights came on, and Hector called 911," Marlee estimated. "The four of them must have peeled out immediately after the gunshot, either before or after the lights came on."

"That really makes them look guilty," Bridget noted, grabbing more pizza and topping off everyone's wine glasses.

"We know that their formal wear was rented at Irene's on Professor Vernon's credit card. If the ripped email note I found in his room is to be believed, then one of the foursome must be the shooter," Marlee said.

"But why the ruse of dressing up and participating in a game?" Bettina challenged. "And how were they to know who would be picked to take part in the game? Besides that, who orchestrated the blackout when he was shot?"

"I don't know why it would need to be so complicated. But if the foursome is involved, then the two who weren't part of the game could have sneaked down to the basement and flipped the breaker. Then, hearing the gunshot, they waited for a minute and turned on the electricity. We've been talking about how none of us saw anyone go down to the basement or come back up. Well, maybe they didn't come back up the stairs. There's a walk-out door that we hardly ever use from the basement. You'd have to know it was there to use it, but it's fully functional," Marlee said.

"Show us," said Bettina, getting to her feet and heading toward the basement, wine glass in hand. The three walked downstairs, where Marlee showed them the electrical box, which was located around the corner from the washer and dryer, a hard-to-see space that one wouldn't think to look at. Then they walked to the far corner of the basement, and she showed them the door. Plastic storage tubs of assorted sizes and colors were stacked beside the door, with one of the tubs tipped on its side.

"Those were all stacked up neatly in front of the door the last I remember," Marlee said. "It's some of Hector's crap, and he promised to organize it in tubs and keep it tidy. That's the only way I let him bring it when we moved here. His beloved deer horns are in one of them."

"Just a thought," said Bridget, realizing she was out of her depth among the police detective and the criminology professor, both of whom either regularly dealt with or researched crime. "While Owl and F were at the dining table, the other two ran down here and flipped the breaker. Then, they flip it back on after the gun goes off. When the lights come on, and everyone is confused, Owl and F run downstairs, too, and all four leave through this basement door. No one would see them leave."

Marlee turned toward her cousin, slack-jawed. "That's brilliant. The four of them could have easily moved the tubs away from the door and left that way. That ensured that the police didn't see them going out the front door. Since they were wearing glittery ball gowns and tuxedos, they would catch the officers' eyes if they exited through the front."

"Then why didn't the officers that arrived on the scene see them walking down the street?" Bettina asked.

"They must have had a car stashed nearby. Maybe in the alley. I'm guessing they didn't arrive on foot. They walked out the basement door, walked to their vehicle, and calmly drove away. I'm betting they changed clothes right away and returned the formal wear that night in the drop box at Irene's," Marlee said.

"It's odd that they would take the time to return the formal wear after killing someone and fleeing the scene. I'm sure they were ready to be out of town as soon as possible. Why take the time to return the clothing?" Bridget asked. "It wasn't even rented under any of their names."

"They didn't think anyone would track down the clothing to Irene's store. But who cares where they received it? If I was on the run after committing a murder, I'd throw the clothes out the car window or in a garbage can at the gas station," Bettina said. "No way would I take the time to return them."

Unable to think of any other explanations for the foursome's behavior, Marlee, Bettina, and Bridget marched back upstairs. As Marlee munched on her third, well fourth, piece of pizza, she remembered something. "Do you know who the two guys were in the Minnesota sports jerseys?" She provided a description of them.

"No, according to Ethan Wiley, they must have left before the murder mystery game even got underway. And I didn't see any names in the guest book that could be theirs," Bettina said.

"Dammit! What's the point of having a guest book if no one is going to sign it?" Marlee was beyond frustrated. If they knew the names of the two Minnesota jersey guys and the foursome in the formal wear, then they would likely have the names of Professor Vernon's killer and the person or persons trying to frame Hector.

She ranted and raved about the poor etiquette of guests who don't sign the guest book for a full minute. Bettina and Bridget let her go. They knew she needed to let off steam, and bitching about guests not signing in for an Open House was innocuous when it came to polite party behavior. Marlee took a deep breath, gearing up for another go-round on this topic, when her phone rang. She didn't recognize the number on the cell. As a rule, she didn't answer unknown numbers, but tonight she had a feeling it could be something or someone important.

It was. It was Hector calling from a burner phone. "They're going to arrest me tomorrow. I'm on my way out of town to follow up on a lead. I'm not telling you anything because I don't want you to get into trouble if this whole thing goes sideways. Don't tell anyone you talked to me. I love you." Click.

As Mother used to say, "Don't let the same snake bite you twice."

Chapter 16

Marlee took a deep breath before turning around to face Bettina and Bridget. She couldn't let them know that Hector was the person who called her since he was on the run and had specifically asked her not to tell anyone.

"You know, it's not even an election year, and I'm still getting tons of robo-calls about being registered to vote," she said, throwing up her hands in mock desperation. "I've had it!" Marlee tried to act nonchalant as she picked up an empty pizza box and folded it into the kitchen garbage. She busied herself in the kitchen and when she returned to the living room, Bettina was leaving.

"Gotta get an early start tomorrow," the detective said as she pulled on her jacket and walked outside. "I'm parked a couple blocks away so nobody would notice my car here. Trying to keep a low profile within my department as far as this case goes."

Bettina was no sooner out the front door than Bridget whirled toward Marlee. "What gives? Who were you talking to a couple of minutes ago? I know it wasn't a robo-call." Bridget knew her cousin well enough to notice when she was lying. Marlee was able to hide her "tells" from most people, but not her cousin.

She was torn. On one hand, Hector told her not to discuss the conversation with anyone and she held dear her promises to him. On the other hand, Bridget wanted to help Hector get out of this situation as much as she did. Plus, it would be nice to have someone to talk to that wasn't in law enforcement. She released a deep sigh and then blurted, "It was Hector. He's on the run because he thinks he'll be arrested soon. You can't tell anybody. Not one person. Understand?"

"I won't say a peep to anyone," Bridget promised, holding her hand up as if swearing to tell the truth, the whole truth, and nothing but the truth in court. "Why does he think Wallace is going to arrest him?"

"He didn't say, but he must think there will be something new that comes to light soon, which will make him the only suspect," Marlee said. "I'm so worried, and I don't know what to do to help him."

"What would be the new development that would further incriminate Hector? Don't get mad at me, but if he's innocent, it shouldn't make any difference what is discovered. And don't get me wrong. I know he's innocent. I'm just trying to understand."

"Hector is innocent. I would bet my life on it. But whoever is trying to set him up has gone to great lengths already. It wouldn't be surprising to find out the real killer planted other evidence that puts Hector in a bad light," Marlee replied.

"Let's think about this logically," Bridget said. "The bottom half of the printed email you found in the professor's things may have been written by someone else and planted among his papers, knowing it would be found. Didn't you say the couple who was on the weekend date heard people outside the professor's room the night before the party? It could have even been the couple who were on their first date. That whole date thing might be a sham. One of them could have brought the ripped email with them and shoved it in his folder of papers. The detectives don't have the professor's medical records yet, so we don't know for sure that he's dying. That whole part may be a farce. Professor Vernon could be in perfect health and had no idea that Saturday would be his last night alive."

Marlee perked up a bit. "You're right. Professor Vernon may have been set up as a victim, too. Thank God Hector wasn't the one who was shot at the party. It never occurred to me that whoever is setting him up might want him dead, too."

"We know that Owl and F left before police could question them. And according to Ethan, the two guys in the Minnesota sports jerseys were already gone before the game started. Any of them, working individually or together, could have authored the email and ripped it up and then planted it in the professor's room. Then, whoever is involved, carries out the electrical outage and shooting at the party the following night."

"That makes a lot of sense. More sense than the professor plotting his own murder and implicating an innocent person. Still, how do you explain Hector being named the beneficiary of his life insurance policy? And how did Hector's service weapon get out of the locked gun cabinet and be used to kill the professor?" Marlee moved to the kitchen and returned with the crime chart and the notes they made earlier about the murder.

"I don't claim to have all the answers," Bridget said. "I don't even know if any of what I said is right, but it seems more logical than the professor orchestrating his own death."

"Occam's razor," Marlee said. "The simplest solution is usually correct."

"There's nothing simple about this case," Bridget said, peering at the crime chart.

Marlee looked at the chart, knowing they likely had everything they needed right in front of them to solve the case and clear Hector. "We still haven't talked to Nadia Deen about what she remembers from the party. I'm going to see if she's at work tonight." She reached for her phone and made a quick call to Perkins and, confirming that Nadia was on duty until 10:00 p.m., the McCabe cousins rushed out the door.

Perkins was a chain restaurant that catered to Midwestern folk with bland palettes and hearty appetites. They were famous for their all-day breakfasts, multitudes of meat and potato dishes, and enormous desserts. Asking to be seated in Nadia's section, they were led to a four-top table in the center of the room. Perkins was mostly empty, so Marlee wasn't overly concerned that they would be overheard by nosy diners. Entertainment options in Elmwood were limited, so listening in on the conversations of others was a refined art form.

Nadia approached their table, not even looking at them when she said "hello" and asked what they wanted to drink. The twenty-something student and server were in a rush even though there were only four other tables of people in the restaurant, and two of them already had their food. Her hair was pulled back in what was once a tight bun, but now several strands of her hair had come loose, giving her a messy look. Adding to her sloppy appearance was a brown stain on her apron that Marlee hoped was beef gravy.

"It's me, Nadia," Marlee said, startling the young woman into paying attention to them.

"Oh, sorry, Dr. McCabe. I've been so spaced-out today," she said with a small smile, attempting to push the loose hair around her face behind her ears.

"That's understandable, given everything that happened at the murder mystery party on Saturday night," Marlee said. "Can you spare a few minutes to chat with us about what you saw?"

"Just a couple minutes. Let me go get your drinks, and I'll be right back." In five minutes, she was back with two cups of hot water and a wooden box with a variety of individually packaged tea bags. She sat in a chair across from Marlee and motioned for her to begin the questioning.

"Did you notice anyone go down to the basement at any point on Saturday night? Or come back up from the basement?"

"No, I didn't even know where the stairs were to the basement until I opened it by mistake thinking it was a pantry. That's when we were looking for more food to serve since most of the appetizers the caterers brought were gone."

"Was the light on when you opened the basement door? Did you hear any noises coming from down there?" Marlee continued.

"No, nothing. I opened the door, realized it wasn't the pantry, and then closed it. It all happened within a few seconds."

"Remember the four people who were really dressed up? Owl and F played the murder mystery game, and the other two watched. Do you know who they are?" Bridget interjected.

"I couldn't see their faces because of their masks, but I don't think I know them. Didn't recognize their voices," Nadia said.

"Did you hear any of them talking other than Owl and F when they were playing the game?"

"Yeah, when I was passing appetizers, I heard them talking. One of the men mentioned another party they were going to that night. Said it was at a cookie house or something like that," Nadia said. "I didn't know we had a place that sold only cookies. It must be new."

"I bet he said Cookie's house, meaning Cookie O'Brien," Marlee said, thinking of the trim, blonde woman who was as close to a socialite as they had in Elmwood. Cookie was an attorney for one of the larger banks in town and made big bucks, which was reflected in the sporty car she drove and the ritzy house where she lived. Cookie made good money and had no problem displaying it, much to the disdain of the frugal people of German and Norwegian heritage that populated Elmwood. Still, she was known for hosting the best parties, and even though people talked about her behind her back, they would be thrilled to get an invitation to one of her splashy soirees.

"Was she having a party on the same day as your Open House? That's tacky," Bridget said, making a face.

"Well, it was Halloween, so I'm guessing there were lots of parties held that night," Marlee said, smiling that her cousin took her side in the battle of the parties.

"Did you hear them say anything else?" Bridget asked.

"That's it. I was busy getting food and drinks for everyone and didn't have time to do much else until you said Ethan and I could play the murder mystery game, too," Nadia said.

"Did you see them leave?" Marlee could not fathom how, so far, no one could account for their departure from the dining room and then the house. Four people in formal wear and masks should not go unnoticed, even at a costume party.

"The last I saw Owl and F, they were standing over the professor's body. I don't recall where the other two were. I have to admit, I thought the professor getting shot was part of the game. At that point, I'm scanning to see who had the gun, and it was your husband," Nadia said, looking at Marlee.

"Boyfriend, not husband," Marlee corrected. "So, you saw Owl and F standing when the lights came back on?"

"Yeah. And then I don't know where they went. About that time, I realized that this wasn't a game anymore and that someone had really been shot while we were all sitting at the table. I kind of lost track of who went where after that," Nadia added. "I hope your boyfriend isn't in trouble. I'm sure he wasn't the one who pulled the trigger. He probably just picked up the gun when he saw it on the floor."

Marlee gave a nod of appreciation at her conclusion. "Who do you think shot the professor?"

Nadia shrugged. "Well, it wasn't me, and I'm sure Ethan wouldn't do it. Or your boyfriend. I guess that leaves the other people at the table, excluding the professor. Unless he shot himself."

"What did you just say?" Marlee asked, although she'd heard Nadia's words clearly.

"Maybe the professor shot himself. Didn't anyone investigate that?"

"I hadn't heard anything about it, but it's possible. It actually makes quite a bit of sense," Marlee said.

A burly man in a grimy apron poked his head out of the kitchen and gave a loud whistle. "You're not getting paid to socialize. The deep fryer isn't going to clean itself," he barked.

"Gotta get back to work before Ziggy has a meltdown," Nadia said, rolling her eyes as she rose to her feet.

"One other quick thing. Did you know the two guys in the Minnesota sports jerseys? Ethan said they were really putting away the wine and appetizers," Bridget said.

"Those two were jackasses. The shorter one asked me for my number. Eww, he sounded like my mom and looked like my dad. And they ate tons of food, like they hadn't seen a meal for days and were catching up on missed calories. Ethan said we might have to cut them off from the wine because they were chugging it. And everyone knows you take your time with wine. You don't chug it like its beer at a frat party," Nadia said with an air of disgust.

Marlee and Bridget exchanged amused looks as they left their table and stopped at the front counter to pay the bill for the tea. "Somebody is really coming up in the world," Bridget said, and they both laughed, remembering how important they felt as college students when they learned something they believed to be highbrow cultural knowledge.

They drove back to Marlee's house and Bridget hopped in her car and went home with another promise not to disclose the earlier phone conversation with Hector. Marlee went inside and wandered around, unsure what to do. Her adrenaline supply was on overload between the murder and now Hector being on the lam. She checked her cell to see if he had texted her but the last text she'd received had been days ago.

I'm sure the cops will track my phone, so I don't know how Hector thinks he can keep his whereabouts secret, she thought as she walked up the stairs to their bedroom. Suddenly, she had an idea. She had her own burner phone that she'd purchased years ago and used when in a pinch. Hector knew she had it, and she had even talked to him using it, but she wasn't sure he had the number. Marlee located it in a junk drawer in their bedroom and plugged it in to charge. While she was waiting, she changed into her pajamas, washed her face, and brushed her teeth. Within a few minutes, she had enough of a charge on the phone to show she'd received a text message from an unknown number in the past half hour. She was terrible with numbers and couldn't recall if it was from the same number Hector had called her on earlier.

Marlee clicked on the text message. It read: *Hope you think of checking this phone.* It was the only text message she'd received in the past few months, so it had to be from Hector. She quickly tapped out a message to him asking where he was and if he was okay.

I'll be OK once this case is solved. DCI is getting involved and I'm sure they're going to arrest me. Marlee knew the Division of Criminal Investigation often got involved in criminal cases when it involved the investigation of a fellow law enforcement officer. The belief was that those in a department would be biased when investigating one of their own or might allow emotion to take over. The DCI was a state-run organization, and although they were law enforcement, too, they had no close connection to individual police departments. Therefore, they could do a more thorough investigation, which would be less likely to be picked apart by defense attorneys.

Hector reiterated that he wouldn't tell her where he was or where he was going in case she was questioned by the DCI. The last thing he wanted was for her to face charges for hiding him and lying to law enforcement. He finished his text, promising to contact her on her burner phone tomorrow.

Marlee backed up to the bed to sit down but missed it and ended up sliding down the side of the bed and onto the floor. Pippa came over and flipped her bushy tail in Marlee's face. She reached over and scratched the cat under the chin and behind the ears as she thought about what to do.

What would she do if Hector was arrested for murder? She couldn't go there. The thought of it was too awful to contemplate. Their whole lives would be upended. Meanwhile, the real murderer would be on the loose.

Marlee went back to the main floor and reached for the crime chart, adding the latest information that Nadia gave them at Perkins. The next person she needed to talk to was Cookie O'Brien. If the foursome in the formal wear attended Cookie's party, she would know who they were. Cookie was a social butterfly, and having guests at her home who were unknown to her was just unheard of. Marlee had to hand it to her; she was a top-notch hostess. Having been invited to one of the parties at her mini-mansion, Marlee gazed at the grandeur of the furnishings of the house and the selection of food and drinks. No beanie weenies and beer for Cookie. She was classy, and it was champagne and caviar for her guests.

Marlee and Cookie were friends on Facebook, much like she was friends with many acquaintances. She reached for her laptop and logged onto the social network, seeing that Cookie was active at that moment. Marlee took a chance and sent her a quick message asking if she'd be available for a quick meeting.

To her surprise, Cookie responded right away, inviting Marlee to come out to her house right now. Even though it was past 10:00 p.m. and she was already in her pajamas, Marlee wasn't going to pass up an opportunity to find out what Cookie knew about the four people in the formal wear. If Cookie would name them, that could aid the cops in interviewing the four unknown guests from Marlee's party. And that could lead to their arrests and Hector's name being cleared in the murder of Professor Vernon once and for all.

The one good thing about delirium is that it has taken my writing into some previously unexplored areas.

Chapter 17

Marlee raced around her house getting presentable to go to Cookie O'Brien's home. She whipped off her pajamas and hastily threw on dressy black pants, a black tank top, and a purple blazer. She topped off her ensemble with large silver hoop earrings and a silver bracelet. Slipping on black boots with a heel over one inch, she felt like she was going to a fashion show, not the home of a Facebook acquaintance. And she hated herself for it. She detested that she felt the need to dress up just to go talk to this woman. Yet, if Marlee showed up in jeans and a sweatshirt, she would feel judged and less than confident. With a touch of mascara and a splash of lipstick, she was out the door.

She drove to Cookie's neighborhood in record time even though it was on the opposite side of town from where Marlee and Hector lived. They were in the historic district, while Cookie lived with the others in town who liked to show off their wealth, whether it was real or not. Her home was located on a cul-de-sac surrounded by tens of thousands of dollars worth of trees, shrubs, and landscaping.

An elaborate chime could be heard outside the house when Marlee rang the doorbell. Cookie answered almost immediately, dressed in an adorable pink velour sweat suit and white baseball cap. "Come in, come in," she urged, grabbing Marlee by the arm and escorting her through the doorway. "Oooh, you look so nice, and I'm a wreck. Just got home from hot yoga and didn't have time to shower and change yet."

"Thank you for letting me come over so late. I wasn't sure if you would remember me," Marlee said.

"Of course, I remember you. How could I forget? You teach at MSU, and you came to one of my parties. I'll never forget that party," Cookie said with a smile, yet she didn't articulate what had made the party so memorable. Marlee thought it might have been something she had done and then she realized that's exactly what Cookie wanted. She was a game player and Marlee wasn't, which made Marlee a target for exactly that type of thing. "Now, what can I get you to drink? Wine? A cocktail?"

"I'll have whatever you're having," Marlee said, a comment that she would soon regret when Cookie led her through the foyer and into a den with a wet bar and began mixing various kinds of hard alcohol in a shaker of ice.

"Here you go. It's my own concoction. I'm thinking about having it patented, so I can't tell you what's in it," Cookie said with a wide grin.

Marlee took a sip of the multi-alcohol drink, which was devoid of any mixer. It tasted like a cross between lighter fluid and gasoline with a hint of bug spray. "Mmm, you should go on *Shark Tank* with this idea," she said, hoping it didn't sound snarky.

Cookie took the comment as a genuine compliment and motioned for Marlee to sit in one of the wing-backed chairs near the unlit fireplace. "What brings you out tonight? You mentioned you had something important to discuss. Of course, I was intrigued and knew we needed to speak right away so I could satisfy my curiosity."

"I understand you had a party here on Halloween," Marlee began. "That same night, my boyfriend and I hosted an Open House at our B&B and...."

"You're absolutely right," Cookie clutched at her neck. "That was in extremely poor taste, and I should have canceled once I heard about your business party, but the invitations were already sent, and the food was ordered. There was no way I could cancel with such short notice. But I do apologize."

"No, that's not it at all. I didn't even know you had a party until tonight when someone mentioned it. It was Halloween, and I think many parties were going on around town. I didn't expect anyone to cancel their festivities just because of our Open House. You see, at our party, we hosted a murder mystery game and ...."

"Oh, I heard about the unfortunate mishap with the gun and your boyfriend. He's with the police, isn't he?" Cookie asked, sipping her drink.

"Yes, he is," Marlee said, wondering how long it would take before she could finish the story without interruption. "There were some guests at our party who were overheard saying they were coming to your party, and we never caught their names. There were four of them, two men and two women. All were dressed very formally, the men in tuxedos, one woman wearing a blue gown, and the other had on a burgundy gown. All four of them wore masks covering their eyes. Does this sound like a foursome that came to your party?"

Cookie took another slow sip of her drink, enjoying having some information that was unknown to her guest. Then she took another drink and smiled before speaking. "Yes, they were here. I remember them well."

"And? Who are they?" Marlee was ready to wring this lady's neck if she didn't spill the beans soon. First, she prevented Marlee from asking her questions. Now, she was stalling with the answers.

"I'm surprised you didn't recognize them. It was Onna Ramone from the Elmwood Chamber of Commerce and her husband, Franklin. The other couple were their houseguests for the week. Onna introduced us, but I'm afraid I can't remember their names. She will be thrilled when I tell her you didn't recognize her at your Open House," Cookie said.

"I'm not sure Onna knows me," Marlee said. "She probably just stopped by since we're a new business in town. Hector and I didn't get a chance to talk to them before everything went haywire."

"No, she knows you. She mentioned to me that they'd just come from your party. Onna also told me about the incident with the gun but made me promise not to say anything to anyone else at my party."

"Did she realize the professor who was shot actually died? They left before the police could question them."

"Yes, I'm afraid Onna wanted their names kept out of the police record on this type of thing. Said they made a hasty exit."

Marlee had a bitter taste in her mouth that wasn't completely attributable to the ghastly cocktail Cookie made for her. It galled Marlee that Onna felt that she and her friends were above the law and shouldn't have to endure questioning like the other guests. Nothing good could come from sharing these thoughts with Cookie, so she kept it to herself. "Did any of them know who shot the gun?"

"It was your boyfriend, wasn't it? Onna said he was holding the gun."

She nodded reluctantly. "He picked up the gun from the floor, and that was when the lights came back on. Hector didn't fire the weapon; he just had it in his hand."

"How theatrical. Sounds like an Agatha Christie book that's been made into a community theater production. A gathering of unknowns for a murder mystery party, an electrical outage, a man shot dead, and the host left holding the gun. I love it!" Cookie exclaimed with a toss of her head.

It was getting harder and harder to bite her tongue. Marlee took a deep, calming breath and said, "A man was killed in my home, and I just want to make sure the right person or people are held accountable."

Cookie had the good manners to look remorseful. "Of course. How insensitive of me. I watch crime shows on television in the evenings, and I get so wrapped up in the stories that I forget real people are involved."

"You said that Onna and her husband were hosting the other couple for a few days. Are they still there, or did they leave?"

"I'm not sure. You'll have to contact Onna to find out," Cookie said, finishing her drink and standing up to make another. She raised her empty glass and raised her eyebrows.

"No more for me, Cookie. But thank you. I can't even finish this one if I expect to drive tonight. And I really need to run home and get ready for class and office hours tomorrow."

Cookie frowned, disappointed that she'd be alone in her large house with no one to drink with. "Do you want to switch to wine?"

"No, I've hit my limit for alcohol tonight," Marlee said, which sort of was the truth if her three glasses of white wine were factored in from supper. But mostly, she just wanted to avoid putting any more of Cookie's god-awful drink in her mouth. "Thanks again for meeting with me."

As Marlee drove away, she saw Cookie standing barefoot on the front step, waving with one hand, cocktail in the other. Marlee shuddered at the aftertaste of the cocktail, and her first order of business at home was to brush her teeth and gargle with mouthwash.

The next morning, Marlee checked her burner phone before she got out of bed. It was 6:00 a.m. She didn't have to be at work for office hours until 9:00 a.m., but there was plenty to do, and she wanted to get a jump on the day. Hector hadn't sent a text overnight, which she suspected since she checked at least four times in the night when she awoke.

She bounded downstairs and made a pot of coffee, forgetting that Hector wasn't there to share it with her. Marlee had been single, and happily so, most of her life. She was an independent woman and had no problem taking care of herself. That's why it was so hard for her to let Hector into her life. Once she did, he became very easy to get used to. They had their share of disagreements and even went through couples counseling for a bit, but they got along for the most part. She loved him with all her heart, and now that he was gone, she felt at loose ends. Marlee shook her head to clear her thoughts. The sooner she figured out who had shot Professor Vernon, the sooner the culprit would be arrested. And that meant Hector would be back home, and life could return to normal. Or what posed as normal for them.

With a full mug of coffee in hand, Marlee jogged upstairs to shower and get ready for the day. She had office hours starting at 9:00, then her Intro to Policing class, followed by more office hours ending at 2:00 p.m. Overall, a fairly easy day.

Before leaving the house, Marlee checked her burner phone again. Still no text from Hector. She sent him a brief text with the identities of Onna and Franklin Ramone and their out-of-town friends as the foursome dressed in formal wear. She also mentioned that she would be contacting Onna at work that day.

It was an hour before the Chamber of Commerce office opened, but Marlee was too antsy to remain at home any longer. After pouring more dry food in Pippa's bowl and petting her until she growled, Marlee was off to Perkatory. She didn't have any leads to follow up on at the coffee shop but thought Ethan might be working and she could chat with him.

Perkatory was exceptionally busy at 7:00 a.m. People were getting their caffeine fixes on their way to work, and some students had been there all night studying for exams. Ethan was behind the bar making drinks, so she knew he would only have time to talk to her once the crowd dissipated. She ordered a large black coffee and took it to her table in the back. Instead of facing the wall to avoid people, like she usually did, she sat with her back to the wall so she could watch for someone, anyone she knew. She opened her purse and pulled out a baggie containing her powdered creamer of choice: non-dairy, sugar-free vanilla caramel. After stirring in four heaping spoons of the chemical concoction, she licked off the plastic spoon and put it back in her purse.

As she sipped on her large cup of brew, she mentally kicked herself for not bringing her laptop. At least she could get some work done while waiting for Ethan to have a minute of free time to talk. She had both her personal cell and her burner phone with her, but that wasn't going to help her with her grading. Marlee took her cell and logged into Facebook. Social media was a time suck more than anything, but it had its uses too.

She went to the Elmwood Chamber of Commerce's page and looked at the staff. Onna was front and center in the group photo. Marlee was glad she'd familiarized herself with Onna's looks since it had been some time since she'd seen her. Onna was the woman who identified herself as Owl at the murder mystery party, and the man who went by F had to be her husband, Franklin. She typed in Onna's name and found that her personal Facebook page was open to everyone, so she perused her photos. As she suspected, they were Owl and F. *I wonder why they didn't give their real names. I wouldn't have known who they were anyway unless Onna said she was with the Chamber of Commerce,* Marlee thought.

Ethan hurried over to her table and sat across from her. "I can only chat a minute. Teddy has been extra prickly since his girlfriend dumped him."

"Teddy has a girlfriend?" Marlee wondered who would be interested in that crusty old bastard.

"Had. It was an Internet girlfriend, and she dumped him. She's from Romania. Teddy was getting serious enough about her to go over for a visit. But then she broke up with him. At least she did it before he bought the ticket," Ethan said.

"He told you all of this?" Marlee didn't think Ethan's boss seemed like the type to share any personal matters or feelings with his employees.

"No, he forgot to close out his Facebook account on the computer in the back, and I saw the private messages he and this lady were sharing," Ethan said, glancing over his shoulder to make sure Teddy wasn't behind him. "I'm ashamed to say it, but I got really invested in their story. Teddy saved his Facebook password on the computer, so I went back in for occasional updates."

"You little snoop," Marlee said with a laugh. "I'm never leaving my computer or phone unattended around you."

"Hey," Ethan said, throwing up his hands in mock surrender. "What would you have done?"

"Same." When they finished giggling about their shared love of nosing around in other people's business,

Marlee updated him on her new findings, minus the fact that Hector was on the run.

"Onna and Franklin Ramone? She comes in here sometimes since her office is only a block away. I didn't recognize her at your Open House. Their costumes were good at concealing their identities."

"And now I know why they returned their formal wear right away. It would reflect poorly on Onna if she was late returning her gown. Irene might withdraw as a member of the Chamber and badmouth her to other business owners around town," Marlee said. "What I don't understand is why Professor Vernon rented their tuxes and gowns for them."

"That's a puzzler. Onna can tell you what her connection with the professor is. That should answer a lot of questions," Ethan said. "I wonder if Onna and her husband and their friends knew that there was blood on the clothes they returned to Irene's shop."

"I'll ask Onna when I talk to her. You better scoot. I just saw Teddy look over this way, and he looks grumpier than usual."

Marlee went back to her phone and looked for Franklin Ramone's Facebook profile. Unlike his wife, Franklin kept his profile page closed. Not just anyone could look at his private information. The only thing available to see on his home page was a family photo, which looked to be from a few years prior.

She went to the photos section on his profile and was surprised to see it was open and there were recent pictures. Marlee looked through them, finding most of them uninteresting. That is until she came to a photo of Franklin and Onna along with another couple who looked similar in size and shape to the couple who had accompanied them to the Open House. They had been tagged in the photo. The man was listed as Trent Carter while the woman was identified as Janelle Vernon. Vernon, as in *Professor Vernon*.

Hopefully, the damage I cause will be lessened by the rewards I give. They have to look at the bigger picture.

Chapter 18

Marlee hurried from Perkatory, walking fast along the block to the Chamber of Commerce. It wouldn't be open for another five minutes, but she was willing to wait as long as she could talk to Onna Ramone right away. Fifteen minutes later, a young man in his mid-twenties, already burned out from work life, ambled toward the door and unlocked it with a huge sigh. He gave Marlee a blank stare as if he had no idea why someone would be at their door.

"Good morning," she chirped, intentionally trying to piss him off a little bit with her perkiness. I'm here to see Onna Ramone."

"She isn't here," he said. No reason given. No hint that she would be in soon. Nothing.

"When do you expect her?" Marlee asked, unwilling to let the poorly mannered man off the hook.

"She said she would be in after she stopped at the Post Office," he said with a heavy sigh, looking down at the computer on his desk, uninterested in helping the general public even though that was partially why the Chamber of Commerce existed.

"Are you thinking about fifteen minutes or half an hour before she's here?" Marlee persisted.

He gave her an exasperated look. "That's all she told me at breakfast."

"Oh, she's your mom," Marlee said. Now she knew how someone with absolutely no people skills got the job. Nepotism was alive and well and running the front desk at the Chamber of Commerce.

He ignored her, and she sat in a padded chair near the window and leafed through a People magazine from September. She was partway through an article on Prince Harry's ongoing feud with the British monarchy when Onna burst through the front door, a large white box full of letters in her arms. "Mail collection is going to be one of your jobs from now on," she barked at her son, who continued to look down at the computer. "I hate going to the Post Office." She plunked the box full of mail on his desk, and he ignored it.

Marlee cleared her throat, as this obtuse mother and son work duo wasn't going to help her anytime soon. And she had office hours on campus starting in less than half an hour. "Hello, Onna."

"Oh, hello. Marlee. Cookie texted me and said you'd be coming over today. I didn't realize it would be right away this morning," she said, trying to pull herself together and act professionally. "Please come into my office."

Marlee followed her into the ornately decorated office filled with items common to Elmwood: a stuffed deer head, a mounted walleye, and a wooden hand-carved pheasant. No matter where Marlee sat, she felt at least two or more glassy eyes following her. She chose a chair with the majority of the dead wildlife and replicas behind her and Onna sat across from her, a small coffee table between them covered in brochures touting the praises of Elmwood and its vigorous business climate.

"I didn't realize you were one of the masked people at my Open House on Saturday night. The costumes you and your friends wore were elaborate and kept us all guessing," Marlee began. She needed to start slowly to gain as much information as possible from Onna. If she began slamming her with accusations about leaving before the police came, Onna would likely clam up or tell her to leave.

Onna beamed, happy to have pulled one over on Marlee and the whole party. "That's really saying something, considering that you co-own the B&B with a detective. I fooled a detective!"

"You sure did," Marlee said, lacking the enthusiasm of her counterpart. "I know it was crowded and got kind of wild at the party. Who do you think shot the professor?"

Onna's gaze traveled around the room as if she was seeing it for the first time. She was piecing together her story, Marlee could tell. If Onna had nothing to hide, then she would just blurt out what she thought. "The first time I saw the gun was when the detective had it. I don't know what happened to it after that."

"You didn't see anyone with the gun before you saw Hector holding it? Not even while you were seated at the table playing the murder mystery game?"

Onna shook her head from side to side. "No, I had no idea there was a gun until there was a loud boom, and then the lights came back on. The detective was holding it in his right hand. That's all I saw."

"You were with your husband and another couple." Marlee waited for her to expand on the comment, but all Onna did was nod.

"Who was the other couple?" Marlee continued.

Onna looked around the room again. "Out of town friends. We thought it would be fun to bring them to the parties we attended around town."

"And what are their names?"

"Trent and Janelle." She gave no last names.

"Are they still staying with you?" Marlee persisted. She didn't care if she was late for her office hours. She was going to pull the information out of Onna one sentence at a time if she had to.

"Until Thursday. They go back to Wisconsin then."

"Why did you leave before the police arrived? You must have known they would want to talk to you about what you saw," Marlee said gently, trying not to dissuade the reticent witness from providing details.

"The four of us chatted and realized none of us had seen anything and decided to leave," Onna said, making eye contact with Marlee for the first time during the questioning. "You have to understand. My husband and I both have important jobs in Elmwood. People look up to us. We can't be associated with a shooting. Franklin is running for state senate next year, and we can't have our names brought into a murder investigation."

"So, you decided to sneak out through the basement before the police ever arrived," Marlee said, shooting her shot. "And then you walked to your car and drove to Cookie's party."

Onna reluctantly nodded. "No one was supposed to know. We had a lot of fun disguising ourselves, and I could tell when you stopped by to introduce yourself and welcome us to your party that you had no idea who we were. None of us saw anything. I swear. If we knew who shot that man, we certainly would have spoken up right away."

"How did you know about the exit door in the basement?" Marlee asked. "It wasn't visible, and most people wouldn't even realize it was there."

"Franklin worked as an insurance claims adjustor for years and had been in the house when there was flooding in the basement. He remembered there was a door down there, and that's how we left. I promise we didn't see anything that can help the case," Cookie insisted.

"Maybe you saw or heard something important and didn't even realize it. One of you could hold the key to unlocking the murder," Marlee said, judgment creeping into her voice even though she was trying to keep it under wraps.

"I know, and I feel terrible. We all do. But Franklin can't be associated with this kind of thing. His opponent in the election would bring it up over and over. And who would vote for a candidate who goes to parties where people are shot? Having Franklin associated with the murder would torpedo his political career," Onna said, tearing up. "We had to protect ourselves."

"Where are your house guests now?"

"At the house with Franklin. They were going to have a lazy morning, and then I'm taking off work at 2:00, and we ladies are going to bake kuchen while the guys go to an estate auction in Webster," Onna said. "Why? You're not going to talk to them, are you?"

Marlee looked at her incredulously. "Of course, I'm going to talk to them. I need to know what each person saw and heard while at the party." She refrained from mentioning that the police needed to question them all, too. Onna seemed very entitled to special treatment and would be shocked when the police showed up at her house later.

"Well, okay. As long as the police stay out of it, and you don't mention this to anyone else."

Marlee nodded, having no intention of doing either of those things. She stood and made her way toward the closed office door before thinking of one last question. "How did you come up with your costumes?" She knew Professor Vernon had rented them for the foursome from Irene's, but she wanted to hear what Onna had to say.

"It was Janelle's idea. She thought dressing up in formal attire and wearing masks covering most of our faces would be exciting, so she rented them for us. We had fun getting ready and fooling people at the parties. We went to one at the Elks Lodge before we came to your house. No one could identify Franklin or me there either. It was such fun," Onna said, tears now dried and a smile returning to her face.

"Janelle rented the formal wear? Janelle Vernon?" Marlee asked.

"That's right. Why?"

"Do you realize she is related to the professor who was shot at the party?" Marlee asked.

"Oh, come on. That's ridiculous. She doesn't know anyone here, and neither does her husband. They both work at a college in Wisconsin," Onna said.

"So did Professor Vernon. He taught English and Creative Writing there for nearly thirty years,"

"Seriously? I don't know why she wouldn't have mentioned it."

"Really? Because you four were seen talking with him at my party before the game started. And since your little group didn't talk to anyone else, it seems odd that Janelle would be talking to her uncle and not realize it was him. Especially since he wasn't wearing much of a costume," Marlee said. "Besides, there's a witness who saw Professor Vernon hand an envelope to someone in your group."

"I think you need to leave now," Onna said. "And don't bother going over to my house. I'm calling Franklin right now and telling him not to talk to you. Just leave us alone. You have no idea what kind of problems you're causing."

Cell phone in hand, she pushed Bettina's name and waited for her to answer. "Come to my office as soon as you can. I have a bunch of new information."

"So do I," said Bettina and clicked off without further ado.

The parking gods were on Marlee's side, as she flew into the lot nearest her building on campus and found a parking spot up front. She raced to her building, taking the elevator to the third floor, and arriving for office hours at 9:02 a.m. She looked around and was relieved that no one was waiting for her. Mostly, she was worried about her dean getting on her. Even though she was a Full Professor now, he seemed determined to make her life miserable. He often walked by her office, even though it was well out of his way. If she were ever late, it was brought to her attention in a sternly worded email. He and others in the MSU administration received bad press due to their own actions brought to light by Marlee the previous year. Since then, the dean was quick to point out her every fault even though there was little he could do to get her fired at this point in her career.

She dropped her things in her office chair and ran to the restroom, returning to find Bettina in her office. "Oh my god, you're never going to guess what I found out," Marlee said, not pausing for Bettina to get a word in edgewise. "The four people dressed in the formal wear were Onna and Franklin Ramone from here in town and their friends, one of which is named Janelle Vernon and is the niece of Professor Vernon. Onna admitted that they left through the basement door because Franklin is running for state senator next year and didn't want his reputation tarnished. Janelle is the one who suggested they dress in formal wear and masks. She was the one who rented them. Janelle and her husband are still here in town for another couple of days and are at the Ramone's house right now." She collapsed into her chair, moving her coat and book bag out of the way as she sat on them.

"When did you find out all of this?" Bettina asked with a frown, no doubt irritated that Marlee hadn't reported the information to her immediately so she and the other detectives could carry out the investigation.

"I pieced together some clues yesterday, but it just came together this morning. I called you right after I talked to Onna Ramone," Marlee said. It was mostly true. She didn't need to bog down the flow of the story with how she learned the identity of Onna and her group. They could discuss it later when they had more time.

Bettina stepped out of Marlee's office and into the hallway to make a call. She came back and announced, "Wallace and Quigley are on their way over to talk to Franklin and the others. Hope they haven't lawyered up by the time they get there."

"Well, it's possible," Marlee said, not feeling the need to bring up the fact that Onna had kicked her out of her office and told her she was going to call her husband and direct him not to talk to her. She assumed neither he nor Janelle and Trent would be talking to the police either.

"What's your big news? You said you'd learned something new about the case." Marlee hoped to get Bettina off track.

"I do, but you're not going to like it. DCI took over the case as of this morning and are looking for Hector. They're going to take him into custody and charge him with the murder of Professor Vernon."

I've lived a good life. I worked hard and paid my bills. I loved my career, especially teaching students how to write. Writing my own work was my first passion, and teaching was my second. My third passion—well, it was a recent development—involved standing up for people who couldn't stand up for themselves.

Chapter 19

Hector had been one hundred percent right. The Division of Criminal Investigation had stepped in to take over the investigation from the Elmwood Police Department since it was believed his fellow officers would not or could not conduct a thorough investigation of Professor Vernon's life and death. And now Hector was being charged with the professor's murder.

"What we need to know is," Bettina continued, looking Marlee straight in the eye, "where's Hector? We've been by the house, he isn't answering his phone, and no one has seen his Jeep. You need to tell us where he's at. Things are only going to get worse for him if he avoids us. He knows that."

"I don't know where he is," Marlee said, holding Bettina's gaze. It was true. She didn't know Hector's whereabouts because he had not told her. And now she was glad he withheld his location because there was no way she would've been able to flat out lie to Bettina for any length of time. Sure, she could tell half-truths, spin stories, and conveniently leave out details, but not lie. Not to her friend who happened to be a seasoned detective.

Bettina squinted as she continued to stare at Marlee. "When did you last see him?"

"Yesterday. When Wallace and a uniformed officer came to talk to him at the house and then hauled him down to the station."

"You never thought to mention that he never came home last night?" Bettina continued.

"Why would that be noteworthy? Besides, I asked you when you were at my house last night if Hector had been arrested, and you said he was done at the station and was probably meeting with his lawyer. I assumed the same thing," Marlee said, holding her ground.

"Seems mighty suspicious to me that with all the news you had to share with me this morning that Hector not coming home last night didn't make the list," Bettina said.

"What was I supposed to say? I mean, you are already looking at him like he's the main suspect. And now I guess he is since the DCI is going to arrest him. He probably realized that and it's why he didn't come home," Marlee said.

"If you know where he's at and you're not telling me, you're in big trouble and can be arrested. This case is out of our hands now. The DCI doesn't play around," Bettina chastised.

"I'm not lying. I seriously don't know where he is," Marlee said. "I wish I did know where he was. Then I'd know if he was safe,"

"You need to let me know if you talk to him. Right away, not a day or an hour later. Right away. Understand?" Bettina asked.

"I will let you know right away if I talk to him. I promise," Marlee said. She intended to keep her promise and hoped that communication between her and Hector remained through texts on their respective burner phones. But if it came down to keeping her promise to Hector or to Bettina, she would choose Hector. Every single time.

After Bettina left, Marlee met with a student who stopped by to talk about internships. Her head and her heart didn't care about students or internships or anything right now other than Hector and making sure he was not arrested. She provided some half-assed information to the student and sent her on her way with a promise to update her when she knew more about internships in the local probation office. Her Intro to Policing class did not go much better. Marlee could not stay focused on her lecture, and after engaging the students in small group discussions, she excused class early.

Marlee still had over two hours of office hours and didn't feel right about leaving, even though she wanted to keep looking for new information on who killed the professor. She texted Bridget, and to her surprise, her cousin agreed to come over.

Bridget arrived in Marlee's office thirty minutes later with two giant slices of hot pizza in individual to-go boxes. "I went through the drive-through and grabbed these. I'm guessing you haven't had lunch."

"Thanks, Bridget," Marlee said. It was a testament to how worried she was that she hadn't even realized that she was hungry. She brought her cousin up to speed, first with what she'd found out at Cookie's house last night and her discussion with Onna Ramone that morning. Then she detailed her meeting with

Bettina and Hector's impending arrest by the Division of Criminal Investigation.

"That's exactly what Hector was afraid of, right?" Bridget asked.

"Yep. He knew what would most likely happen with the state investigators involved. That's why he's hiding. Hector's trying to find out who killed Professor Vernon and get his own name cleared. But he can't very well do that if he's tied up in an investigation room explaining himself. Or in jail."

Bridget groaned. "Does the DCI really think Hector intentionally killed Professor Vernon? Or is it a territorial dispute between the Elmwood Police Department and the investigators with the state DCI?"

"It could be political. The DCI probably thinks the Elmwood PD has been protecting Hector because of his position there. Or they may think the EPD isn't competent enough to handle the investigation, whereas DCI investigates various types of murders all over the state. Who knows what they're thinking? There's a ton of pressure on them to solve the case. For the third day in a row, Hector's name and our B&B have been front-page news. If I were a regular citizen reading the paper, I'd think Hector was guilty too," Marlee replied, bitterness creeping into her voice. "I was called by reporters from the Minneapolis Star Tribune and the Chicago Sun-Times yesterday. And then there's the local TV stations and online newspapers. Sure, the evidence is damning. Hector's service weapon was used to shoot Professor Vernon, and Hector was holding the gun when the lights came on. And then, for whatever outlandish reason, the professor names Hector as the beneficiary of his life insurance policy."

"But come on," Bridget said as she licked the last of the mozzarella cheese off the pizza container. "How dumb would you have to be to use your own gun during a party and then be caught holding the gun? Nobody would be stupid enough to carry out a murder that way. And Hector certainly isn't stupid."

"Nor is he a murderer," Marlee added as she collected their oily napkins and empty pizza containers and threw them in the trash can. "I think the insurance policy is where we need to start this afternoon. We need to find out the name of the company issuing the policy and call them. Maybe they can tell us how long Hector has been listed as the beneficiary. Hector swears he never met Professor Vernon before he came to stay at our B&B, so how this all came together is a complete mystery."

Bridget took a deep breath, choosing her words carefully. "Has Hector ever talked to you about his parents? Is there any chance the professor could be his father?"

Marlee began to laugh. "That's all we need, Hector discovering he's the love child of his mother and Professor Vernon." She continued to laugh until tears leaked from her eyes. It wasn't that funny, but a good release of emotion. Once she'd collected herself, she responded to her cousin's question. "I've seen photos of Hector's parents. He's the spitting image of his father, so I doubt Professor Vernon is his dad."

"Maybe Professor Vernon had a fling with Hector's mother and believed he was Hector's father," Bridget suggested.

"I would be very surprised if that were the case," Marlee said, stifling a giggle.

"So, what's the connection between Hector and the professor?" Bridget asked, a bit miffed that Marlee had laughed at what she thought was a reasonable explanation.

"No clue. Professor Vernon must have sought out our B&B since Hector is the co-owner. But why? According to Hector, the professor never made any contact with him other than to ask if he could burn a candle in his room. When Hector told him he couldn't because it was a fire hazard, the professor accepted it and that was that."

"I know you have no reason to doubt what Hector told you. I don't doubt him, either. But there must be some connection between the two men. Professor Vernon didn't just pick Hector's name out of the blue to be the beneficiary of his life insurance policy and then stay at his B&B and somehow arrange for his own murder."

Marlee gazed out the streaked window at the late afternoon sun. "You know, why would the professor have his murder all planned out but have his stay at the B&B booked for three weeks? He'd already been here a week before his death. If we're going with the theory that he hired someone to kill him, why have it happen randomly during a three-week period? That's an awfully long time to be on edge about someone killing you. I can't believe I'm even saying it. The professor hiring his own hitman, because he was dying, is nuts. Who would do that? And even if he did, why here? Why now? Why involve Hector?"

Bridget nodded in agreement. "If he wanted to die before his disease left him debilitated and in pain, he could have taken a bunch of pills at home. Or shot himself. There was no reason to go through this much effort to bring about his death."

"Unless Professor Vernon was trying to make some type of point," Marlee said, raising her eyebrows.

"Like what? That euthanasia should be legalized?"

"I don't know. And there certainly would be less convoluted ways to protest the euthanasia laws in the country," Marlee said and then paused. "But maybe that's it. Maybe he needed something so messed up and unexplainable to draw attention to him and his right to decide how and when to die."

Bridget sighed. "You said yourself that the professor's murder has been front-page news since it happened and will likely continue for some time. I talked to a friend from Denver yesterday, and she knew all about it. I think the more details come out about the professor's death, the more news coverage it will get."

"And that right there was the whole point Professor Vernon was trying to make!" Marlee jumped up from her chair and reached for her cell. She called Bettina Crawford and told her they were on their way to the police station. Office hours be damned. She wasn't accomplishing anything on campus anyway. For the second time that day, Marlee and Bettina were going to meet to discuss the murder at the B&B.

"Have you two been drinking?" Bettina asked as she showed Marlee and Bridget into an empty meeting room at the police station. "You made absolutely no sense when you called."

The McCabe cousins took turns laying out their theory that Professor Vernon orchestrated his own murder to bring attention to the federal prohibition against euthanasia. "The longer the investigation takes and the more scandalous it becomes, the more news coverage and the more people will follow the story," Bridget said.

"And the more attention the matter gets, the more likely people are to vote to legalize euthanasia. Professor Vernon is a sympathetic victim, one that people will relate to. It's actually pure genius on his part to use his illness and his desire to die on his own terms," Marlee added.

Bettina handed Styrofoam cups of coffee to Marlee and Bridget, giving the detective time to consider their claims. "Interesting ideas. Don't think I've ever heard of that type of motive for a case like this. It still doesn't explain the professor's connection to Hector but is worth looking into. But don't get your hopes up. It's a far-fetched theory, and I doubt I'd get any support from DCI to pursue this lead."

Marlee's face fell as she realized Bettina couldn't do anything with the new spin on the evidence. "So, we have to wait around until the DCI comes up with this idea on their own?"

Bettina nodded dejectedly. "I can suggest it to them, but Karstens is in charge, and he likes to throw his weight around. Anything Wallace and I have told him has been dismissed. He says they are starting over from square one with the investigation since they can't be sure mistakes weren't made."

"If they're starting over from scratch, then why are they looking for Hector with such determination?" Marlee asked.

Bettina lowered her voice, glancing at the door to make sure it was closed. "It's a two-pronged investigation. Karstens and his team are pursuing Hector as the killer, while another agent and her team are looking at everything with fresh eyes. It's not that they actually think someone else is guilty, but they want to explore all avenues to help solidify their case against Hector. If this goes to trial, Hector's defense lawyer will put everything under the microscope that our PD and the DCI did in the investigation. You two should probably get out of here before they see you. You might be tied up for hours giving your statements again."

Bridget jumped to her feet, sliding on her coat. "What should we do now?"

"Not much you can do. Stay out of the DCI's way, and if you know where Hector is, you better tell them. He's already in deep shit, and I'm sure he doesn't want you two to get into any trouble because of him."

Marlee grimaced as she gave a brief nod. Bettina was right, but they all knew Marlee wouldn't give up any information on Hector even if it meant being charged with a crime herself. She took a deep breath and let it out. "Has anyone checked into Professor Vernon's insurance policy? That could hold some clues as to why he selected Hector as his beneficiary."

Bettina rolled her eyes. "That's on hold, too, from what I hear. And it's a shame I can't look into it right now since The Quartermain Insurance Agency sells policies from Massachusetts National and has a branch office here in Elmwood. Downtown, a block off Main Street." Bettina quickly slapped her hand across her mouth. "Oh, no. I shouldn't have said anything about that. You can't go there or say anything to the DCI about me spilling the beans."

Marlee and Bridget's eyes grew wide with this added information, but they promised to forget what Bettina just told them. Marlee reached for her coat, and the two of them left the police station with a new source of information to investigate.

As they piled into Marlee's CR-V, Bridget said, "I can't believe Bettina let it slip that there's an insurance agency here in town that sells policies from Massachusetts National."

Marlee grinned. "Bettina didn't let it slip. She told us, knowing that we'll go check it out. Her hands are tied now that the DCI is overseeing the case. She has to follow the DCI's directives, but we don't."

House of Games

Nobody takes a stand anymore. At best, they write a check or post a meme on social media. But to fully put themselves out in support of the cause? No way. I'm not sure which is worse: being oblivious to the problem or knowing but ignoring it.

Chapter 20

It took a whole five minutes to drive from the police station to the Quartermain Insurance Agency. The office was one of four storefronts situated in a new strip mall, which now housed a Subway, a nail salon, and a dollar store in addition to the insurance office. Marlee parked out front and they walked in, noticing a sign on the door indicating the office was open until 4:00 p.m. that day. She glanced at her phone, noting that it was 3:30 already. With fingers crossed, she approached the reception desk and asked to speak with an agent about an urgent matter.

Marlee didn't know if it was a slow day at the office or if the agent's curiosity got the better of him, but they were led into an agent's office right away. On the drive there, Marlee and Bridget rehearsed what they thought was the best way to elicit information about Professor Vernon's life insurance policy. Chances were slim that they'd get any helpful information, but they had to try.

After introducing themselves, Marlee sat up straight in the chair and squared her shoulders. "My husband has been named the beneficiary of a life insurance policy held by this company, and I have some questions." Bridget looked at her cousin as she began.

Claiming that Marlee and Hector were married wasn't part of the original plan.

"Of course, it would be best if your husband could be here right now. There's a limit on what I can disclose to anyone other than the beneficiary, but I can probably give you a little information," the agent said. "May I see some ID?"

"Of course," Marlee said, relieved she hadn't been tossed out of the insurance office already. She fished through her purse and handed over her driver's license, hoping the agent wouldn't challenge her on having a different surname from Hector's. Or her weight, which was obviously thirty pounds less than her actual weight.

"I kept my birth name," Marlee said self-consciously. "It made no sense to change it since we were only recently married, and I have established myself and my career under McCabe." She could hear herself babbling but was unable to stop.

Bridget took the opportunity to jump on the nervousness bandwagon. "Yeah, I think a lot of women in our age group opted to keep their names when they married. I've heard the younger generation is leaning toward the name change again. That's if they get married at all. The marriage rate has been decreasing. I just read an article about the decrease in the number of marriages in Scandinavia, and it seems the Unites States is following that trend."

Marlee, now in control of herself, could recognize Bridget's babbling was overkill. It sounded like something a guilty person would say. She nudged Bridget's foot with her own, and the two sat in silence as the agent looked at the driver's license.

"Very good," he said. "I must tell you that I'm not a permanent agent at the Elmwood office. I'm just temping while the business gets started, but I'm hoping to be hired full-time eventually. A bank official from our headquarters in Minneapolis will be here starting on Monday, so if you need anything detailed, you'll have to come back then. Now, what is it you want to know? I cannot release any money to anyone but the beneficiary. And it's a process that takes some time."

"Oh, that's fine. I didn't come to collect the money. I was wondering if there's a record of why Professor Vernon would've made my husband the beneficiary of his life insurance policy. To the best of my knowledge, they'd only met on Saturday. That was the day he... died," Marlee gulped.

The agent tapped on his keyboard while keeping his eyes on his computer screen. "Ah, yes. The change to the policy was made recently. Very recently. On Saturday morning, in fact. I see that Jerome A. Vernon met with a manager at this office and filed a change of beneficiary form for his life insurance policy."

"Who was the beneficiary before my husband?" Marlee asked, nearly choking as she referred to her long-term boyfriend as her spouse. Hector wanted to get married, but Marlee insisted that she didn't want to wed. Ever.

A few more taps on the keyboard revealed the name of Janelle A. Vernon. "Looks like Mr. Vernon switched the beneficiary from his niece, Janelle A. Vernon, to Hector G. Ramos on Saturday, October 31st. The policy owner doesn't have to give a reason but sometimes the agent will make a note. Let me check on that," the agent said. More tapping and then the answer. "No, I'm sorry. I don't see any reason noted for the change or any connection Mr. Vernon has to Mr. Ramos."

"But what if—" Marlee began before she was interrupted.

"Just a minute," he said, his tone of voice changing. "I see this policy is flagged because of the suspicious nature of Mr. Vernon's death. And I also see a note showing that Hector Ramos is a suspect in the death." The agent peered over the top of his reading glasses. "I think we're done here."

Before they knew what happened, Marlee and Bridget were escorted out of the insurance office by a stern woman, whom she vaguely recognized as a former non-traditional student who had flunked her classes. The cousins were in shock and said little on the way back to Marlee's house.

"First, I can't believe anyone can waltz into an insurance agency and claim to be the spouse of a beneficiary and get that much information," Bridget said as she grabbed the wine from Marlee's fridge and poured them each a glass of Sauvignon Blanc. They settled in at the dining room table with the crime chart splayed before them.

"What gets me," Marlee said, taking a healthy sip of wine, "is that the professor's niece was set to inherit $100,000 when he died, but then he changed the beneficiary the same day he was killed. What prompted him to do that? There must have been a falling out between Professor Vernon and his niece. What would make you mad enough at someone to remove them as your beneficiary when you die?"

Bridget thought as she topped off their wine glasses. "If someone lied to me or tried to cheat me, I wouldn't go out of my way to do them any favors."

"So, let's say Janelle lied to her uncle. What would be a big enough lie to turn him against her?"

"It could be a family secret. Maybe someone in their family killed another person, and everyone kept it secret, but then Janelle decided to tell, and the professor didn't want his family legacy ruined," Bridget guessed.

"Or maybe she knew something about her uncle and was going to reveal it. He couldn't do anything to stop her, but he could make sure she didn't receive any of his money upon death. That might be the closest thing to punishment he could do to her. And I wonder if Janelle knew she had been removed as her uncle's beneficiary. Or if she was ever aware that Professor Vernon had chosen her in the first place." Marlee swirled the wine in her glass, silently vowing not to drink too much tonight.

"Maybe Janelle knew she was set to inherit, and she and her husband were the people who visited Professor Vernon's room on Friday night. They may have come to confront him or try to change his mind about having himself killed," Bridget said. "If it was them, it must not have been violent, or I'm sure the other guests would have noted it."

"You know, Professor Vernon and Janelle both worked at Badger State University. Maybe the rift had something to do with one or both of their careers. I wonder if Janelle knows of her uncle's charge in Georgia that landed him on the sex offender registry. What if she was spreading it around on campus and trying to make it seem much worse than a drunken public urination charge?" Marlee reached for her laptop and found her way to the university's website. Within a few clicks, Janelle Vernon's smiling face popped up. "She works in the Public Relations Department. A prominent position, but hardly someone who could get her uncle into trouble at the university. He's a tenured, full professor with thirty-five years at the institution, while she's only been there twelve years and holds a position of lesser status."

Bridget smiled. "Ah, but you're forgetting the power of the rumor. High status is no protection from malicious gossip and carefully planted lies. She may be causing him problems, and he found out."

"Good point. And when everyone heard "sex offender," they would react and not take the time to find out that the charge is much more innocuous than it sounds. Like any college, I'm sure there are plenty of rumors at Badger State University. I wish I knew someone who worked there. The university isn't going to put its gossip and dirt online, but I have yet to find an employee who won't happily discuss what's going on behind the scenes," Marlee said.

"I don't know anyone on faculty at Badger State, but I have a former student who went on to get her master's degree there. Maybe she'd have some dirt." Bridget grinned, realizing this could be the big break they needed in the case.

Marlee squealed with delight. "Oh, this is awesome! Grad students always know the good gossip."

After twenty minutes of poking around online, Bridget found her former student and made contact.

After a quick phone call, Bridget relayed her findings. "Yasmine said it's well known that Professor Vernon has been slipping. And not just the regular amount of slipping that's tolerated for seasoned profs. He's been known to present false information in class, embarrassed himself at faculty orientation this fall, and has, on occasion, needed help locating his office."

"That's serious stuff. But if he's tenured, then what can be done to get him out of the classroom?" Marlee asked, unaware of any clause that would allow a university to terminate the employment of a tenured professor in this type of situation.

"Apparently, this sabbatical was awarded to him to get him off campus while the administration figures out what to do. They've been encouraging him to retire, but he refuses. Yasmine said his niece has been trying to get him to retire but has had no luck. There was a blow-up at a faculty meeting not that long ago, and there's been tension between them since then," Bridget said. "No mention of his sex offender status, though."

"Wow, so the connection between Professor Vernon and Janelle deepens. I'm sure it was embarrassing to her as a spokesperson on campus to have an uncle who's losing it in such a public fashion. It would tarnish her reputation, too. It's looking more and more like Janelle could've killed him. Why else would she have come to Elmwood at the same time as her uncle and then attended a party at the B&B where he was staying?"

Pippa chose that moment to saunter into the dining room and jump on the table, planting herself squarely on the crime chart. Bridget leaned in to pull the poster board out from under the cat, but Pippa had other ideas. She launched herself at Bridget with a demonic screech, stopping only a fraction of an inch from her face. Bridget jumped back and shrieked. "My god, that cat is the devil."

In her haste, Bridget had knocked over her own glass of wine. Rather than save the crime chart from getting damp, she looked to Marlee to solve the problem. "I'm not going near that thing."

"Oh, Pippa," Marlee said with a little smile as she grabbed the persnickety Persian with one arm and the crime chart with the other. "She hasn't been getting much attention lately and is acting out." She placed the cat on the floor and reached for a dishtowel to mop up the spilled wine.

"Like hell she is," Bridget shouted. "That cat is always evil, and you're the only one who can't see it. Everyone is afraid of her. Even Hector. He hates her. He told me so himself."

Marlee let the negative comments roll off her back. She was used to her family and friends not understanding what a sweet, albeit sometimes irritable, cat that Pippa could be. "Speaking of Hector, I need to check my burner phone. There weren't any new texts from him last time I checked." She rummaged through her purse, dejected, when there were no voice messages or texts from Hector. "I just want to know that he's okay."

Bridget, immediately disavowed of her anger, moved to put an empathetic arm around her cousin. "I know. I do, too. As soon as we can figure out what's going on with Professor Vernon's insurance policy, I think the case will be wrapped up."

"Get off me, Bridget. I'm not a hugger," Marlee growled as she shook off her cousin's comforting arm. "I don't know how we're going to find answers if the Elmwood Police and the Division of Criminal Investigation haven't figured it out yet."

Bridget took a step back. "Listen to me. You've figured out things in the past way before the police did. We need to buckle down and focus on what we do know. And then we need to find a way to get the information we don't have yet."

"You're right." Marlee took a deep breath and looked toward the dining room table. "Let's get back to work."

With rolled-up sleeves and newly filled glasses of wine, the McCabe cousins continued to pore over the crime chart. "We've talked about the professor's possible motives for removing his niece as beneficiary, but let's come back to why he would name Hector as the recipient of a life insurance payout. Why name somebody so random as the co-owner of the B&B where you've been staying for a week? He hadn't even met Hector until the night of the party. If he was going to randomly assign a new beneficiary, it should have been me since I'd talked to him a few times," Marlee said with a grin.

"Then you'd be the prime suspect in his murder." Bridget looked over the top of the reading glasses she pulled from her purse.

"Let's brainstorm any connections, no matter how unlikely, that there may be between Hector and Professor Vernon. Something so insignificant that a trained observer like Hector wouldn't even notice at first. How might their paths have crossed in the past?"

Bridget scrunched up her nose. "You're certain there's no family connection? Not everyone knows the details about their lineage. We're told a story, and we believe it unless shown otherwise. Maybe Hector was adopted, and it was never disclosed, even to him. Or the professor could be the member of the family that no one ever mentioned, so the younger generations have no idea they even exist."

Marlee scooted her chair back from the table and returned, holding a black photo album. She flipped through the plastic-coated pockets holding yellowed Polaroids of Hector's family. She pointed to a photo of Hector, around age twenty, and his parents in their fifties. "Still think he's adopted?"

Bridget laughed as she focused in on the picture of a young Hector and what looked like Hector in the present. "He looks exactly like his dad. I don't think there's any doubt about his paternity, but what about the professor as a relative who was cut out of the family decades ago? Or maybe Hector's mother or father was cut out of the family and never mentioned anyone else from the old days."

Marlee flipped to a page depicting Hector and around twenty first cousins. Another page showed his father with his adult siblings and a final picture revealed Hector's mother with her sisters. "I suppose it's possible that Professor Vernon was cut out of Hector's family, but I don't think Hector's parents were cut out of his. As you can see, both parents have several siblings. His parents are dead, but he stays in touch with a few cousins. In fact, they're planning a family reunion on his father's side next summer."

"Well, shit," Bridget said as she closed the photo album and pushed it to the side of the table. "Did Hector ever live in Wisconsin? Did he go to Badger State University or live in La Crosse? Maybe he attended a police training there and somehow met the professor."

"No, I'm not sure he's ever been to Wisconsin other than just driving through to get to another state. And from what I've found from a cursory search of Professor Vernon's background, he never worked or lived in South Dakota. I'd still like to know what brought him here to Elmwood. Why choose our B&B? We're new and have no track record. I can see if we'd been in business for a while and have several rave reviews on Yelp, but that's just not the case. At least not yet."

Bridget took a deep breath. "Now, don't get mad or take this the wrong way, but maybe he wanted to stay at a new place. A B&B where the proprietors really didn't know what they were doing. A place where some details would be overlooked until the reality of running the operation was clear and those small things were fixed."

Marlee felt her temperature rise but bit her tongue. As much as she hated to admit it, there might be some truth to her cousin's assertion. "Like what?" She heard the bite to her voice and tried to keep it under control.

"The lack of a security camera in the back stairway is the main one that comes to mind," Bridget said. "I also noticed that you were leaving your front door unlocked, even when you weren't home."

"The security camera was supposed to be installed, but Hector hadn't gotten to it yet. And the B&B websites that I've looked at recommend leaving your front door unlocked so that guests can come in if they have a problem. Not everyone wants to call or text; they want to talk face-to-face with the owners. We lock the door when one of us isn't here and hang up a sign with our cell numbers."

"I'm not criticizing, I'm just pointing out that Professor Vernon may have knowingly searched for an unestablished B&B and decided to take advantage. That's if he was really trying to plan his own murder."

Marlee shrugged. "It's as good of an explanation as any. I'm still wondering if Hector's job as a police detective has any connection to the professor. Other than Professor Vernon being a registered sex offender in Wisconsin, I don't know what connection a police detective would have with an English professor."

"Did he have to fill out any paperwork to come to South Dakota for three weeks?" Bridget asked.

"No, I already checked on that, thinking maybe the professor's paperwork had made its way to Hector's desk somehow, but it didn't. And Hector doesn't have anything to do with approving travel requests to the state anyway."

"So, what the hell is the connection?" Bridget shoved the crime chart away from her and removed her reading glasses.

Marlee closed her eyes as thoughts whirled around in her mind. She knew the pieces of the puzzle were there, but she couldn't figure out how to put them together. "Maybe we're looking at it from the wrong angle. Hector has investigated a ton of cases over the years, everything from murder to sex trafficking to drugs. It could be that someone connected to Professor Vernon was a victim of a crime Hector investigated."

She opened her eyes to find Bridget looking at her with her mouth wide open. "I bet that's it! Professor Vernon's friend or relative was raped or killed by someone Hector helped send to prison. It's the professor's way of paying him back."

"Except for one small problem," Marlee sighed. "No one rewards civil servants for doing their job. Not monetarily, anyway. Victims shouldn't be expected to give money to the police, EMTs, or anyone else who helps them in a time of crisis. Besides, the professor just changed the beneficiary of his will from his niece to Hector. It seems his decision might be more of a knee-jerk reaction to something rather than a reward for Hector's past crime-solving. Besides, Hector doesn't investigate as a lone wolf. More than one person works on a case from the time the incident is reported or discovered until the matter is handled. He's one of several who's involved in investigating any given crime."

"What now? What else can we do?"

"We need to go put the squeeze on the professor's niece. I think Janelle Vernon is the key to finding out what happened."

As long as it doesn't get lost, everything will work out fine in the end. But until then, it might be a rough few days.

Chapter 21

"Yeah, right," Bridget groaned. "How are we going to get access to Janelle Vernon? She's staying at Onna and Franklin Ramone's house, and I'm sure they all lawyered up. There's no way Onna will let us get access to Janelle even if Janelle is willing to talk to us."

"Then we won't go through Onna to get to Janelle. We need to lure her away from Onna's house under false pretenses. We could call her acting as if we're from Irene's formal wear shop and ask her to come down to the store to take care of something to do with her credit card." Marlee tapped her chin as she thought about the perfect ruse to get Janelle Vernon alone and willing to talk to them.

"What if she comes to Irene's and brings Onna with her?" Bridget asked, blowing a car-sized hole in her cousin's plan.

"I was thinking we could suggest that there was something wonky with her credit card. Like maybe Janelle is over her limit because of the fees charged for the damage done to one tux and one dress. She wouldn't want to discuss private financial matters in front of her friend, would she? That's something I'd want kept private."

After twenty minutes of back and forth and what ifs, Marlee and Bridget formulated their plan to talk to Janelle Vernon. Marlee grabbed her burner phone and called Irene's, posing as someone from the police department. After obtaining the phone number associated with Janelle's credit card, she called the professor's niece.

"Hello, Ms. Vernon? This is Mary with Irene's formal wear store. You rented two tuxes and two dresses from us a few days ago and the credit card company is declining payment of the fees we added for cleaning the garments. As you'll recall, you signed a document when you rented the formal wear indicating a $1,000 fee per garment that needed deep cleaning or repair. Your credit card is denying payment because you are over your credit limit. Can you please come to the shop right away to get this sorted?"

There was a long pause on the other end of the line as Janelle, no doubt, thought about her credit limit and the best way to handle it. "Here, I'll just use another credit card and give you the number over the phone. That should take care of it."

"No, ma'am. We need you to come back to the store to take care of it in person. Besides, we found something in one of the garments that is, um, of a personal nature that I'm sure you want back," Marlee said, hoping against hope that Janelle wouldn't push her for more information. "And please use the back entrance in the alley since the store isn't open for business right now."

Again, another long pause. "I can't imagine... well, I mean, it shouldn't... I have no idea what... Fine.

I'll be there in fifteen minutes," Janelle snapped as she ended the call.

The cousins raced to Marlee's vehicle and drove to the alley behind Irene's. "What personal item of Janelle's do you have?" asked Bridget.

Marlee grinned. "I don't have anything of theirs, but when I mentioned having something, it sure prompted Janelle to agree to meet me right away. That tells me something. I don't know what, but it's a clue."

They parked next to the dumpster that Irene's shared with the other businesses on the block. Luckily, the formal wear store was closed, so they wouldn't have to worry about Irene or one of her employees getting involved. As they waited for Janelle to arrive, Marlee's cell rang. It was Bettina.

After a quick phone conversation, Marlee relayed the information to her cousin. "Bettina says that the red stains on Onna and Franklin Ramone's costumes weren't blood after all. The lab determined it was a fine mist of red wine. There wasn't any gunshot residue or blowback on their costumes, either. I guess that rules the two of them out as the shooter," Marlee said dejectedly as two more suspects were in the clear while Hector was on the run.

Before Marlee and Bridget could process the latest information, Janelle rolled into the alley, driving an older model BMW with Wisconsin license plates. She jumped out of her car and raced to Irene's back door which was locked. She was ready to pound on the door before Marlee intercepted her. For all they knew, Irene and her employees might be inside, and she didn't want them disrupting the ruse.

"Janelle?" Marlee asked as she approached from the side.

"Yes, can you open this door so we can go inside and take care of this matter right now?" Janelle stomped her foot as she spoke.

"We just had word of a gas leak in the building and were forced to evacuate. This happened two weeks ago and now it's happened again. Irene really needs to update her building," Marlee said, posing as an irritated employee. "But I grabbed my paperwork and waited for you out here in my car since you were making a special trip to get the matter cleared up." She gestured to her Honda CR-V.

Janelle gave Marlee a bewildered look but followed her to the car and sat in the passenger seat, vacant now that Bridget had moved to the back. "So, what's this all about? She began rummaging in her oversized designer purse knock-off, looking for her wallet. I'll just use another credit card, and we can get on with it. And I need that item of mine that you found with our costumes."

"It's not that simple," Marlee said, ignoring Janelle's demand for the item found in the pocket of the returned formalwear since no such object existed. She started the car to turn on the heater and locked the doors in the process. "We're looking into the death of your uncle and want to know why you showed up here in Elmwood at the same time he was here?"

Janelle gasped and took a long look at Marlee. "Wait, I know you. You're the lady from the party at the B&B. How are you involved in all of this? And you work at Irene's, too?"

Marlee let the last question remain unanswered. The less Janelle Vernon knew about her and Bridget, the more cooperation she hoped to receive. "Yes, it was my B&B where your uncle was killed. Why did you, Onna Ramone, and your husbands come to the party?"

"It was an Open House. We thought it would be fun. Trent and I were here to visit Onna and Franklin, so we decided to go all out with our costumes and hit a bunch of parties here in town. I never imagined there would be a problem with us attending your party. Onna said it was advertised as 'open to the public,' after all."

"It's not about the party." Bridget leaned into the discussion from the back seat like a small child, asking how long until they reached their destination. "Why was your uncle staying at the B&B?"

Janelle craned her neck to look at Bridget. "And you work at Irene's, too?"

"No, I'm her cousin." Bridget pointed her head in Marlee's direction. "And I was at the Halloween party too."

"Oh, yeah. Now I remember. You were the big fish."

Marlee chuckled in spite of herself at Janelle's comment. There was nothing she enjoyed more than having skinny little Bridget taken down a peg.

"I was a mermaid," Bridget said with a frown as she crossed her arms in front of her and settled back against the seat.

"Anyway, your uncle," Marlee began, steering the conversation back on track. "We know people at Badger State and have heard he was in a bit of hot water at the university. But what we don't understand is how he ended up here in Elmwood to work on his sabbatical research."

Janelle took a deep breath. "My uncle is losing it. Very few of his decisions make sense anymore. He was only given the sabbatical to remove him from campus for a few months. Uncle Jerry has become an embarrassment to BSU and to me since I work there, too. Why did he choose Elmwood and your B&B? I don't know."

"He booked a three-week stay here. Do you know where he planned to go after that?" Marlee asked.

Janelle shook her head from side to side. "Like I already said, his actions didn't make much sense anymore."

"Did you have any influence over him?" Bridget asked. "Could you reign him in?"

"I tried, but with little success. That's the main reason Trent and I are here. We came to talk him into moving in with us when he gets back to La Crosse. I've investigated getting guardianship of Uncle Jerry since his cognitive function has declined so much."

"What caused this decline? Was it even safe for him to be on his own?" Marlee questioned, trying to keep the judginess out of her voice.

"I started hearing rumblings on campus about nine months ago in February. Uncle Jerry was going off on unrelated tangents in class, disrupting faculty meetings that he wasn't even supposed to attend, starting arguments with his dean that nearly resulted in violence, embarrassing admin during public events, and so on. There were complaints from students and faculty in his department. Some professors tend to get a little nutty toward the end of their careers, so I didn't think much of it. I figured it was partially true but exaggerated by the time the information made it through the grapevine to me. Then, I was called into a special meeting with the President, the head of Human Resources, and the dean of Uncle Jerry's department. They let me know how dreadful things were, and they were seeking to terminate him on the grounds of creating an unsafe environment for students, colleagues, and staff."

"Did anyone know the cause of his erratic behavior?" Marlee asked, wondering to what extent Janelle and others at Badger State University knew about Professor Vernon's medical diagnosis.

"My husband and I tried getting him to a doctor, but he refused. Uncle Jerry insisted he just had a medical check-up and was fine." Janelle shook her head back and forth as she recalled their many conversations. "He wouldn't let us help him."

"Was he aware of his troublesome behavior on campus? Or did he think everything was fine?" Bridget asked.

"I think he understood some of it was a problem, but his main worry was that the university was trying to get rid of him just because he was old. And, of course, it's not legal to terminate someone for age."

"So, you knew Professor Vernon was coming to Elmwood and decided to come here too?" Marlee said. "And that's why you attended the party?"

Janelle nodded. "We decided to stay with my friend Onna and use that as our excuse for being here at the same time. I found handwritten notes in my uncle's office, so I knew where he was going and when."

"Who wanted your uncle dead? I understand he caused problems for himself and Badger State University, but none of it seems to rise to the level of murdering him," Marlee said.

"I don't know. There's no one I can think of who wanted to hurt him. We all just wanted him off campus. That's all. I'd hoped he would move in with me and Trent, at least until we could find a placement for him in an elder care facility." Janelle reached inside her purse and pulled out a glossy brochure featuring an elderly woman seated on a flowered chair with a doting middle-aged couple gazing fondly at her. "We have a tour scheduled next week. I guess I need to call and cancel that now." A lone tear slipped down her cheek, and she wiped it away with the back of her hand.

Marlee gave Janelle a good, long look. Was she truly a grieving relative who tried to help her uncle but failed? Or was she trying out her acting chops? "I know you weren't seated at the table playing the murder mystery game when your uncle was shot. Where were you standing?"

"By the side of the table. Directly behind where my uncle was sitting. My husband, Trent, was right beside me. We both thought it was part of the game when the lights went out, and there was a gunshot. The lights came back on, I saw Uncle Jerry on the floor bleeding, and it was pandemonium. No one knew what to do."

"Was that the point when you and your husband, along with Onna and Franklin Ramone, decided to leave immediately?" Marlee chose her words with care. She had much more information to extract from Janelle and this might be her only chance to do so.

Janelle looked down toward her feet and nodded. "I'm not proud of it, but Onna said Franklin couldn't be linked to a shooting at a party, and we needed to get out of there right away. They led us down to the basement and out through a side door, and we went to our vehicle."

"Did you know your uncle was dead?" Bridget asked.

"I assumed so. He wasn't moving, and there was a lot of blood. I didn't think there was anything I could do for him. I just acted without thinking when Onna pushed us toward the basement."

"And then?" Marlee asked.

"Franklin said we needed to get to another party ASAP so no one would know we were at your party when Uncle Jerry was shot. We could tell anyone who asked that we were there but left before the shooting. This all came back to keeping a clean image for his senate campaign. We went to a fancy party at the home of Onna's friend and stayed for a bit then went home. We changed out of our costumes, and then Franklin took them back to the formal wear store and put them in the overnight depository."

"You were wearing the blue dress?" Bridget interjected.

"Yes, I had the blue one, and Onna wore the dark red gown."

"What did you, Trent, and the Ramones talk to your uncle about that night at the party?" Marlee recalled Ethan saying he saw the four of them engaged in conversation with Professor Vernon prior to the start of the murder mystery game. "Someone saw him hand a note to one of you."

"I didn't think he would recognize us since we all wore masks with our dresses and tuxes. I wanted to keep an eye on him for a few hours. He was lucid that night and picked Trent and me out of the crowd right away and summoned us over. The four of us went to talk to him, and he said he wanted us to leave him alone. He realized I was following him, and he was irritated. Uncle Jerry wasn't angry with me; he just wanted to be left alone."

"Was he angry with you when you met with him in his room in the B&B on Friday night? Other guests said they heard arguing, and your uncle was the only other guest besides the two who told me about it."

Janelle wrinkled her face. "I didn't go to his room. The Open House was the first time I was ever at your B&B. And I certainly never went upstairs to the room my uncle was renting. Who was he arguing with?"

"That's what we're wondering, too," Bridget said, giving Janelle a sour look behind her back. "No one else in Elmwood knew your uncle, so who would be arguing with him?"

Janelle turned her whole body around to face Bridget. "I don't know who was arguing with him, but it wasn't me!"

Marlee waved her hands as a symbolic clearing of the air. She still had several more questions for Janelle and didn't want her to become defensive and refuse to answer. "We can come back to that. Do you know how your uncle knew my boyfriend? His name is Hector Ramos, and he was dressed as a lumberjack at the party.

He swears he doesn't know Professor Vernon, yet your uncle seemed to know Hector."

Janelle shrugged. "I don't know all the people my uncle knows. Uncle Jerry may have just made his acquaintance since he's been staying at your B&B."

Marlee took a deep breath as she launched into what she suspected would be the conversation-ender. "Not according to my boyfriend. He said the party was the only time they talked, and that was very brief. Did you know that your uncle made Hector the beneficiary of his life insurance policy?"

Janelle whirled to face Marlee. "How do you know anything about my uncle's life insurance?"

"I heard it from reliable sources," Marlee said, leaving it vague. No need to bring to light the information from the police department that Bettina Crawford had been sharing with her all along.

"Well, your sources got it wrong. I'm Uncle Jerry's sole beneficiary for his life insurance and his will. He's told me over and over that I get everything, even though it's not a lot," Janelle insisted. "I cannot imagine him giving anything over to someone else, especially someone he just met."

"I checked with the insurance company, and on the morning of the party, the professor went to the local Quartermain Insurance branch and filled out a change of beneficiary form. He designated Hector to get the $100,000 payout when he died. You had been named the beneficiary before that, so it suggests he acted out of anger by cutting you out," Marlee said.

"This is ridiculous," Janelle said as she fumbled with her purse and the door handle. "And I'm not giving you my credit card to settle the outrageous cleaning fees for the formal wear. I'll come into the store tomorrow and talk to the manager. She needs to know how unprofessional and irresponsibly her employees are acting. And I'm also calling the police!"

"That's good," Marlee shouted at Janelle before she slammed the door. "Because I know they really want to talk to you!"

House of Games

And then there's Janelle. Leave it to her to back out on her promise. She's unreliable and a liar, just like her mother, rest her rotten soul.

Chapter 22

"Do you believe Janelle? Were her tears real?" Bridget asked her cousin as she moved from the back of the SUV to the passenger seat.

Marlee shrugged. "I don't know. At times, she seemed like a concerned relative who was trying to do right by her uncle. At other times, I got a scammy vibe from her. How about you?"

"Same. She could be telling the truth about some things and lying about others."

"That might be the best explanation for now. Janelle realizes her uncle is in cognitive decline but didn't know the extent of his impairment. It's not unusual for someone to keep a diagnosis like that from their family and friends, especially if they think others will insist on a treatment path they don't want. Professor Vernon may have hated the idea of living with Janelle and Trent or going to a nursing home. If that's the case, then no wonder he didn't share his medical status with them." Marlee drove through the alley and onto a semi-busy street.

While waiting at a stoplight, the cousins silently pondered their interaction with Janelle Vernon. Bridget tugged off her coat underneath the fastened seat belt, noting the rising temperature in the vehicle. She reached over and turned the heat to a lower temperature. "She seemed genuine when she denied being in her uncle's room on Friday night. She insisted it wasn't her arguing with him, yet both of the other guests said they overheard two people arguing with Professor Vernon that night. If not Janelle and her husband, then who?"

Marlee nodded. "That's right. Didn't Paul and Leanne say they heard two voices besides the professor's? A male and a female?"

"That's what I remember. Let's go to your house and review the crime chart. There are so many moving parts, and I can't keep everything straight."

Marlee parked in their B&B driveway and took a long look at the future she and Hector hoped to build. This was not just their home but a project for them to work on together while receiving an income to pay for updates and renovations. The couple had talked about the B&B being their retirement plan should they decide to retire soon. Hector had enough years in with the police department that he could retire whenever he wanted. Marlee, on the other hand, had another five years before her pension would kick in. Both had previous service from other occupations that counted toward their overall years toward retirement. But now, what would they do? Hector was on the run and facing a possible murder charge. They would lose all their equity in the house in paying Hector's legal bills. Losing their home and declaring bankruptcy were very real options.

She shook her head to clear away the negative thoughts. There was plenty of time to deal with all of that later. Right now, she and Bridget needed to focus on discovering the real killer and clearing Hector's name.

They walked into the house and, as usual, grabbed a bottle of wine from the fridge and a box of snack crackers from the kitchen counter. As Marlee peeled off her coat, Bridget grabbed clean wine glasses from the dishwasher and was generous in her pour of the Sauvignon Blanc. The crime chart was still on the dining room table from the last time they consulted it.

"The thing I can't get past is that no one really has a motive to kill the professor except for Janelle and her husband. Although she seemed surprised that she was no longer the beneficiary of his life insurance policy, she said she would be inheriting everything named in her uncle's will," Marlee said as she took a giant gulp from the wine glass.

"Who knows? Maybe he changed his will too."

"He would've had to do that before he came here. His attorney must be back in Wisconsin, so he wouldn't have been able to make a snap decision on changing the will as he did with his life insurance policy," Marlee pointed out.

"Unless he found another attorney and made a whole new will." Bridget raised her eyebrows as she reached for a handful of cheese crackers, popping them in her mouth one by one. "And the newest will invalidates any will made prior to that time. It's a standard clause in most wills. I just had mine made out recently."

"The professor totally could've done that," Marlee said, hitting her forehead with her palm. "Now we need to find out if he met with an attorney here and devised a whole new will. And there are dozens of attorneys here in Elmwood. It'll take forever to talk to each one. And they're attorneys, so they won't offer up the information as easily as the average person might."

"Could your friend Denny Harlow find out for you?" Bridget finished off the last of the crackers, finding only cheesy dust in the bottom of the cellophane bag.

Marlee snorted. "He's hardly a friend. He's represented me before when I was suspected of a crime, and he's Hector's attorney of record right now. Still, it wouldn't hurt to put a bug in his ear and see if he can do some checking. He'd have a better chance getting this information than I would."

Denny Harlow was a listed contact in her phone, but Marlee doubted she could reach the alcoholic attorney. It was well past happy hour, so he was no doubt already drunk and quite possibly passed out by now. If he wasn't passed out, then Denny was probably in the arms of some new love interest, the name of whom he would not recall in a few hours. She texted him a brief message detailing the conversation she and Bridget had with Janelle that evening and their question about a possible will change for Professor Vernon in Elmwood.

Less than a minute later Marlee's phone rang. It was Denny, and he sounded sober. "Denny, I thought you might be out on the town. Glad I was able to reach you."

He gave a wheezy cough before speaking. "I'm doing a sobriety thing. Not my choice, it was a suggestion from the court system. I'm at home going nuts watching reality television. It's so bad it would drive someone to drink if they weren't already a drunk." Denny chuckled at his own self-deprecating joke.

Marlee wasn't sure how to respond. For as long as she'd known Denny, which was over twenty years, he'd been a chronic alcoholic. He was under the influence about half of the time she talked to him, so to hear of his attempt at sobriety was shocking. "Uh, well, good for you, Denny. It's always great to work on self-improvement. I just started a new diet, so I know how hard it can be." She glanced at Bridget who made a face at her, urging her to get to the point.

"So, you heard my message. What do you think about Professor Vernon drawing up an entirely new will while he was here in Elmwood? He was here a week before he was killed, so that's time enough to get it done, especially if he didn't have much in the way of assets."

"It's possible. Since he amended his life insurance while he's been here, maybe he made up a new will, too." Denny stopped talking and coughed for a full minute before resuming the conversation. "Sorry about that. I may have stopped drinking, but I've doubled my smoking."

"Can you use your connections to find out if Professor Vernon used a local attorney to prepare a new will?" Marlee asked.

"Yeah, I'll do some checking. Anything to get me out of this apartment and away from reality TV."

"Denny, have you heard from Hector? I haven't seen him since Wallace hauled him down to the station. You were there when they questioned him. Did he say anything about where he was going?" Marlee knew the chances were slim that Hector's attorney would provide any information on their latest contacts or his whereabouts. And if he did, it most certainly would not be on an unsecured phone line.

"No, I haven't. Hoping he turns up soon," Denny said unenthusiastically. "I'm sure he's just off visiting someone and forgot to tell you."

"Yeah, you're probably right," Marlee said, playing along with the attorney's ruse. If her house was bugged or her phone tapped, then Denny didn't want either of them to make any statements implicating Hector further. Or themselves. She felt marginally better after talking to Denny, knowing he was doing a respectable job for Hector even though, as a defense attorney, he was frequently at odds with the police department. And apparently now under some sort of court directive to quit drinking.

"What now?" Bridget topped off their wine glasses and searched the pantry for more snacks.

Marlee stood at the dining room table, peering down at the crime chart. "This would be so much easier to figure out if we knew who the real focus was. Was Professor Vernon the main target or was he just a convenient victim used to set up Hector for a big fall?"

Bridget flipped the chart over, revealing the connections they previously named in relation to Hector being the prime target. "If the professor was killed only to implicate Hector in his murder, then we can eliminate several of the people who were playing the murder mystery game. The couple who was staying here on their big date weekend wouldn't have any motive, so we can cross them off the suspect list."

Marlee's hopes soared as she listened to her cousin make cuts to the suspect list. "You're right.

Leanne and Paul have no connection and can be discarded. Ethan and Nadia can be crossed off as well. Shelly McFarland was at the table, as was Hector, and we both know they didn't shoot the professor, so cross them off, too."

"Those remaining at the table, besides the professor, are Franklin and Onna Ramone. Would either of them have a reason to kill the professor as a way of setting up Hector for the murder?" Bridget asked. "Does Hector even know them?"

"I don't think so. He didn't recognize them at the party and he's super observant, as you know. He never mentioned knowing either Onna or Franklin, but they've been here in Elmwood for years, maybe decades. Maybe Hector investigated them or arrested one of their kids," Marlee suggested.

"Arresting a child for underage drinking or vandalism is hardly a motive for murder," Bridget countered.

"I said their child I didn't say the person arrested was a child. Maybe their adult son or daughter went to the penitentiary on a drug case. They could be facing a long time in prison based on an investigation Hector did. I don't recall anything in the newspaper or scuttlebutt around town about Onna's kids."

Bridget shook her head back and forth. "But you said Hector didn't investigate anything alone. Every case is a team effort. If Onna and Franklin killed the professor to set up Hector, then maybe they will target other detectives on the Elmwood Police Department too."

Marlee's jaw dropped as she considered her cousin's theory. It was a stretch but not one they could dismiss without further investigation. "I'm calling Bettina and getting her over here right away." She fumbled for her cell and made the call to Bettina's direct number. Before she could share Bridget's theory or offer updates on what they learned from Janelle, Bettina cut her off.

"The DCI found Hector, and they're bringing him in. He's under arrest for the murder of Professor Jerome Vernon."

House of Games

*Sometimes things work out the way you want them to.
But not usually.*

Chapter 23

Marlee's cell phone clattered to the floor before she bothered to end the call to Bettina. Hector was en route, courtesy of the South Dakota Division of Criminal Investigation, to Elmwood and facing a murder charge in the death of Professor Vernon. Now what?

After a quick update to Bridget, Marlee retrieved her phone and placed another call to Denny Harlow. "I'll be at the jail to meet him as soon as the DCI arrives," Denny assured her. "Hector's a smart guy. He knows to keep his mouth shut, even around his fellow officers. They may be his coworkers and his friends, but he will see how fast those relationships change now that he's charged."

She'd never been much of a crier, preferring to keep her emotions inside and dealing with them through overeating, problem drinking, and occasional temper flare-ups, but now, with Hector's murder charge, everything was too real. No amount of food and alcohol could fill this gaping hole of pain that had settled inside her heart. As tears began to flow down her face, Marlee turned her back to her cousin, embarrassed by the uncharacteristic show of emotion.

Bridget, who was all about processing feelings, pulled her cousin into a tight bear hug. "It's going to be

OK. We'll figure this out and get Hector released and the real killer behind bars." Bridget tried to push Marlee's head toward her shoulder as she began patting her cousin's back.

"Dammit, Bridget! You're making it worse," Marlee sniffled, wiping her left eye and her nose on the sleeve of her long-sleeved t-shirt. She rolled her shoulders as if to shake off the very memory of the hug. Before Marlee could chastise her cousin further, a loud and persistent knock at the front garnered her attention.

It was Bettina at the door, out of breath and looking fearful. Two things Marlee never thought she'd see in the fit, competent detective. "Let me in. It's cold out here, and it's starting to snow."

Marlee stepped aside, letting Bettina have enough room to kick off her shoes and toss her coat in the general direction of the hall tree before bombarding her with questions about Hector's arrest. It wasn't that she was being polite; she just didn't want to hear the answers.

Bridget ran toward Bettina, a glass of wine in hand. "I can't begin to get my mind around this whole thing. Hector in custody for murder?"

Bettina gratefully accepted the full glass of wine and took a gulp. "Not too much of this stuff. I need to keep a clear head." She took another gulp and set it down on a decorative table. "My car is up the street in the apartment building's parking lot, so no one knows I'm here. This is a one hundred percent unofficial visit, okay?"

"What the hell is going on?" Marlee finally blurted.

"Hector's a hell of a detective, but he's not great at hiding. The DCI picked him up an hour ago, and he was eating a burger and fries at a Mom and Pop diner in Mobridge." Bettina shook her head in disbelief. "A couple of Highway Patrol officers spotted his Jeep parked out front and ran the plates."

"Are you kidding? Why would he be out in public like that?" Bridget asked. "Did he have a head injury? Maybe he had a mental break because of the stress of the whole situation. That's probably why he took off in the first place." Bridget continued to weave together theories that explained away Hector's irrational behavior and put him in the best possible light.

Bettina furrowed her eyebrows and frowned. "He should've come back and turned himself in. It would look better for him if he self-surrendered rather than wait to be caught. And why was he in Mobridge? I'm not buying any of this. Except maybe the mental breakdown. That's starting to make more sense."

"We don't know that Mobridge is where he's been hiding. I don't know that he has anyone there who would let him hide out at their home. Maybe he was passing through on his way back to Elmwood. Maybe he's just been driving this whole time and only now was he detected," Marlee said. She couldn't piece together Hector's actions either but knew he must have a reason for doing what he did.

Marlee's phone chirped with an incoming text. Denny messaged that Hector was now booked into the Elmwood Jail and had an initial appearance on the murder charge the following morning. He reminded her, unnecessarily, that there was no way Hector would be released on bond. Given the seriousness of the charges and the fact that he'd been hiding to avoid prosecution, anything but remaining in jail was out of the question. There might be a possibility she could visit Hector, but they wouldn't know until tomorrow.

Marlee, Bridget, and Bettina all moved to the dining room table and looked at the crime chart as if, like a Magic 8 Ball, it would reveal all. Bettina had brought her wine glass along with her and was nearing a refill. "Changed my mind," she said with a guilty expression when she caught Marlee's eye.

"No judgment," Marlee said, refilling her own glass for the umpteenth time. "I know you're in a tough situation, Bettina, but do you know anything about the professor's death that will help Hector? If you do, you need to tell us."

"I overheard the DCI agents talking about the professor's medical records. He had a fast-moving brain cancer that would've left him in need of around-the-clock care within a few weeks. The DCI is still giving us very little information. Since they took over the case, we've been shut out," Bettina said, shaking her head from side to side.

"Hey," interrupted Bridget. "We forgot to tell Bettina about our conversation with Janelle Vernon today. That was the reason you called her in the first place."

Marlee nodded and, in as few words as possible, detailed their meeting with Janelle Vernon, leaving out how they obtained her phone number and the credit card ruse they used to get her back to Irene's. "Janelle knew her uncle was having difficulty at the university where they both work, but she didn't seem to be aware of his brain cancer diagnosis. She detailed his odd and unprofessional behavior and said she and her husband, Trent, had come to Elmwood to keep an eye on him. Janelle planned to ask the professor to move in with them until they could find him suitable care for his deteriorating cognitive function."

"Really?" Bettina asked. "What did she know about the transfer of the beneficiary of the life insurance policy from her to Hector?"

"She denied knowing anything about it. According to Janelle, her uncle told her previously that she was the sole beneficiary of everything in his will, including the life insurance policy. She seemed to be in disbelief that he had changed the life insurance beneficiary while he was in Elmwood." Marlee reached for a tissue to clean her smudged eyeglasses.

"Was she being truthful or throwing a bunch of bullshit your way?"

"Parts of what she said seemed genuine, but other times, neither one of us was sure," Bridget said. "I think she truly cared about her uncle's future, but whether it was really about his well-being or about his money, I don't know."

Marlee nodded in agreement. "And when I asked her about going to Professor Vernon's room on Friday night, she denied it. Said she never went to his room at the B&B. She only saw him there at the party, where he recognized her and Trent and told them to leave him alone. I told her that the professor changing the beneficiary on his life insurance policy the very next morning, while out of town and on a Saturday, no less, seemed like a strong reaction to something she had done or said. That's when she stopped talking about the case and said she was going to call the cops on us."

"What did you do that made her want to call the police?" Bettina frowned and took turns giving the McCabe cousins a hard look.

"No need to get into that. Just a little misunderstanding," Marlee said quickly as she searched for something to get Bettina onto another topic. "But what's important is that she is denying having any contact with her uncle before the party. Yet, she's the only one with a motive to kill him."

"Based on what we know so far," Bridget corrected. "I mean, it could be anyone, but right now, Janelle appears to have the only motive."

"If we're still assuming the professor was an intended victim," Marlee challenged. "If the whole plan was to get Hector in legal trouble, then any one of the guests could've been the murder victim that night."

The three continued to discuss who would want Hector thrown in prison for a crime he didn't commit. "Any new information on Detective Wallace?" Marlee asked. She knew Bettina was protective of her fellow detectives, but she held no one in higher regard than Hector.

"Nah, he's not getting any updates from DCI either. Other than I'm sure they called to tell him they arrested Hector. Just to rub our noses in it." Bettina's voice was thick with disgust at the state agency that had not only treated the Elmwood PD like bumpkins but also arrested Hector.

"Any follow-up on the piece of paper that I saw Wallace take from Professor Vernon's room when he thought I wasn't looking?"

"I've checked a few times and nothing so far. And if he tried to enter something into evidence from Saturday night, it would face a great deal of scrutiny by Hector's defense team. The paper was improperly seized, it wasn't bagged and tagged, and it never made it to the evidence room. The chain of custody has been broken." Bettina said.

"You know what I just realized?" Marlee asked, not waiting for a response from either her cousin or Bettina. "Remember the couple who stayed here on their first date? Paul and Leanne? Paul said he was from the Mobridge area."

"That's right. He has a ranch outside of town and plans to turn it over to his son in ten years," Bridget said. "I think that's one of the big reasons Paul and Leanne were poorly suited for each other. She lives in Fargo and expects him to move closer to her, while his plan is to remain on the ranch for at least another decade."

Bettina gave Marlee a quizzical look. "You think Hector briefly meeting Paul here at the B&B was enough of a connection for Hector to go to Mobridge? You think Paul agreed to hide Hector?"

"Hmmm..., I hadn't thought of that. I thought maybe Paul is somehow connected to the case and Hector wanted to talk to him."

"You think Paul shot Professor Vernon?" Bridget asked. "Why?"

"No, I don't necessarily think that. I'm wondering if Hector needed to follow up on what Paul and Leanne told him. Remember, they are the only ones who reported that two people were arguing with the professor in his room on Friday night. No one else was around to hear it. We've been taking their word all along that it really happened," Marlee rambled, unsure where her thoughts were taking her.

"Why would Leanne and Paul make up something like that?" Bettina questioned.

Marlee didn't have an answer. Until she did. "Maybe they were the two people arguing with Professor Vernon on Friday night."

Regrets? Only one. I wish I'd punched Dean Spangler in the mouth when I had the chance.

Chapter 24

"Why would Paul and Leanne argue with Professor Vernon?" Bridget asked.

"I have no idea, but if they did and wanted to cover their tracks in case Hector and I heard them, then claiming they overheard people arguing with the professor makes total sense." Marlee gave a satisfied nod. "They didn't know until we met them for lunch at Pizza Ranch on Sunday that we can't hear what happens on the third floor."

"I don't think we have much on Paul and Leanne. Wallace interviewed them after you had lunch on Sunday. He was pissed that Hector had already talked to them. And Wallace was beyond pissed that Hector tipped him off that they were planning to return home without giving interviews at the PD." Bettina smirked as she recalled the former lead detective's ire at Hector's involvement.

Marlee reached for her laptop and Googled "Paul Rowley Mobridge, South Dakota." Nothing strange popped up, mainly farm and ranch-related news articles, his son's junior varsity wrestling scores, and an award for exemplary public service. Paul appeared to be exactly who he had said he was: a rancher, a dad, and a man with strong ties to his community. No surprises. At least none that showed up on a basic internet search.

Leanne Desmond from Fargo, North Dakota, was another story. No one with that name showed up in the Fargo area. Marlee then excluded Fargo and expanded the search to statewide. Still no Leanne Desmond. "Maybe she just got divorced and went back to her birth name," Marlee suggested.

"Or she could've moved from another state and hasn't gotten established yet in Fargo," Bridget offered.

"Do you still have her phone number?" Bettina asked. "If so, we can run a reverse phone check to see if the number matches the name."

"Great idea." Marlee scrolled through her phone and found Leanne's number, typing it into the reverse number look-up on her computer. "Hmmm...the number is registered to Leanne Dalton. Let's see if that name pops up on a Google search." A few keyboard taps later, they had their answer. Their Leanne Desmond was otherwise known as Leanne Dalton in Fargo.

"She probably uses Desmond for her dating profile so she can avoid weirdos," Bettina said. The other two women nodded in agreement, a silent acknowledgment of their own previous online dating experiences gone awry. "It's easier to avoid someone if they don't have your real name."

Marlee typed in the new surname they had for Leanne and the first three search results all dealt with her criminal convictions in Cass County, North Dakota. One of the hits was a newspaper article about her sentencing for a financial scam against elderly people in Fargo. The mugshot showed a younger Leanne with a different hairstyle, but it was clearly the same woman who'd been a guest at the B&B. Leanne had been placed on two years of probation and required to make $7,000 in restitution to the victims. The two additional top search results revealed other convictions for Leanne, also for financial crimes but on a smaller monetary scale.

"Looks like our Leanne is a crook," Marlee said, not bothering to continue looking at the remaining search results. "Maybe that's why she uses a different name. If her potential internet dates do a search on her they would see what we did. But under the surname of Desmond, nothing shows up, which is a little suspicious since most people have some digital footprint."

"I bet poor Paul didn't know anything about her background," Bridget said, sad for the lonely bachelor looking for love in all the wrong places.

"I bet poor Paul was another intended victim," Bettina surmised. "When he told her he ran a ranch, she probably had dollar signs in her eyes. Then, upon meeting him, she found out that he co-owns it with his parents and will pass it on to his son. Most likely, any money Paul has will go back into the operation of the ranch."

"Yep, and once she realized this, she was done with him," Bridget said. "She quit trying to impress him and was going to enjoy some free meals and entertainment over the weekend."

"Maybe she was done with Paul but set her sights on Professor Vernon. He was of retirement age, and Leanne may have thought he had a nest egg socked away. A few months of dating him, and she'd probably devise a way to separate him from his money. Or she would at least have figured out if there was any money she could get from him," Marlee said.

"You don't think Leanne shot the professor, do you? What's her motive? Unless he was traveling with a lot of cash or valuable objects that she could steal, there would be no reason for her to kill him. He's worth more alive than dead to her. If they had been dating for a few months, and she managed to worm her way into his will, then that's another story. At that point, she'd be a prime suspect," Bridget said, breaking down the case point by point.

"Nah, I don't see a reason for her to kill the professor either," Bettina said.

"But you're forgetting the printed email I found in Professor Vernon's room. It was ripped at the top, so we don't know who sent it, but it specified the details of the professor's death. Remember?" Marlee asked. "We sort of discarded the idea because he teaches creative writing. Hector thought maybe he was working on a screenplay or even a novel."

"You think the professor hired Leanne to be his hitman and kill him at the party?" Bettina asked. "This case is getting wilder by the minute. How would they have even met? I mean, Professor Vernon wouldn't have approached Leanne upstairs and casually asked if she'd shoot him during the party."

"No, probably not," Marlee agreed. "But what if they had that part planned before they arrived at the B&B? If the professor was intent on having someone kill him, for whatever reason, then he could have lined that up on the dark web. You can get about anything done on the dark web, from what I hear."

Bettina shot her a look. "How much time have you spent on the dark web?"

"None. I'm kind of afraid to go on there. I don't want my email linked to any murder-for-hire or sex trafficking sites," Marlee confessed. "As interesting as I think it would be, I'm more scared than I am curious. How about you?"

"Yeah, had to a few times for a task force I was on last year. It's beyond disturbing. You can find a buyer or a seller for any type of crime, kink, or fetish that you can imagine." Bettina shook her head back and forth to wipe away the memories of what she'd seen.

Bridget started laughing. "Let me get this straight. The new theory is that Professor Vernon went on the dark web and hired Leanne to meet him at a B&B two states away and kill him at a party? Anyone think this sounds far-fetched?"

"Is it any more far-fetched than a guest staying at a B&B gets shot at a murder mystery party where they know no one, yet the gun of the host was used in the shooting, and the guest leaves the host $100,000 in life insurance benefits? Oh, and the guest may or may not have put out a hit on his own life." Marlee smirked as she upped the ante.

"I don't think we can cross anyone off the crime chart at this point," Bettina said. Bridget reluctantly nodded as she uncapped a purple marker and added Paul and Leanne's names to the crime chart.

Noticing the time, Bettina left for a scheduled appointment. With a promise to contact Marlee if anything developed, the detective was out the door, marching down the street toward her car.

"It is getting late. I should probably go too," Bridget said. "Unless you want me to stay. If you're afraid, I can stay."

Marlee's feathers were ruffled by that comment. If there was one thing she hated, it was being treated like a damsel in distress— unless there was no other way to get what she wanted. "I'm not a child, Bridget. I'll be fine. I've lived by myself most of my life."

"Fine. Just thought I'd be nice and offer," Bridget snapped as she pulled on her coat and slid into her shoes.

Marlee moped around the house after Bettina and Bridget left, wishing she had taken Bridget up on her offer to stay overnight. She wasn't afraid, just lonely. And kind of afraid. She didn't think she was in any danger by herself at the house, but she worried what would happen to Hector. Given the charged crime and that he had to be tracked down by law enforcement, Hector would not be released pending trial. His new home for the next several months would be the county jail, a place he'd helped send a multitude of criminals over the years. If convicted of the murder, then he'd be spending the rest of his life behind bars.

On the other hand, Marlee sensed Hector had an ace up his sleeve. When he was nabbed by law enforcement, he was in plain sight, almost daring someone to arrest him. She hoped he had pieced together more of the puzzle. Maybe enough to get the prosecutor to withdraw the murder charge against him. It was a long shot, but right now, that's all she had.

She got into her fuzzy fleece pajamas and sat on the couch downstairs to watch television until she became sleepy. Stephen Colbert was on, yet she couldn't focus on the monologue or the guest interviews even though one of her favorite stars, Jason Momoa, was the main guest. Marlee's mind was a whirl as the details of the last few days flew by in no particular order. She turned down the volume on the television and moved to the dining room table to take another look at the crime chart. The deeper she dug, the more suspects and motives were added. As Bettina said earlier, they really couldn't discount anyone as the killer now.

Since she couldn't talk to Hector yet, Marlee had no idea what he'd learned while on the lam. But the fact that he was apprehended in Mobridge and one of the B&B guests was from that area had to be more than a coincidence. With that thought in mind, she raced to her office on the second floor and accessed the records for the B&B. Within a few clicks, she had Paul Rowley's telephone number and address.

It was late and Paul had made a big deal at the party about how he was an 'early to bed early to rise' kind of guy. That was all well and fine, but Marlee had to do everything in her power to get Hector out of jail and free from the murder charge. And if Paul Rowley had anything to share, she was going to make sure it was given to Denny Harlow who could decide how to best use it in Hector's defense.

On the fifth ring a sleepy voice said, "Hello? Who is this?"

Marlee identified herself and apologized for the late hour call. "I need to know if you met with Hector Ramos in the last day or so. I think he was coming to

Mobridge." She let the question hang in the air while Paul took a moment to revive himself.

"Uh, yeah. It was the weirdest thing. He came out here to my place. I live nine miles outside of Mobridge, and it's not exactly some place you'd stumble upon. He asked a lot of questions about Leanne, the gal I had the weekend date with at your B&B."

"Yes, I remember," Marlee said, urging him along. "What did Hector want to know?"

"If Leanne and I were still in contact. I answered that question with a big N-O. She acted one way online but totally different in person. Did you know she was a vegetarian?" Paul snorted as if it were the worst moral failing one could possess. "I raise cattle for Chrissake."

"And what else did Hector ask about?" If there was one thing Marlee wanted to avoid, it was a discussion over the vegetarian versus carnivore debate.

"He asked about the two people we heard go into the professor's room the night before the party."

"And?"

"And I told him what I'd said before. Leanne told me she heard two people, a man and a woman, talking with the professor and then they all went inside his room. I didn't hear anything because I was asleep. But Leanne said she heard them arguing, and then the voices quieted down. She never heard them leave," Paul recounted, the grogginess leaving his voice. "Her room was a little closer to the professor's. Plus, she was a night owl. I have crops and animals to take care of and that means getting up early and going to bed early."

"Did you know Leanne has a criminal record?" Marlee threw it out to see if Paul had any reaction to that statement.

"Hector told me she did. I was shocked. She was strange, for sure, but I didn't see her as a criminal. I'm glad to be done with her. I'll be a lot more careful with online dating from now on. Maybe I'll just stick to meeting ladies at church and VFW dances like my mom suggested. This Internet stuff is nuts!"

"Leanne is a scammer. After I found that out, I wondered if she targeted you, thinking you had a lot of money since you own a ranch."

"Yeah, it crossed my mind, too, after Hector told me about her. I really dodged a bullet," Paul said before he realized the weight of his words. "Oh, sorry. Didn't mean it like that."

"Did you know that Hector has been charged with the professor's murder? He didn't do it, of course, but he's being charged." Marlee wasn't sure why she'd offered up this information. Probably because she needed someone to talk to about her boyfriend's legal situation, and no one else was around.

"He told me when he was here. Said he was following up on some leads before he turned himself in," Paul said. "Is he in jail now?"

Marlee gave a brief update on Hector's detention and, after a few more minutes of conversation, thanked Paul for his time and apologized again for waking him. She made her way down the stairs to the first floor to turn off the television before attempting to sleep. The lights were off, but she knew her way back up the stairs to the bedroom she shared with Hector.

Just after clicking off the television, she felt cold steel against the back of her neck.

"Don't move one fucking muscle or you're dead!"

House of Games

Perhaps I misjudged her.

Chapter 25

Marlee's heart was beating so fast that she feared the onset of a heart attack. It happens to rabbits all the time. They were nervous little creatures who could be frightened into heart failure, and that's exactly what she thought would happen to her.

The gun pressed even harder into her neck as she took tentative steps forward.

"Keep moving. I'll tell you when to stop," the voice croaked. Was it a familiar voice? The person was obviously disguising their voice, so it could be someone she knew. At this point, Marlee was unsure of the gender of her assailant. All she knew was that someone had a gun trained on her, and they meant business.

"What do you want," Marlee asked. "I have some cash in my purse, maybe seventy dollars."

"I'm not here for money. You know what I want," the voice rasped. "Hand it over."

"Hand what over?" For the life of her, Marlee had no idea what had been promised to who. Although the house was dark, the streetlight across the street provided illumination as they walked through the living room into the kitchen. She saw the reflection of the person holding the gun, and although she couldn't identify the person by their outline, Marlee felt confident the person was female. What female did she make a promise to? And what was the promise about? Or was this a random break-in by a drug-addled person looking for something to steal and then turning into cash for more drugs?

"My dress," the voice snapped.

Marlee turned to see a figure, clad head to toe in black clothing, including a face-covering ski mask. It was the same person she and Bridget had met earlier that evening, but she bore little resemblance to her earlier self. Before her stood a desperate woman. With a gun.

"Janelle, I don't have your dress. I just said I had something of yours to give you more reason to meet with us to talk about your uncle. I don't have your costumes or anything from the pockets of your formal wear. I don't even work there." Marlee's only hope was to tell the truth. At least as much of the truth as would keep her alive.

"I don't believe you. That's a big coincidence, and I don't believe in coincidences," she spat. "Just hand it over and I'll be out of here."

Marlee faced Janelle head on with only a few feet between them. She had lowered the gun away from Marlee's head, but it was still pointed at the middle of her body. "What if I tell you I don't have it, but I can get it for you?"

"Now!" The gun resumed its earlier position, aimed at Marlee's head.

"I know who has it, and I can get it for you, but not until tomorrow," Marlee said, hoping her bluff would pay off. She knew the Elwood detectives had seized the dresses and tuxes worn by Janelle, Trent, and the Ramones. But Janelle didn't necessarily need to know that. If she thought Marlee could get the dress for her, then maybe she would be on her way.

"How can I trust you to get my dress? And why isn't it here now?" she asked, confusing Marlee further.

Was Janelle drunk or on drugs? Why would she think Marlee had her dress? And why would she want the dress anyway unless she thought it might have blood spatter or some other type of evidence on it. Maybe the police hadn't informed her yet that there was no evidence on the dress of her involvement in the shooting. The only reason Janelle would want her dress back was because she was somehow linked to the crime. She may not have pulled the trigger, but she knew who did.

"I'll have it here for you tomorrow," Marlee promised.

"Not here. You think I'm stupid? You will have an army of cops waiting for me. I'll text you the location tomorrow."

"I'll have it. I promise," Marlee said, feeling less confident in her plan now that the fictional hand-off of the costume would be at an undisclosed location.

"If you don't, I'll track you down and kill you," she said. With that statement, the dark figure turned and exited the house through the back door.

The bonds that unite us are the ones that hurt the most when severed. No one can hurt you like those closest to you.

Chapter 26

Marlee's sleep that night was fitful at best. She was still in shock from Janelle breaking in and holding her at gunpoint. And how could she keep Janelle from shooting her once she realized Marlee didn't have her blue dress? She also worried about Hector. His initial appearance on the murder charge would be in a few hours, and she needed to attend, not just to show support for her beloved but to suss out any other information on his case. She hadn't realized how much she relied on Hector and Bettina's inside knowledge and connections in the police department. Without their help, she floundered as she struggled to make sense of the case.

Her stomach roiled as she downed a second mug of black coffee. She didn't have the appetite for breakfast yet needed the caffeine jolt to compensate for the lack of sleep. Marlee drove to the county courthouse and proceeded through security to the courtroom. She was early, and the only people in the courtroom were the stenographer, two court security officers, and the judge's law clerk. The four employees of the court system bustled around readying themselves and the courtroom for a display of grand theater: a local seasoned detective making his initial appearance on a murder charge.

Denny Harlow walked through the back doors of the courtroom and gave her a wink. He reeked of cigarette smoke, but she didn't smell alcohol on him, which was a surprising new trend. After placing his briefcase on the defense table, he walked back to Marlee. "Just met with Hector, and he's keeping his spirits up. He's preparing for a long fight on this."

It was hardly the news she wanted to hear from Hector's defense attorney. She wanted to hear that it was all a big mistake, a miscarriage of justice, and that her boyfriend would be released from jail this morning. She yearned to hear of another arrest in the murder of Professor Vernon. Or at least the presence of another viable suspect. Denny was unable to offer her any of those things as he backed away and returned to his table before she could tell him of the break-in at her house just hours earlier.

Bettina Crawford edged in next to Marlee and gave her a half smile. There was nothing she could do for Hector but show support for her trusted colleague and good friend. Marlee wondered how many other detectives and officers would be in court today to support Hector. They were in an awkward position. Depending upon the outcome of the initial appearance today and subsequent court hearings, Hector may not have any support from within his department. In fact, supporting Hector might have a detrimental effect on the careers of those supporting him in the police department, especially in the event he was found guilty of the charges.

Marlee needed to clear her head before the hearing started. She hurried down the hall to the restroom and splashed cold water on her face. As she dried her face with a paper towel, Janelle Vernon entered the restroom. When they made eye contact, Marlee couldn't hold in her rage.

"You have some nerve breaking into my house last night and holding me at gunpoint! You're lucky I don't have you arrested." Marlee threw the damp paper towel in the general direction of the garbage bin.

"I don't know what you're talking about," Janelle said in a cool tone, unperturbed by Marlee's outburst. "I don't have a gun, and even if I did, I wouldn't point it at anyone."

"Bullshit! You threatened me because you thought I had your dress. Besides that, I think you hired someone to kill your uncle," Marlee spat.

Janelle whirled around and shoved Marlee with both hands, throwing her to the floor. "I said I had nothing to do with my uncle's death. Leave me alone!"

"Or what?" Marlee challenged as she looked up from the hard tiled bathroom floor, her backside aching from the hard fall.

"Fuck around and find out," Janelle snapped as she spun on her heel and left the restroom.

Marlee returned to the courtroom, still shaking from her second showdown with Janelle in the past nine hours. And after their most recent encounter, she didn't know if Janelle would still be contacting her tonight about retrieving her blue gown.

She heard a faint, clanking sound, which became louder and louder. Marlee turned to see Hector, dressed in an orange jumpsuit, being led into the courtroom. He was handcuffed and his legs were shackled, allowing him to take only little shuffling steps. Marlee covered her mouth, afraid that a combo of coffee and bile was about to spew forth.

Hector shuffled toward the defense table and was guided by a law enforcement officer into the chair next to Denny. He never looked up to make eye contact with Marlee or even see that she and Bettina were both there in support of him. His eyes were focused downward. There was no way of knowing what was happening to him, other than through communication with Denny. Marlee didn't know when she'd be allowed to talk to him, but it probably wouldn't be anytime soon. Tears came to her eyes as she understood the gravity of the situation. She might not talk to Hector again for a very long time.

By this time, several more people had filtered into the courtroom. Marlee glanced around and saw Bridget sitting with Diane and Kathleen from Supper Club. In a pew closer to the front were Janelle Vernon and her husband, Trent. Noticeably absent were their close friends, Onna and Franklin Ramone. *Still keeping their distance to protect their precious reputations and careers*, Marlee thought bitterly. Since Hector's reputation and career, as well as his freedom, were all on the line, Marlee didn't have much sympathy for the Ramones. And she gave zero fucks about Janelle and her husband.

Denny Harlow, seated next to Hector at the defense table, leaned in to offer words of comfort to his client before the hearing began. Today's hearing was perfunctory. Hector would be advised of the charges against him and advised of his rights. Denny would probably ask that Hector be released on bail even though everyone present knew it was never going to happen in this case. Then Hector would be escorted back to jail, where he would remain until his next court hearing.

Marlee knew all about the stages of court proceedings, having attended hearings when she was a probation officer and also teaching about them in her classes. But what she couldn't have known was what would happen when a rail-thin woman in her seventies breezed into the room. She was impeccably dressed in a vintage pink and gray Chanel suit with dark shoes and a coordinating handbag. Her silver hair was offset by the bright pink silk scarf knotted around her neck.

"Who is that woman?" Marlee asked Bettina.

"It's Irene from the formal wear shop on Main Street. Don't you know her?" Bettina looked at Marlee questioningly.

"No, I only talked to her on the phone. Why do you think she's here?"

Bettina shrugged. "Probably just following along with the case like everyone else in town. Or maybe she thinks she'll learn something about the break-in at her shop."

Everyone in the courtroom stood as The Honorable Douglas B. Trembly entered the room and seated himself behind the bench. "Please be seated," he said with a light rap of the gavel.

"Judge," Denny Harlow began. "May I please approach the bench before we get started? It has a bearing on the whole case."

"I object, Your Honor," said the prosecutor. "This is highly unusual at an initial appearance."

"I agree, it is unusual, but you will want to know about the critical information I just received," Denny insisted.

The judge shook his head side to side, but his curiosity got the better of him and he motioned for both Denny and the prosecutor to approach the bench. Denny proffered a letter for the judge to read and within moments, the hearing had been adjourned while the judge, Denny, and the prosecutor retired to the judge's chambers to discuss the secretive matter. Hector was escorted into the chambers by court security. As the defendant, he was entitled to be present during discussions about his case.

The clock hanging above the bench showed that only fifteen minutes had passed, but it seemed like hours. The courtroom was abuzz as everyone tried to figure out what was going on in the judge's chambers. Marlee found herself holding her breath at times, wondering what Denny had to present to the judge. She'd been to many court hearings in the past, and she'd never seen one interrupted before it even began. She crossed her fingers and hoped that Denny had evidence which would allow Hector to be released on bail. His situation would still be dire, but it would be so much better if he could remain at home rather than in jail while they awaited further hearings.

When the door to the judge's chambers burst open, no one was expecting what would come next. Denny, a huge grin on his face, returned to the defense table while a shell-shocked prosecutor stumbled toward his seat. Hector was escorted back out by court security. He looked downward at the carpet, no expression on his face whatsoever. Everyone rose again as Judge Trembly entered the room and seated himself.

"Well, I've never had this happen before," he said. "Given the information I was just provided, we are going to postpone this hearing until 4:00 p.m. today. And at that time, we will either proceed with the initial appearance as usual or the prosecution will... um, make other arrangements." The judge rapped the gavel and walked back to his chambers, leaving a stunned courtroom.

"What the hell just happened?" Marlee whispered to Bettina.

She threw up her hands and gave a puzzled look. "Talk to Denny and find out what he said to the judge."

Hector was escorted out of the courtroom while other court personnel hurried off to their respective offices. Marlee was the only person left in the courtroom as Denny walked past. "You're wondering what just happened?" he said with a smile.

"Yeah, what did you say to the judge?"

"I showed him a letter that Irene gave me. She was cleaning at the shop and found a letter under the returned clothes depository. It had fallen out of someone's returned garments, but she didn't know when. She opened the letter and realized it pertained to this case. I've known Irene for years, and in fact, we had a little thing back in the day," he said, waggling his eyebrows suggestively. "So, she called me right away, and here we are."

"It's the letter Janelle was looking for when she broke into my house last night," Marlee said, more to herself than Denny.

"Janelle broke into your house?" Denny asked.

"Yes, saying she wanted her dress. I think she was on drugs or something because she wasn't making a lot of sense. I'd met with her earlier and insinuated that I had something of hers," Marlee explained. "She kept demanding her dress. Maybe the letter was inside the dress? Was it the same letter that the Professor handed to one of the men in the tuxes?"

"It's written by Professor Vernon, and he lays out the whole thing. He was dying of brain cancer and wanted to end his life on his own terms. Euthanasia is illegal, and he thought by making a huge spectacle of his situation, he could get the laws overturned. The professor arranged to have someone kill him while he was in Elmwood. We don't know who, and I don't think the professor even knew who it was. It was all lined up secretly online. The Professor even noted how he saw Hector's keys unattended and then found the gun cabinet. He made it clear that Janelle would not receive his life insurance benefits as previously promised."

"We don't know who did it, but soon everyone will know it wasn't Hector who shot the Professor," Marlee said, again holding her breath.

"Well, the reason the hearing was postponed until later this afternoon is that the professor sent copies through the mail to the police department and to Hector. As soon as the letter reaches the police department and can be verified, then we'll know that the professor put everything in motion to bring about his own death. That includes finding Hector's keys and using them to open the gun cabinet and steal his gun," Denny said. "He changed the beneficiary of his insurance policy to Hector because he knew Hector would be a suspect in the murder. He wanted to compensate him for all the trouble. I expect Hector will be released this afternoon."

"Oh my god, Denny. Thank you!" Marlee wrapped the smoke-laden attorney in a giant bear hug.

"I have to get over to the jail to talk to Hector. We'll touch base later. I'll text you if I have anything new." Denny hurried toward the door exiting the courtroom.

"Wait!" Marlee exclaimed. "Who shot Professor Vernon?"

"We still don't know."

Marlee stumbled out of the courtroom and into a small group of her friends. She repeated the story Denny had just relayed to her; that Professor Vernon had arranged his own murder to bring attention to the laws against euthanasia and to prevent himself from suffering a debilitating and painful death from brain cancer.

"So, who shot the professor?" Bridget asked, eyes wide as she awaited the answer they all wanted to hear.

"We don't know yet. I guess the professor didn't even know who was going to shoot him. Or at least he didn't name them in the letter," Marlee said. "I'm still not clear on all of it. Denny had to talk to Hector at the jail and do some other things on the case, so I didn't get all the details. But apparently, we're still looking for the person who shot Professor Vernon."

"And the person who flipped the breaker before the gun was fired," Bettina said.

As children, my sister and I played a game called "Liar Liar." She won every time. My niece favors her, not just in looks but also in personality.

Chapter 27

"That's right," Marlee said, slapping her forehead. "Two people are involved in killing Professor Vernon. At least two people, maybe more. We don't know who he had lined up to kill him. He must have known after he wrote the letter because he had to give them Hector's gun to use at the party."

Bridget made a face. "Was the gun handed off to someone at the party? Or did the professor meet with them earlier to give them the gun? And why did he provide the gun? If he hired a professional killer, they should have their own weapons."

"All good questions. And I don't have the answer to any of them," Marlee said as she quickly updated the small group about Janelle breaking into her home last night and demanding her costume. "I think she wanted her dress because the letter was in her pocket. The same letter that Denny just told me about. The one that exonerates Hector. Janelle wanted it in her possession so Hector could be blamed for shooting the professor, letting her off the hook for any involvement. And it would, thus, allow her to keep all of her uncle's assets."

"Janelle is not a nice person," Bridget said, recalling the conversation she and Marlee had with the woman. "I wonder what she's going to do when the letter is found to be credible. It wrecks her whole plan."

"She's a terrible person!" Marlee exclaimed, detailing the break-in again but leaving out the part about connecting with Janelle later that night to retrieve her dress that she mistakenly thought Marlee could produce.

"She might not be the one who shot the professor, but she could have hired them," Bettina said. "I think it was the two guys wearing the Minnesota sports jerseys."

Marlee shook her head from side to side. "No, I don't think so. Again, if the assailant was hired, then why did Professor Vernon need to provide them with a gun?"

"Unless the shooting had to be carried out using Hector's gun," Bridget mused. "We've been assuming that the professor saw Hector's keys unattended and, after snooping around your house, found the locked gun cabinet and helped himself to the gun. This theory sounds like he just bumbled along, and lo and behold, there's a firearm."

"What was his plan if he couldn't get his hands on a gun? Did he have another way the hitman was to kill him?" Marlee asked. "Like poison?"

"What do we know about the professor's timeline so far?" Bettina asked.

"He checked into the B&B one week before the Open House. He was booked for two more weeks. During the past week, we know he spent time at Perkatory and the community library besides hanging out in his room. I hadn't heard anything about him being on the MSU campus or anywhere else around town," Marlee said.

"But during a week's time, the professor could have been all over town and even traveled to other towns in the area. We don't know everything he was doing," Bettina replied.

"I wonder if some of his actions are without rational explanation. He had brain cancer and had been suffering from behavioral disturbances caused by the disease. Many of the things he'd said or done could be a byproduct of the spread of his brain cancer," Marlee said.

"Yeah, maybe he just had a general plan and thought he'd get it all thrown together in the three weeks he was in Elmwood," Bridget said. "None of it seems that organized. The most organized thing he did was book a room at your B&B and then stay there."

"The few times I saw him, he seemed to be in his right mind. I just thought he was an eccentric old man, much like many people his age. Nothing he said or did caused me to have any concerns about him," Marlee said. "Of course, I wasn't looking for any problems either."

"None of this is getting us any closer to who shot Professor Vernon and who tripped the breaker in the basement," Bettina grumbled. "As soon as a copy of the same letter Denny showed in court is delivered to the police department and can be authenticated, we'll know that Hector is innocent. But it still doesn't help us figure out who shot him and who helped pull off the crime by cutting the electricity."

With no new ideas, the group decided to disperse but meet up later that afternoon to hear the official findings from Professor Vernon's letter.— and, hopefully, celebrate Hector's release from jail.

"I'm going over to the jail to talk to Denny when he's finished meeting with Hector. I can't wait until later this afternoon to find out the rest of the details that were in the professor's letter." Marlee pulled on her coat and left the courthouse, walking two blocks over to the jail.

She was in luck, as Denny Harlow was walking out the front door of the jail as she approached. "I need to talk to you. I have to know what else is going on," Marlee pleaded.

Denny frowned. "I've told you what I can. The shit's gonna hit the fan, but I can't talk to anyone other than Hector, and he asked me to keep it quiet until the hearing this afternoon. And he's my client, so I have to follow his wishes."

"But why...?" Marlee sputtered. Why was Hector keeping her out of the loop? What was so top secret that she had to be kept in the dark?

"I'm sorry, but I can't," Denny said as he moved past her and walked down the street toward his law office. "I'll see you back in court at 4:00."

Marlee knew it was useless trying to talk to Hector while he was in jail. There was no way he would be allowed any visitors other than his attorney. With her mind swirling and her feelings hurt, Marlee walked back to her vehicle and drove home.

Instead of parking in the garage, as she normally did, Marlee left her CR-V parked in front. As she walked toward the house, she began thinking about the door to the basement. Onna and Janelle had both admitted that they, along with their husbands, left through the basement exit on the night of the party. Onna said

Franklin had been to the house numerous times in the past and knew there was a basement exit.

Marlee moved toward the exit door, which was partially hidden by landscaping. It wasn't visible to the average person approaching the house from the outside since it was located on the side, and there was no sidewalk leading up to it. *I wonder how many people know about this door.* She stood looking around her property trying to determine if the person who flipped the breaker entered the basement through the inside of the house or if they came in through the basement exit door.

She groaned out loud with the realization that whoever flipped the breaker and cut the electricity could be someone who never showed their face at the party. And if that was the case, then the suspect list grew larger by the minute. All they had to do was use a credit card to slide between the door frame and the locking side of the door. The card would slide between the beveled interior side of the bolt and the door frame, popping open the door. She did it all the time in college when she forgot the keys to her apartment. It was a handy trick, and she knew it could be done by about anyone in under a minute.

Marlee used her keys to open the exit door from the outside. She swung the door open and peered into the basement. Nothing looked any different than usual. Before she pushed the door shut again, she gave a hard look at the lock. It was a deadbolt, which could only be unlocked from the outside with a key. The credit card method wouldn't work to open a door with a lock like this. She slammed the door and locked it, walking up to the front door of the house. *So much for anyone being able to access the basement door from the outside. You need a key to get in.*

That's when it hit her. Someone else had a key to the basement exit door and had let themselves in on the night of the party. After flipping the breaker off and then back on, they fled through the basement exit and ran to their car.

But who else had keys to their house? After Marlee and Hector moved in, they had all the locks changed, except for the basement exit door, since it wasn't readily visible unless one knew where to look. They'd forgotten about it and never took the time later to have the lock changed on that door. The previous owners had lived in the house for over forty years before they died. They could have given keys to any number of people. But who among them would want to help kill an elderly professor from Wisconsin?

Marlee went inside and sat down in the living room. Pippa crawled onto her lap and began to purr. The more she thought about someone having a key to her house, the madder she became. She thought back to the little Spanish style home she purchased before she met Hector. Marlee had loved that house and hated to sell it, but when Hector moved in it was obvious they needed more room for the two of them and Pippa. As she recalled fond memories of her previous house, she realized she still had keys. She'd turned over three sets when she sold the house but, later on, discovered another set. And she'd never bothered discarding them or taking them over to the new owners. By that time, they may have changed the locks anyway.

"You know who else had keys to my old house, Pippa?" Marlee asked as the picture began to get clearer. "One of my neighbors. We exchanged keys to each other's houses just in case we needed someone to look in on things if there was an emergency." Marlee assumed the previous owners had done the same with this house.

Marlee shooed Pippa off her lap and dashed out the door and over to the home of their next-door neighbor. She pounded on the door and rang the doorbell at the same time. "Charles, I know you're home. I want to talk to you!" she shouted.

Charles DeYoung flung open the door, nearly knocking Marlee off the doorstep. "What do you want?"

"I know you have a key to our basement door, and I know you used it on Saturday night," Marlee said, looking him straight in the eye even though she wasn't one hundred percent sure that's what happened.

Charles merely looked at her and blinked, not saying a word.

"I want to know who you're working with," Marlee demanded.

"I'm retired. You know that," he growled.

"Who were you working with to kill Professor Vernon?"

Brenda Donelan

What if I wasn't dying? What if there was a cure? What if I had ten or twenty more years to live? I don't think I'd change a thing.

Chapter 28

Charles DeYoung stood at his front door staring at Marlee, words failing him for what seemed like an hour. "I didn't kill anyone. I want a lawyer," he snapped and then pulled the door shut.

Marlee ran back to her house and called Bettina. "My next-door neighbor was part of the plot to kill the professor. He had an extra key and let himself in through the outside basement door and cut the power so the shooter could remain anonymous. I just went over to his house and confronted him, and you should've seen the look on his face. He denied it and then said he wanted a lawyer." Marlee's words spilled out in a jumble as she struggled to communicate what she'd learned.

"Why would he want the professor dead? He's not a professional hitman. And I don't see him hanging out in murder-for-hire chatrooms on the dark web," Bettina scoffed.

"I don't know why, but he's involved. And I think if we put the squeeze on him, he'll tell us who fired the gun and killed Professor Vernon," Marlee insisted. "Come over now!"

"I can't do that. I don't have any legal authority to put the squeeze on anyone. And I'm not even working on this case anymore. The DCI took over. You know that,"

Bettina said. "I think you're grasping at straws. You've been under a ton of stress and probably haven't had much sleep in the past few days. It's all taking a toll on you and distorting your thinking."

"Fine," Marlee said. "I'll handle it myself." She clicked off the phone and stuffed it inside her jacket pocket. She paced back and forth in the living room as she planned her next course of action. She knew in her heart that Charles from next door was mixed up in the professor's murder. The look on his face confirmed his involvement. She just didn't know *why* he took part.

Marlee marched back over to Charles' house and pounded on the door with both fists. He clearly had been expecting a return visit because he opened the door almost immediately. "I don't want to talk to anyone," Charles said but remained standing in the doorway.

"My boyfriend's freedom and reputation are on the line. You don't get the luxury of staying silent," Marlee shouted as she forced her way past Charles and into his living room. She felt as if she'd traveled back in time to the 1940s by the look of his flower-print furniture.

"I beg your pardon," Charles said, although the tone of his voice didn't carry much authority. "I'll ask you to leave at once, or I'm calling the police."

"And tell them what? That you broke into our basement during the Open House and flipped the breaker so we wouldn't have electricity for a couple of minutes? And that you're working with the person who shot Professor Vernon? I'm sure the police would love to hear what you have to say."

"I don't know anything about that poor man getting shot. I would never, ever be involved in something like that," Charles said, making direct eye contact with Marlee for the first time.

She didn't believe him but decided to back off the murder accusation for now. She would start small. Get him to admit to lesser offenses before he copped to being an accomplice to murder. "Why were you in our basement the night of the party?"

Charles avoided looking at Marlee. "I was here the whole time. I don't know what you're talking about."

"Bullshit. You were in the basement. An eyewitness has come forward and described you to a T." Marlee hoped her voice wasn't wavering as she bluffed her way through the story.

"Who was this mystery witness?" Charles asked.

"Someone who knows you very well, Charles," Marlee said, letting her gaze move across the street to the homes of the neighbors. "No use denying it."

Much to her surprise, the grumpy neighbor burst into tears, sobbing so severely that his words could not be deciphered. After the crying subsided and he'd blown his nose, he sunk to a green flowered armchair and began to speak. "I didn't have anything to do with shooting that man. All I did was use the key the Knutsons had given me over twenty years ago when we became neighbors and then friends. I gave them the keys to my house as well. We watched each other's homes when one of us was away. All I was trying to do in the basement was cut the electricity so your Open House would be a flop. I thought the more embarrassment and disappointment you had now, the less likely you were to stay in business."

"This was all about wrecking our business?"

"You know very well that the Historic District is no place for your upstairs motel. City Hall should know that too, but I suspect they bent the rules because your boyfriend is a detective." Charles became more indignant as he stood his ground on preventing businesses from operating in the Historic District. "But I had absolutely nothing to do with the murder."

"It seems awfully coincidental that moments after you flipped the breaker, Professor Vernon was shot. I don't think you and the gunman could have timed it any better," Marlee said.

Charles DeYoung shook his head back and forth as he looked at Marlee. "No, you have to believe me. I don't know anything about the shooting. My plan was to flip the breaker, leave it off, and come back here to my place. By the time someone went to the basement to check the breaker, several minutes of darkness would've passed. And I'd hoped it would prompt your guests to leave. But once I heard the gunshot, I was so shocked that I flipped the breaker so the electricity would come back on. And then I ran out of there and back here."

Marlee studied him for a minute. As much as she hated to admit it, he seemed believable. "Okay, let's say that's what really happened. What did you see when you got back here? I'm sure you were looking out the window."

He nodded. "I stood by the window with my lights off. I saw two ladies in ballgowns and two men in tuxedos run out of the basement door and across the street to a car. Then they drove away. About three minutes later, the whole neighborhood was abuzz with lights, sirens, and police officers. I watched for a long time as the police and your guests left the house. Then, a bunch of people wearing hazmat suits arrived with all kinds of equipment. I saw you drive away, and later, I saw the body bag brought out on a stretcher and placed into the back of an ambulance. I kept watching until there was no more activity outside, although I knew there were still people inside collecting evidence. Then I fell asleep on the sofa."

"Had you ever met Professor Vernon? Do you know any of the people who were at our party?" Marlee asked.

"I don't know the professor, and I'm not sure if I know anyone from your party since I wasn't there. I'm guessing there probably wasn't anyone there I knew. I think we run in different circles," Charles said, looking down from his high horse.

Marlee chose to overlook his condescending attitude. Instead, she listed the names of as many guests from the party as she could remember. "Do any of those names sound familiar?"

"I've heard of Franklin and Onna Ramone but don't know them personally. I don't know any of the others you mentioned."

She'd rattled off the names of fifty people from the party. There had been a few unknowns, but then their identities were later discovered to be the Ramones, Janelle, and Trent. The only two people unaccounted for were the two men in their thirties who wore Minnesota sports jerseys. Marlee gave a description of the men and watched as Charles's eyes widened. "Did you see them enter or leave the house?"

"Yes, they entered your house at 7:00 p.m.," Charles said with certainty.

"Wow, you really were keeping close tabs on everyone who came and went," Marlee said, annoyed and impressed at the same time.

"Not everyone, just them," Charles said.

"Why them? Do you know those two men?"

"Of course, I know them. I lived next to them while they were growing up. It's Derek and Luke Knutson. They are the ones who sold you their parents' house. They stopped over to say "hello" before they went to your party."

Marlee's jaw dropped as she learned the identities of the last two unknown guests from the party. "Why on Earth did they come to the Open House? And what are they doing in Elmwood? They live in New York. They didn't even come back to sign the papers for the sale of the house."

"They hadn't been back in years. They remembered how much they liked pheasant hunting as kids. Their dad always took them out to hunt. I was invited, too, but I'm not a hunter by any means. Anyway, they reached out to a few old friends from high school and came back for a long weekend of hunting. They heard from one of their friends that you were operating an upstairs motel, and they wanted to stop by and check it out. When they found out it was an Open House, they realized they could come in and look around without having to talk to you or tell you who they were," Charles said.

"Why didn't they want to meet us?" Marlee was confused. The two men took the time out of their fun hunting weekend to stop by the home where they grew up yet didn't want to talk to the new owners.

"Derek said they weren't sure how they would feel about your operation. They thought it best to visit anonymously in case they didn't approve. You and your boyfriend already bought the house, so there wasn't much they could do about it, even if they didn't like your changes."

"Are they still in town?"

"Doubt it. They planned on driving back to Minneapolis on Monday and flying home to New York that night."

Marlee took a deep breath, unsure how to proceed. "Charles, you've been a real shithead to us since we bought the place. I understand that you didn't like the idea of a B&B operating next door, but we followed the city's rules and have been doing everything by the book. If you hadn't broken into our basement and cut the electricity, then the shooter might not have taken that opportunity to kill the professor at that time. It was only under the cover of darkness that they knew they could shoot the professor and get away with it."

Charles looked mildly ashamed, most likely because he was caught rather than because he thought he was in the wrong. "Are you going to press charges?"

"I don't know what we're going to do. Hector has a court hearing later this afternoon, and I want you to come with me. If necessary, you can tell the court that it was you who flipped the breaker in the basement," Marlee said.

"Me? No, I'm not going to do that," Charles said. "Why would I implicate myself in this mess?"

"Yes, you are. You owe us that much," Marlee said. "I'll expect you at the courthouse at 3:45. If you're not there, I'm going to the police station and tell them all about you breaking in."

"Well, what difference does it make if I tell the story or if you report me? It's coming out either way," Charles said. "And I know you two will try to get me locked up over this."

"Not necessarily. We don't have to make a big deal out of you using the key you were rightly given decades ago. We don't have to call it breaking and entering. Let's say you thought it would be a fun prank to cut our electricity, and maybe you didn't use the best judgment," Marlee said, showing lenience toward Charles since she needed him as much as he needed her.

With some reluctance, Charles nodded his head. "Okay. I'll be there."

Marlee wasn't sure she could believe him, but she didn't have many options at this point.

Just when you think you know what's going on...

Chapter 29

Marlee was glad she arrived early since it was standing room only in the courtroom by 3:30. It seemed everyone in town wanted the latest news regarding Hector and the charges against him. Glancing around, she saw several on- and off-duty police officers, members of the community, the local press, and most of her friends. The one person she wanted to see, Charles DeYoung, was not in attendance. Marlee fussed with the Kleenex in her hand, unsure what to do if the next-door neighbor was a no-show at the hearing.

With two minutes to spare, a reluctant Charles DeYoung peered tentatively through the swinging courtroom doors. Marlee caught his eye and waved him toward the empty space she'd been saving for him. "Thanks for coming," she whispered as he sat beside her. She wasn't feeling very gracious toward him, but they needed each other— at least until the charges against Hector were dropped and he was released from custody.

Charles gave a curt nod, eyes forward. He was a loose cannon, and Marlee knew it. Her whole plan could easily blow up in her face. She needed Charles to tell the story of his involvement so their lives could return to normal. With dismissal of the murder charges and an absolution by the judge, Hector should be able to return to work as usual. But too many mistakes on his part left his career in jeopardy. He had failed to install security at the B&B, left his keys unattended, and kept his gun cabinet on the main floor which was accessible to others. Each one of these actions and inactions put the detective in a poor light.

Judge Trembly entered the courtroom at exactly 4:02 and directed everyone to sit. The room was bursting at the seams with spectators, yet not one sound could be heard after everyone was seated. This was the best show in town right now, and no one wanted to miss a thing.

"This is by far one of the most unusual cases I've presided over," said the judge after making note of Hector as the defendant, the case number, and the charge. "And I've been on the bench for fifteen years. Believe me when I tell you I thought I'd seen everything. We've reconvened in light of new information that was presented to the prosecutor earlier today. The Court has received a notarized, handwritten letter from Professor Jerome A. Vernon, which arrived in today's mail. I've reviewed the letter, and both the prosecution and defense have had time to read it and verify its authenticity. Considering the information provided via Professor Vernon's letter, what does the prosecution have to say?"

All eyes turned toward the prosecutor as he stood. "The state moves to dismiss the murder charge against Hector Ramos," he said with a red face.

A spontaneous cheer went up from the crowd but was soon silenced by the pounding of Judge Trembly's gavel. "I will clear this room of all spectators if there's any more disruption!" After everyone had settled down, he announced, "The charge is dismissed. Mr. Ramos, you are free to go. Court adjourned."

"That's it?" Charles asked, rising to his feet, likely looking to bolt from the courtroom.

"Not so fast. Hector is no longer charged with murder, but we still have to figure out who killed the professor. And that's where you come in. Someone will eventually be charged, and we need your explanation for cutting the power in the basement. Let's talk to Denny." She grabbed the arm of his tan corduroy blazer and led him to the defense table where Hector and Denny stood, all smiles.

Marlee leaned into hug Hector, and they shared a long kiss before he would be taken away by court staff to process his dismissal paperwork and return him to his own clothes. "Who killed the professor? And why? I know you've figured it out."

"Not here, not now," he whispered, looking around to see who was listening in. "What's he doing here?" Hector asked, looking at their obnoxious neighbor standing beside them.

Marlee rolled her eyes. "Guess who cut the electricity in the basement during the party?"

"What?" Hector's mouth dropped wide open.

"Charles says he didn't have anything to do with the murder. He thought it would be funny to flip the breaker and ruin our party and hopefully wreck our business."

"I still had a key that the Knutsons gave me when they owned the house," Charles interjected. "I don't know anything about the murder. When I heard the gunshot, I turned the electricity back on and got out of there."

Hector shook his head in disgust, unable to comment further before he was taken back to the jail to be processed out. Denny Harlow, who had stayed to listen in on the conversation, suggested they all go wait at the jail for Hector to be released and decide on the next move.

Both Denny and Charles got into Marlee's SUV and the three drove the short distance to the jail. On the drive over, Marlee updated Denny on Charles having the key to their home and the plan for him to talk to the police about it being a prank.

Denny shook his head. "I can't hear any of this. You do what you think is best as long as it keeps my client out of jail. I can't be involved in any false narratives given to the police, or else I'll be sitting in jail."

"I wouldn't call it false, just a creative retelling of the truth," Marlee said, realizing she could run for political office if she continued talking like that.

Half an hour later, Hector exited the jail and hopped into Marlee's SUV. "Let's go home. I want to shower this jail smell off of me."

On the drive home, Marlee reiterated Charles's involvement in the events at their party on Saturday night. "That means that there could be only one person involved in the professor's murder."

"If what he says is true," Hector growled as he glared at his neighbor.

"Everything I said is true," Charles insisted. "I had no reason to kill anyone. I just wanted you to stop running that ludicrous upstairs motel and destroying the neighborhood."

As she parked in their driveway, Charles hastily exited the vehicle and bolted toward his home.

"Not so fast," Marlee said. "You're coming inside with us and helping us figure this out."

Marlee, Charles, and Denny gathered around the dining room table while Hector took a quick shower, returning in clean clothes and a beer in hand. "I want to hear from Charles exactly what he did." Hector plunked down the beer bottle and drove a hard look at their neighbor.

"It's just as I told you before," Charles stammered. "I still had a key from when the Knutsons lived here. I heard about your big party and thought I'd try to dissuade people from your upstairs motel by causing a disruption. I thought I'd try the key to the basement to see if it even worked. The locksmith changed some of your locks when you moved in, but I never saw them go to the basement exit. It seemed like it was worth a try. The key still worked, and I used the light on my phone to find the breaker box. I flipped it to cut all the electricity to the house and was going to leave, thinking that would be a huge disruption to your party and put your business in a bad light. But then I heard a gunshot, and I got scared. It didn't sound fake to me. It sounded like a real gun. So, I flipped the electricity back on and ran back home. Then all the police cars and ambulances started arriving."

"What was your connection to the Ramones, Janelle, and her husband?" Marlee asked.

"I've known Onna and Frank since I moved here, but we're not friends, just acquaintances. I've never met the professor's niece and her husband. I only know about them because of the media coverage," Charles said, throwing up his hands. "Seriously."

Hector sat at the table with a smirk, not saying a word as he listened to Charles. "I believe you, Charles. You've been an asshole since we moved in, but I believe you when you say you had nothing to do with the murder of the professor."

"Tell them how you know," Denny urged Hector.

"Because I know who did it and how it was done," Hector stated with a smile. "There were at least two people involved in the shooting."

House of Games

I just remembered one other regret. I forgot to write a review for the B&B. I'd give them four out of five stars. They're off to a good start, but there's plenty of room for improvement.

Chapter 30

The trap had been set. She still wasn't one hundred percent sure how Hector had figured out who shot the professor, but there would be plenty of time later to dissect the case. Marlee continuously checked her phone to see if Janelle had texted her about the location of their meeting. The text arrived shortly after the sun went down. It read: *Meet at Lily Park by the carousel. Come alone. If anyone is with you, I'll shoot everyone, starting with you.*

Marlee knew the park well. Even though it was mainly for kids and families, she regularly went there for walks in the summer. The park hosted a variety of rides and attractions suited for small to middle-grade children. Halloween was the final day the park was open for the season, so meeting there tonight ensured no one would be around to witness the hand off of the blue dress. She and Hector had put together a plan, and Hector had pulled some strings with the police department. Nonetheless, she held her breath as she pulled her SUV into the parking lot and walked toward the carousel in the middle of the park. In her hand, she carried a white trash bag, ready to hand it off to Janelle. Hector had assembled the bag, knowing exactly what Janelle sought.

Her heart was racing, and she was sweating despite the crisp November air. She took a deep breath to clear her mind and steady her shaking hands. Marlee walked to the carousel which would be out of use until the following spring. She walked around the carousel, hoping to see Janelle, but she wasn't to be found.

Marlee's phone pinged with an incoming text: Walk to the old barn at the far end of the park.

She gasped. How would the police be able to track her if they didn't know her new location? She walked as loudly as she could across the park, crunching the fallen leaves with every step. Once she arrived at the old barn, Marlee received another text: *Leave the park through the south exit and walk into the trees surrounding the golf course.*

Marlee shivered as a combination of cold wind and fear struck her at the same time. She knew this constant moving from one spot to another could continue all night. She also knew she might be walking straight into her own death trap if she entered the dense tree belt. As scared as she was, Marlee knew she had no choice. This might be their only chance to catch Janelle red-handed and put her away for the death of her uncle.

Looking more confident than she felt, Marlee threw back her shoulders and marched into the trees. She waited until she was in the center before she stopped and waited for another ping on her phone. She waited for what seemed like an hour before she heard a snapping branch.

Marlee whirled around to face a figure clad in dark clothing and a full-coverage ski mask. "Drop it," she growled, and Marlee did as directed.

"I did as you asked. Now I just want to leave, and this will all be over," Marlee said, disgusted that her voice trembled as he spoke. "No need for anyone to get hurt."

She snorted as she moved toward the trash bag and picked it up. The light from her cell phone shone on the blue contents within. "Is everything here?"

"Yes," Marlee said, unsure what she meant by everything.

"Who did you get it from?"

"I think you can guess," Marlee said, bluffing.

"Ah yes, your beloved boyfriend, the detective," she snorted as she rifled through the sack to make sure all her belongings were inside. Once satisfied, she turned and walked away. Over her shoulder, she said, "Count to one hundred, then go back to your car and go home. I'd like to shoot you, but I don't need the cops running out here when they hear shots fired."

Marlee counted to one hundred as quickly as she could then fast walked to her car which was over a mile away. To her surprise, the entire park area was swarming with police cars within minutes, all of them had their lights flashing. On the ground was the figure clad in black, the white garbage bag by her side. Hector cuffed her and helped the woman to her feet. Two DCI officers whisked her away to a waiting car and sped off.

Dean Spangler will be receiving something special in the mail from me. I made sure to have it shipped well after my death. I hope he enjoys the giant box of horse manure.

Chapter 31

It was nearing 3:00 a.m. when Hector, Marlee, and Bettina gathered back at the B&B. Marlee called Bridget to come over, even though it was the middle of the night. She arrived within minutes in her yellow flannel pajamas and her long, dark hair twisted up into a messy bun. With the suspect in custody, they could now put the remaining pieces of the puzzle into place.

Hector pulled his chair a little closer to the table as he launched into what he found out when he was on the run from the law. "Initially, I thought it had to be the professor's niece and her husband. They had the most to gain from Professor Vernon's death since she was the sole heir in his will. But then I realized she would be inheriting everything regardless of whether he died by gunshot now or in a few months from his disease. The risk was too great, and it didn't seem that Janelle and Trent were in financial hardship. In other words, there was no incentive for either of them to kill the professor now versus let his brain cancer take its course in a few months."

"Then who shot the professor?" Marlee demanded.

"Leanne Desmond," Hector stated matter-of-factly as he awaited everyone's reaction.

"Then why did Janelle want her dress? Did she hire Leanne?" Marlee asked.

"No, Janelle wasn't involved at all. That was Leanne on the ground. She broke in here and threatened you. And she was the one with the gun in the trees tonight," Hector reported, stretching out the story.

"But how?" Bridget asked, rubbing the sleep from her eyes.

"Yeah, how?" Bettina echoed.

"We were right early on when we talked about Professor Vernon hiring someone to kill him. He trolled for information on the Dark Web, and Leanne responded. I'm not exactly sure how they made initial contact and set up the deal. She's the only one who said she heard two loud voices from the professor's room the night before the party. We trusted her account because there was no reason to suspect her. She got the gun from the professor and was going to use it at some point while she was staying there. She just didn't know when the opportunity would present itself."

"Why would she show up to kill someone without her own gun?" Marlee asked, still not fully buying into Hector's theory. "And what does Leanne get out of this? You're the beneficiary of the life insurance policy and Janelle Vernon inherits the rest of the professor's estate."

"She did have her own gun. It's what she pointed at you last night and tonight. But the professor gave her my service weapon after he was able to get it out of the lockbox in the first-floor closet. Remember, the professor wanted as much interest in his death as possible to bring the issue of euthanasia to light. A random shooting doesn't hold the public's interest like what actually played out: the gun of a detective used to kill someone in the detective's own home, and then said detective is the newly named beneficiary of the professor's life insurance policy."

"Then, after it's all settled, we learn that the detective was initially set up, but only temporarily. That's why he was rewarded with the proceeds from the professor's life insurance policy," Bettina finished. "The public is going to lap this up!"

"The press has been going nuts over what they know, or think they know, of the case so far. They will lose their minds when they hear this was all planned by Professor Vernon," Hector added.

"But we still don't know if or how Leanne was compensated. I assume it's money, but how was she paid?" Marlee insisted. "I mean, if we can't show a direct link between payment from the professor to Leanne, then I don't think there's much of a case against her."

Hector smiled, knowing he was about to drop a bomb. "Blue fibers were found on the professor's body. At first the lab thought they were from Janelle's blue dress since she was standing behind him during the murder mystery game. But testing showed they didn't match. Leanne was wearing a blue Disney princess dress, but those fibers didn't match either."

Marlee threw up her hands. "That pokes a hole in your theory if the blue fibers didn't come from Leanne."

"I said they didn't come from her blue dress. They came from the long blue gloves she was wearing with her costume," Hector said.

"She wasn't wearing gloves," Marlee said as she reflected back on that evening. "Was she? I don't remember seeing any gloves."

"Leanne had long blue gloves on when she first came into the party with Paul. She must have taken them off soon after arriving, because I don't remember seeing them again," Hector said. "She had them with her and put them on when she shot the professor. That's why there weren't any fingerprints on the gun other than mine. After the Professor handed off the gun to Leanne at some point, probably prior to the party, she wiped it clean and only handled it from there on out with her gloves on. Since she kept the gloves off most of the party, we didn't remember seeing her with them."

"Her dress really was big and poofy. I suppose she could've hidden both a gun and gloves somewhere in the folds of the dress. Maybe it has pockets," Hector suggested.

"So, where are the dress and gloves?" Marlee asked. "You said the fibers from the gloves match those found on the professor, so I assume they're with the police."

"Yep, at the lab," Hector said. "I found them with a little help from Paul Rowley, the guy who was at the B&B on a date weekend."

"So that was your connection to Mobridge!" Marlee shouted. "I knew you had a reason for going there to talk to him."

"The more I thought about that night, the more I remembered. That's when I realized Leanne came into the party wearing gloves. I don't recall her wearing them the rest of the night, but I do have a memory of her holding her drink with a gloved hand. I went to talk to Paul to see how much he knew about Leanne. He already had her pegged as a gold digger but knew nothing about her criminal record. I asked him about her Disney princess dress and gloves, and he actually had them with him in his pickup."

"No way!" Marlee shouted.

"When the police arrived here after the shooting, everyone had to vacate after they were released from initial questioning. Paul and Leanne were allowed to grab their possessions from their rooms, and Paul drove them to a Super 8, where they each got a room. The next day, he was going to take Leanne back to our place to get her car, but Wallace arrived at the Pizza Ranch and drove them both to the station for further questioning," Hector said.

Marlee nodded along, remembering how Paul and Leanne told them at Pizza Ranch that they were leaving for their respective homes after lunch. Hector's quick call to Detective Wallace tipped him off that the two witnesses were intending to leave town without having been properly interviewed.

"They checked out of the Super 8 before lunch and had all their belongings in Paul's pickup. Wallace interviewed them separately at the station. Paul was finished first, and an officer gave him a ride back to his pickup at Pizza Ranch. He was told Leanne would be taken to her car when she was done with questioning, so Paul drove home, forgetting Leanne's things were in his vehicle."

"When did Leanne realize that Paul had her things?" Marlee asked.

Hector grinned. "Not until later that day. She called Paul, frantic about getting her stuff back. Paul said she was really bitchy about it, so he saw no rush in shipping her things to her in Fargo. Lucky for me, he still had her travel bag and a trash bag and gave it to me. I peeked inside the garbage bag and saw the blue princess dress and gloves, and it was then I knew for sure that Leanne was the shooter."

"Then why were you arrested?" Bridget asked. "That doesn't make any sense."

"Because I was afraid that Leanne would take off if she knew she was under suspicion. And I couldn't let my whole department know since Shane Wallace's actions in Professor Vernon's room called his loyalty into question. I called a fellow detective who had been keeping me informed on the case, turned the clothes over to him, and explained everything. We cooked up the idea of the arrest to divert Leanne's attention until the dress and gloves could be tested at the lab," Hector said.

"You willingly went along with the murder charge and being locked up in jail?" Marlee was incredulous that anyone would take solving a case to this level.

"I did because I knew Leanne would soon become suspicious when Paul didn't ship her suitcase and things to her. If she knew I was under arrest for the professor's murder, then she could rest easy for a few days while she waited for Paul to return her belongings, and she could dispose of the dress and gloves," Hector said. "As long as she destroyed them, there would be no link between her and the professor. Anybody who watches crime shows knows there's likely to be evidence on the body and clothes of the shooter. After I was arrested, I had Denny run to Walmart and buy an identical blue princess costume and that was what we used as a decoy tonight. And I couldn't tell you," he said, turning to Marlee. "Like I said all along, I didn't know how this was going to turn out, and I didn't want you involved in the off chance I was still charged with the professor's death."

"Leanne was the only one involved in the murder?" Bettina asked. "I thought you said there were two people."

"Leanne was the only one directly involved, but Professor Vernon put the whole plan in motion. We suspect he directed Leanne to shoot him at the party or afterward when he gave her my service weapon. Charles flipping the breaker in the basement gave her the perfect time to do it," Hector said, glaring in the direction of his neighbor's house.

"It sounds like the professor was going to get shot that night or shortly thereafter regardless of whether the electricity was cut, but Chuck's actions made it easy to carry out. And caused me a whole lot of headaches in the process," Hector grumbled.

"How did Leanne and the professor make contact before they came to our B&B? And how did he pay her?" Marlee asked, still dumbfounded by Hector's revelations.

"We're still sorting that out," Hector answered. "The blue fibers on the gun and the professor's blood on Leanne's gloves and dress are enough to charge her. But we have a lot to figure out. We'll need to search her home and her computer to find any links between the two."

When the foursome had talked through every nuance of the case, they decided to call it a night. The sun would be up in a few hours, so there wouldn't be much sleep for any of them. Bettina and Bridget left while Marlee and Hector remained seated at their dining room table. They smiled at each other as they looked around their big house, still adorned with Halloween and fall decorations. Home. It was a word and a concept they would never take for granted again. Hector reached for Marlee's hand as they walked upstairs to their bedroom. "We need to get the lock changed on that basement door right away, so Chucky isn't over again uninvited."

Marlee nodded, her mind elsewhere as she thought about all the ins and outs of what had happened to them over the past week. "I know it's insensitive to ask, but do you think you'll get to keep the insurance money?"

"I don't know. And even if the insurance company agrees to award it to me, I'm not sure I'd feel comfortable accepting it," Hector said, giving it some thought.

"I can understand that, but he did want you to have it for all the trouble it caused you: being accused of and then arrested for murder, thrown in jail, and having your name smeared in the press. I don't think anyone would blame you if you decided to keep it," Marlee said. "But it's your decision, and I'll stand by whatever you want to do."

Marlee paced around the bedroom, unsure why she was still so unsettled. Finally, it occurred to her. "Hector," she called out.

He poked his head around the doorway to the bathroom, toothbrush in hand. "Yeah?"

"We never found out why Detective Wallace stole the piece of evidence from Professor Vernon's room when he searched it."

"I talked to him before I was released from jail. He came to see me, and I asked him point blank about it. He said he's trying to quit smoking and has been chewing nicotine gum. It gives him a headache and he can only chew it for a short time. Wallace said he needed to get rid of the gum when he went into the professor's room but didn't have anything on him, and he didn't want to throw it in the trash since it was a crime scene. He ripped off a blank sheet of paper from a legal pad and used it to wad up his gun and then tucked it inside his suit jacket," Hector said.

"And you believe him?" Marlee asked, skeptical of Shane Wallace's explanation.

Hector shrugged. "For now. But you can be sure I'll have my eyes on him from here on out."

Afterword

The Elmwood Police Department and the Division of Criminal Investigation joined forces to investigate Leanne Desmond's involvement in the murder for hire. The Federal Bureau of Investigation also joined the investigation since the offense involved using a computer to plan a murder. The fact that three states were involved in the planning and implementation of the professor's death; South Dakota, North Dakota, and Wisconsin, also served to justify the involvement of the FBI.

The investigators were able to prove that Leanne Desmond responded to a request in an Internet chatroom on the Dark Web. She agreed to shoot Professor Vernon in Elmwood, South Dakota, during the three weeks he was there. Upon his death, she was to receive a payment of $25,000. Investigators were unable to track this payment, as it was locked by codes on the Dark Web. Somewhere, $25,000 awaits Leanne Desmond when and if she ever gets out of prison.

Janelle Vernon and her husband, Trent, had the professor's body returned to La Crosse, Wisconsin, to be buried next to his sister, Janelle's mother. Janelle was the sole beneficiary of her uncle's will, which included his belongings and his car. The one hundred-thousand-dollar life insurance payout that she'd been expecting was not earmarked for her. Professor Vernon had a modest amount of money in savings, which perplexed Janelle as she thought he would have saved much more during his lifetime as a frugal man. She was unaware of the money he paid to Leanne for shooting him.

Hector installed security cameras in the back stairway to the B&B rooms, as well as the exterior of the house. He also moved his gun cabinet to his office on the second floor, which was not accessible to anyone now that they kept the front door locked at all times. The insurance company had not decided on whether or not Hector should get the payout from Professor Vernon's life insurance policy. Denny Harlow, their attorney, had told them not to hold their breath. In messy cases like this, the insurance company always rules in its own favor.

Professor Vernon got his wish. His actions brought a tremendous amount of attention to the issue of euthanasia, with a national patients' rights group having started collecting signatures in five states in hopes of getting the legalization of euthanasia on the ballot in upcoming elections. Local and national press swarmed Elmwood for over a week following the announcement of Leanne Desmond's arrest and the professor's involvement in arranging his own death.

If only he could have seen the final chapter of his story come to a close.

At times the plan made sense. Other times it didn't. The longer I waited, the harder it would be to distinguish between truth and delusions. That's why I had to act as soon as possible. For sure, I thought Janelle and her husband would agree to kill me, but I was surprised when they turned out to have a conscience after all. The one and only thing I ever asked of that girl, and she failed me.

I saw Janelle and Trent following me around Elmwood. Those two stood out like a sore thumb. I knew they were there to take me back to La Crosse and put me in an old folks' home, and I wasn't having it. That's why I wrote the letter and handed it to them at the party. They needed to know this was the end of my story. And that they would not be receiving the insurance benefits upon my death since they both refused to help end my life. The Dark Web turned out to be much more intriguing than I could have imagined. After a bit of bumbling around, I located a chatroom and asked about hiring a hitman. I'd done enough research to know you didn't use words like murder and hitman. The request had to be coded and much less obvious in case the police were monitoring it. I messaged a few people, and they either couldn't take care of it right away or wanted more money than I could pay.

Leanne was a good fit. She lived in the region and seemed an unlikely suspect. My main objective was to get her to kill me, but I also wanted her to get away with it. She would be doing me a favor, and I had no intention of her even being a suspect in the shooting. I sent her the details of when and where to meet and put down a deposit on the shooting. We went through a third-party payment system, kind of like PayPal, but for murder. The remainder of the payment was already waiting for Leanne upon the confirmation of my death. The hardest part of the plan was finding a location. I knew it needed to be out of state to bring more attention to the shooting. And it needed to be in a place that had not been in business for very long. I hoped their security would be lax and it would be easier to carry out the shooting. As a professor of creative writing, I knew how to set the scene for this story. A rented room in an old house and at Halloween. The Open House at the B&B and the murder mystery party just fell into my lap. There was no amount of planning that could have made that come about.

Leanne and I met at the B&B the first night she stayed there. We put the finishing touches on my plan, and I gave her some cash to buy a Halloween costume that could conceal a gun. That was when I turned over Hector's gun to her. She said she brought one with her, but I wanted his to be used to add more drama to the story of my death. Getting his gun was a stroke of luck, too. He'd left his keys on an end table. I walked in the front door and heard him talking on his phone. I nosed around for a bit, not intending to take anything. Just occupying myself until Hector finished his call and came to the front room.

He must have forgotten about his keys because I heard Hector run upstairs while still talking on the phone.

When I saw the locked cabinet in the closet, I knew his gun was likely inside. I'd done my research on this couple and knew he was a police detective. I used the key to open the cabinet, took the gun, and locked the cabinet. I threw the keys back where I found them and left with the gun tucked in my waistband, just like in the movies.

I was nervous that night because I knew it would be my last. But I was more excited than scared. Being allowed to choose my own manner of death was frightening, but not nearly as much as suffering from increasing dementia and a painful death from cancer. I knew I would be shot on Halloween night at the party, but I didn't know how Leanne would do it. Again, luck was on my side when we were both selected to play roles in the murder mystery game. And who could have predicted that the electricity would go out during the game? I couldn't have planned this any better. Am I lucky or what?

Brenda Donelan

Acknowledgments

A great big "thank you" goes out to my beta readers; MaryJo Bullard, Dayle Tibbs Angyal, and Audra Bonhorst Hawkinson. Their watchful eyes helped me to fix a few problems in the manuscript that slipped right past me.

Brian Schell, my editor, is to be credited for his diligent work in editing my book. As long as I live, I'll never figure out when to use a comma. But with Brian on my team, I guess I don't have to.

Cecile Reynolds, my proofreader, has a keen eye for detail. I want to acknowledge her hard work and dedication.

Samantha Lund Hillmer has been my cover designer since the first book. I love her work and fell in love with this cover for House Of Games as soon as she sent it to me.

I would also like to acknowledge Geerati for the cover photography, courtesy of iStock.

In addition, Michelle Maupin Barrett Photography is credited for the author's photo.

So much of House of Games centers around the B&B that Marlee and Hector operate. I really didn't have much knowledge of how they are run, so I stayed at two of them and interviewed both proprietors. Many thanks to Catherine Hieulle in Plainfaing, France. I enjoyed staying at her lovely, picturesque inn (Mon Eden Vosgien) and was glad to hear about the operation from an international perspective. Also, thank you to Deb Schuetzle from Pierre, South Dakota who operates the Hitching Horse Inn. She provided a helpful overview of what it takes to run her comfy and welcoming B&B. Any errors related to Inns and B&Bs in the book are entirely mine.

And finally, I want to thank the readers. I wish I could come to each of your homes and talk about books. But friends have told me it would be strange if I did that, so I guess I'll settle for thanking you here in this book, through online communication, and in-person events. Also, I'm kind of an introvert, so I probably wouldn't make it to very many homes. Thanks again for reading my work. Readers are what make the book world go 'round!

Did You Enjoy This Book?

Reviews are the most important way to get my books noticed by other mystery lovers. If you've enjoyed this book, I would love for you to leave a review on the book's Amazon page. The review can be as brief or as detailed as you like.

Without reviews from readers like you, my books will be less visible on Amazon. Honest reviews of my books help bring them to the attention of other mystery lovers around the world.

Thank you so much!

Brenda Donelan

About The Author

Brenda Donelan uses her past work experiences as a social worker, probation officer, investigator, and college professor as inspiration for creating the settings and scenarios in her mystery novels. She is a life-long resident of South Dakota. She grew up on a cattle ranch in Stanley County, attended college in Brookings, and worked in Aberdeen as a probation officer and then as a college professor. She now resides in Sioux Falls and writes mysteries while her two lazy cats nap nearby.

The author can be reached by email at brendadonelanauthor@gmail.com. For more information on Brenda Donelan, books in the University Mystery Series, and tour dates, check out her website at brendadonelan.com or find her on Facebook at Brenda Donelan – Author.

Photo credit: Michelle Maupin Barrett Photography

Also by Brenda Donelan

Day Of The Dead

When a college professor is found dead on campus, rumors and innuendo begin to swirl at Midwestern State University. The police department and the university are mysteriously secretive about the professor's background and the ongoing investigation. Marlee McCabe, a professor of Criminology, is unwittingly pulled into the investigation leading her to question the integrity of the police department and her university. Despite warnings, Marlee uncovers information on the professor's death, making her the next target of someone who has nothing left to lose.

Holiday Homicide

Criminology professor Marlee McCabe is thrust into a criminal investigation when a janitor is murdered at Midwestern State University. Marlee's sleuthing leads her to the Lake Traverse Indian Reservation and into the dangerous underworld of trafficking Native American artifacts and sacred cultural items. Those involved are not afraid to use threats, violence, and even murder to keep their secrets buried. What will they do to keep Marlee from exposing the truth?

Murder To Go

On the second day of a week-long class trip, a body is discovered in a motel room. Criminology Professor Marlee McCabe struggles to continue the tour of prisons and juvenile correctional facilities while uncovering the truth behind the life and death of the victim. As she protects her students from harm, Marlee begins to suspect the killer has ties to her university. What steps will the murderer take to hide the truth and prevent Marlee from revealing it?

Art Of Deception

A million-dollar antique is stolen from an art show in Elmwood and Professor Marlee McCabe jumps into the investigation when her cousin, Bridget, is arrested and thrown in jail. Marlee steadfastly defends her cousin until secret details of Bridget's life call that loyalty into question. As Marlee struggles between dedication to family and the pursuit of justice, she is forced to make decisions which may destroy the rest of her life.

Fatal Footsteps

Get ready for a wild ride as Criminology Professor Marlee McCabe looks back to her earliest adventure as an amateur detective. It's 1987, the time of acid wash jeans and big, permed hair. When a college dorm mate is found dead in the snow outside a party house, Marlee puts her newly learned Criminology knowledge to use as she strives to find out who killed the co-ed and why. The more involved Marlee and her roommate become in the investigation, the more deadly it becomes for them and their friends. As the body count rises, Marlee fears she's next on the killer's hit list.

Blood Feud

When an unexpected teaching assignment whisks Marlee McCabe off to New Delhi, India, she lands right in the middle of an ongoing family dispute and an academic firestorm. Before long, Marlee is faced with the most difficult decisions of her life, causing her to choose between her life back home and a new life in India. Without the familiarity of the Midwest, she's dependent upon the good graces of strangers. But are these new acquaintances really who they pretend to be? Sacrificing her career and her own safety, Marlee struggles to unravel the mystery of who murdered her only friend in India. Can she unmask the killer before she becomes the next victim?

Sinner Or Saint

An unexpected visitor forces Professor Marlee McCabe to delve into the underground world of international jewel smuggling. She battles to save her new friend from deadly consequences in both Dublin, Ireland and the sleepy college town of Elmwood, South Dakota. Lies and half-truths make Marlee question her beliefs on good and evil. Can she sort the good people from the bad before it's too late? Does Marlee hold the key to solving the mystery or is she just a pawn in someone's sinister game of cat and mouse?

In Search Of Sierra

What do a missing student, a tattoo parlor, a pack of mean girls, and a box of family secrets have in common? That is the puzzle Professor Marlee McCabe struggles to solve when she's pulled into the search for Sierra Prince, a former student who has vanished without a trace. The deeper Marlee digs, the more she discovers about Sierra's dysfunctional past and her stalker on campus. The clock is ticking. Can Marlee figure out what happened to the young woman before it is too late?

Deadly Reality

When a controversial professor dies on the set of a reality show filming on campus, Marlee McCabe searches for answers. As she digs deep into the case, she discovers a professor with shady connections, several disgruntled students, and a Hollywood director with dreams much bigger than reality television. Can Marlee solve the mystery before an innocent person is prosecuted for murder? Will Marlee's recklessness bring about the demise of her beloved university?

Made in the USA
Columbia, SC
02 December 2024

48274572R00202